Finding STORM

SAMANTHA TOWLE

OTHER BOOKS BY SAMANTHA TOWLE

STAND-ALONE NOVELS

River Wild

Under Her

Unsuitable

Sacking the Quarterback (BookShots Flames/James Patterson)

The Ending I Want

When I Was Yours

Trouble

THE GODS SERIES

Ruin
Rush

THE WARDROBE SERIES

Wardrobe Malfunction
Breaking Hollywood

THE REVVED SERIES

Revved
Revived

THE STORM SERIES

The Mighty Storm
Wethering the Storm
Taming the Storm
The Storm

PARANORMAL ROMANCE NOVELS

The Bringer

THE ALEXANDRA JONES SERIES

First Bitten
Original Sin

Visit my website at www.samanthatowle.co.uk
Cover Model: Colton B.
Photographer: Wander Aguiar
Cover Designer: Najla Qamber Designs
Editor and Interior Designer: Jovana Shirley,
Unforeseen Editing, www.unforeseenediting.com

ISBN-13: 9781687661692

1

STORM

"We're Slater Raze. And you've been fucking awesome!"

I'm already walking offstage before Raze has finished speaking, handing off my guitar to one of the roadies.

I'm just not feeling it tonight. Actually, I've not been feeling it at all recently.

I'll always love the music. But something's missing. I have this hollow feeling inside of me. And no matter how much coke I take, weed I smoke, whiskey I drink, or pussy I fuck, nothing is filling it.

I'm twenty-four years old and starting to wonder if I'm already burned out.

Now, wouldn't that be an LA fucking tragedy?

Not that I'm saying I didn't give those people a good show because I did. I always show up and give my all.

Just lately, my all is more of an act than reality.

I swipe an unopened bottle of water off a passing table, downing it as I walk toward our dressing room.

I let myself in the room, savoring the peace that won't last long.

I sit my ass down on the sofa and light up a cigarette when Raze comes striding in.

He pulls off his shirt, tossing it aside, and grabs a clean one that's been left in here for him, pulling it on. Raze always sweats like a motherfucker onstage.

Fuck knows why 'cause all he does is sing.

He grabs one of the chairs from a dressing table and pulls it over. He turns it around and sits down on it. "Sup?" he says to me.

"Nothing."

I toss my pack of smokes and lighter to him. He catches them and takes a cigarette out, putting it between his lips.

Before lighting it, he pulls his long hair back off his face and ties it up, using a band from around his wrist.

He takes a drag of his cigarette. His words come out with the smoke. "Good show?"

It sounds like a question. But all I answer with is, "Yep."

"You left the stage pretty quick."

I shrug.

"Something happen?"

"Nope. Just needed a smoke."

He's watching me. Thing about Raze is, he's a smart motherfucker, and he knows me well.

He's my best friend. Has been since I moved to LA.

I met him because his dad used to be a producer for The Mighty Storm—biggest band in the world and my official and unofficial adopted family.

Raze was always at the studio with his dad. I was there because Jake, Tom, Denny, and Smith were there, and where they went, I went.

My biological father was Jonny Creed.

Jonny used to be the guitarist in The Mighty Storm. He died in an automobile accident when I was about five years old.

Not that I ever knew him.

And he never knew me.

My mom kept me a secret from them all.

But when she was diagnosed with incurable cancer when I was thirteen, she reached out to Jake.

My mom used to be a TMS groupie. She'd slept with both Jake and Jonny around the time she got pregnant with me.

Back then, Jake's and Jonny's lifestyles were very similar to how I live mine now. Women, drugs, drinking, constant partying, and nonstop traveling.

Mom didn't want to raise a baby around that.

It took me a long time to understand why she'd kept me away. Living the life I do now, I get it.

So, she moved away and kept me secret. Until she was dying.

There was a DNA test, but it was set on that I was Jonny's kid.

I look exactly like him.

So, it was no surprise when the results came back that I was a Creed.

Jake moved me and Mom to LA. When Mom passed, I moved in with Jake and his wife, Tru, and their kids JJ, Billy, and Belle. My grandpa, Jonny's dad, moved in too.

Grandpa died three years ago though. He had a stroke that he never recovered from.

The last of my blood gone.

Even though I had my grandpa back then, Jake and Tru adopted me. My mom had asked them to. She wanted me to have a legal guardian after she was gone.

I had a ready-made family. And I love them all. I do.

But, really, music was always my home.

I never felt more comfortable than I did when I was at the studio with them.

But Raze eventually stopped coming around the studio when his dad decided that he preferred drinking to working.

Now, the asshole just spends his days getting wasted and leeching off his only son.

But that's a story for another time.

Raze and I continued being friends though. I didn't have many friends around that time, so I wasn't letting go of the one I had.

Raze and I were friends long before we formed our band, Slater Raze.

Speaking of our band …

"Where's Cash and Levi?"

Cash is our drummer, and Levi plays bass. I've known them almost as long as I've known Raze.

I met them both at high school. Eventually, I introduced them to Raze. The four of us created Slater Raze when we were fifteen. We've been together ever since.

"Cash got distracted."

I laugh. Cash gets easily distracted. Usually by women.

Who am I kidding? It's always by women.

"Levi?"

"Taking a piss."

I take a long pull on my cigarette. Letting the smoke out slowly, I watch it curl upward toward the ceiling.

"What's eating at you?"

I bring my eyes down to Raze.

I shrug.

"You think you played shit?"

I laugh and take another pull on my smoke. "You know I didn't."

"Then, what the fuck's wrong with you?"

I lean forward and put my cigarette out in the ashtray on the coffee table sitting between us. "Since when did you become my shrink?"

"Fuck off. I'm concerned."

"I'm fine."

"Is it the Jonny stuff again?"

I get compared to Jonny. *A lot.*

Hell, even my and Raze's friendship has been compared to Jonny and Jake's.

Does it drain me? Drive me nuts?

Of course it does.

Hearing how I'll never live up to the musical standard or success that Jonny had sucks ass.

Think Kurt Cobain. Jonny has been immortalized in the exact same way.

His face and talent frozen forever in time.

Unfortunately for me, unlike Kurt's offspring, I'm a musician. I play the same instrument as Jonny did.

Therefore, every aspect of my life is measured against his.

My talent, my private life, *everything.*

Jonny died young. So, I guess if we're going the same route, I have a few years left in me before my car takes a nosedive into a ravine.

I know; I'm fucking hilarious.

I shrug again. "I don't know, man. I'm just tired."

The door flies open, banging against the plasterboard wall.

"Motherfuckers!"

It's Cash.

"What the fuck are you two pussies doing in here? Braiding each other's hair?"

I flip him off, and he just laughs.

"Greenroom. Now. There's pussy waiting to be signed."

That raises my brow. "Signed?"

"Sorry." Cash grins. "I meant, fucked."

Both Raze and I laugh before getting to our feet and following him out into the hall.

The three of us walk into the greenroom, which is already filled, mostly with men I do know—roadies, producers, and the like. And women I don't know.

Levi is already here. He hands me a beer as I approach.

Cash is off, already beelining for some Asian-looking chick who's sitting on one of the sofas. I'm guessing she was his earlier distraction.

She'll last for the night, and then he'll move on to the next.

Like we all will.

Raze is talking to one of our sound guys.

"Good show," Levi says to me. His words don't sound like a question because, unlike Raze, Levi doesn't probe. He's just chill. The most laid-back motherfucker I've ever met.

"Yeah. Good show," I say to him.

I take a swig of my beer and let my eyes drift over the room.

One table filled with food. Another littered with booze. There'll be drugs here too, just not on show.

Music playing in the background. Women here, hoping to hook up with one of us.

Same shit. Different night.

Yawn.

Shit. If fifteen-year-old me could hear me now, he'd probably punch me in the nuts.

And I'd deserve it.

Maybe I was right earlier. Maybe I am burned out.

Maybe I just need a break. From everything.

I go to my pocket for my cigarettes and remember that I left them in the other room.

For fuck's sake.

"Just gonna head back to the dressing room. Left my smokes in there," I tell Cash.

Taking my beer with me, I walk back, taking my time. I'm in no rush.

Pushing open the dressing room door, I cross the room and grab the pack and my lighter off the table.

I take one out and light it up, inhaling the smoke. I pocket the pack and lighter.

When I turn around, bottle still in hand, I'm only half-surprised to see a girl in the doorway.

Well, when I say girl, I mean, woman. I'd say she's about my age.

I don't recognize her. But then again, she could have been coming to the after-parties for months, and I still wouldn't recognize her.

I'd have to care to remember, and as of late, I care about very little.

"Hi." She smiles and bites her lip, giving me a shy look. "You're Storm, right?"

This chick is anything but shy. She wouldn't be here, about to proposition me for sex if she was.

And no, that's not me being a presumptuous asshole.

That's from me being in varying scenarios of this exact same situation far too many times to remember.

A woman who doesn't work for the label or the band, standing in my doorway after a show, is here for one reason only.

To fuck me.

But she's going for the coy angle, and I'll play along. It's not like I've got anything better to do.

I don't say anything. I just let my eyes drag down the length of her while I take another drag on my cigarette.

She's pretty.

Tall, like I like my women. Long legs. Shoulder-length blonde hair. Short skirt. Low-cut top. Tan skin. Pouty lips, which aren't natural. The tits aren't real either.

I've seen enough to know the difference.

Hey, I'm not judging. A girl wants to make some changes to what the genetic gods gave her, then all the power to her.

If I could cosmetic surgery out whatever the fuck is going on with me at the moment, then I would.

She's probably a nice girl.

But it also doesn't take a rocket scientist to know what she's here for.

I wouldn't say she wants to fuck me specifically. Hell, maybe she does. But, usually, these girls just want to screw any guy from the band.

Whether it be for bragging rights or because she's hoping more will come from it, I've no clue.

I'd like to think she's not that stupid.

Me and the boys definitely aren't known for being the settling-down type.

She twirls her hair around her finger and bites her lip again, looking at me from under false lashes. "I'm Nina."

"I'm not in the mood to talk."

Okay, that was a bit assholish, but it's also the truth. The last thing I want to do right now is talk. And I definitely don't care what her name is.

"Okay. So, no talking. Are you in the mood to fuck?"

And there it is.

Am I in the mood to fuck?

Good question.

It's not like I have anything else going on right this second.

But the prospect of screwing this girl doesn't exactly get my blood pumping either.

I guess I could go home and sleep. I do have an interview first thing tomorrow morning.

I almost laugh out loud.

Go home and sleep.

Some fucking rock star I am.

I bet Jonny wouldn't have ever turned down the chance to fuck a hot chick.

And now, I'm comparing my libido with my dead father's.

That's some Freudian shit right there. My shrink would have a fucking field day with it.

I flick the building ash from my cigarette into the ashtray on the table.

"Can I have one?" She gestures to the smoke in my hand.

Pulling the packet from my pocket, I get one out and hold it out to her.

She crosses the room, letting the door close behind her. Her heels click loudly on the wooden floor.

She takes the cigarette from me, purposely running her nails over my hand.

I feel absolutely nothing.

Not even a flicker of interest.

But that's nothing new. Not as of late anyway.

She puts the cigarette between her lips. I hold the lighter out. She steps closer, and I light it for her.

She doesn't move away. She's so close, I can smell her perfume.

And see right down her top.

And still, I feel nothing.

I watch the smoke slip out of her mouth with her next words. "I've heard things about you … good things. My friend Mel said you have a magical tongue."

That does make me laugh.

So, I've banged her friend. Not surprising. I've screwed a lot of women.

She smiles, looking pleased.

"I have a magical tongue too," she tells me.

"That so?" I wonder if I sound as bored as I feel.

"Yep." She reaches out and trails her finger down my chest, my stomach, stopping at the button of my jeans. "I can show you oblivion, baby."

I stifle a laugh this time.

As lines go, that was pretty fucking cheesy.

But, honestly, oblivion does sound better than anything I'm feeling—or not feeling—right now.

Her hand moves down, and she cups my dick through my jeans and squeezes.

I don't even flinch.

But my dick does finally perk up and show some interest.

Maybe I should just fuck her. It's not like I have anything else to do.

Jesus. Is this what my life has come to?

Lifting my beer bottle to my lips, I drain it.

I put the bottle down on the table beside me. Take one last drag on my cigarette and drop the butt inside the empty bottle.

I stare at her a moment.

She licks her lips.

Guess I could fuck her. Beats sitting around, stuck in my own head all night, trying to figure out what the fuck is wrong with me.

Decision made, I take her cigarette from her hand and drop that in the bottle too.

"You got a condom?" I ask her.

She reaches a hand inside her bra and pulls one out. She taps me on the nose with it. "I was a good Girl Scout. I always came prepared."

A feeling of boredom almost overwhelms me. She really needs to stop talking.

She reaches for my zipper, but I catch her wrist, stopping her. I stare down into her pretty face.

"Like I said before, I ain't in the mood to talk. So, if we fuck, that's all we do. Quietly. Then, we're done. Or this ain't happening."

Her smile dims, but she quickly covers it up, forcing her smile to go wider than before.

But I don't feel bad.

I'm nothing if not honest.

"No talking." She makes the zip motion across her lips. "Got it."

I let go of her wrist.

She nudges me backward until I sit my ass back down on the sofa I was sitting in not ten minutes ago.

She gets on her knees between my legs and smiles up at me. "You want me to be quiet, rock star? Then, you'd better keep my mouth full."

She yanks down my zipper.

I shut my eyes, let my head fall back, and wait for that oblivion she promised to take hold.

2

STORM

Consciousness pushes at the fringes of sleep.

I love that moment when you're just leaving a dream, slipping out of your mind's fiction and cruising back into reality.

Although my reality isn't feeling too great at the moment.

I'm pretty sure I was hit by a liquor truck.

That, or I just got absolutely shit-faced last night.

I'm guessing it was the latter.

Groaning, I run my tongue over my teeth.

Feels like something up and died in my mouth.

Blindly, I reach out to my nightstand in the hope I had the forethought to bring a bottle of water.

My hand collides with a lamp.

I don't have a lamp on my nightstand.

I force open one eye.

Yep, definitely not my nightstand. Or wall.

I'm not in my bedroom.

Where the hell am I?

I force open the other eye and slightly turn my head to survey my surroundings.

Hotel room. Well, suite by the looks of the size of it.

Guess I was feeling generous last night.

Not like you can't afford it, Slater.

Yeah, and it's also Jonny's money.

Was Jonny's money.

Money that went to my grandpa when Jonny died, and when Grandpa found out about my existence, he had the money put in a trust for me, which I got when I turned twenty-one.

Grandpa and I used to disagree on it all the time. I'd tell him I didn't want the money. He'd say it was mine by right. I'd say it was his. He was Jonny's dad after all. Jonny might have been my father by blood, but I never knew him.

Grandpa would always say to me, "Well, I ain't taking it to the grave with me. So, it's yours whether you want it or not."

I stare at the wall, my head pounding.

I don't even remember checking into the hotel. I'm guessing making it home must have been out of the question for me.

At least I'm not in some strange chick's house. Always a plus. Because leaving a woman's house is always awkward as hell.

I'm always up-front that I'm only in it for the night, but not all women listen, and that makes the morning after not worth the night before.

On a few occasions, I have encountered some women who are basically using me as much as I'm using them. Which is awesome. Whether it's just for sex or so they can tell their friends that they fucked the guitarist from Slater Raze.

Although, that one time, there was a woman—a lot older than me, but fit as fuck—who only had sex with me because she was obsessed with Jonny.

I know; it was creep factor one hundred.

Waking up in a room covered in pictures of Jonny Creed after a night of screwing someone was quite possibly the creepiest thing that has ever happened to me.

And there I'd been, thinking she didn't want to turn on the bedroom light because she was shy.

No, it was because my biological father was plastered all over her fucking walls.

A feminine sigh from behind me has me turning my head all the way around.

Seems I didn't come here alone.

Dark brown hair is splayed over the white pillowcase.

Brown hair?

I screwed a blonde last night. I know that for sure. I was sober when I did it.

We banged on the sofa after she finished sucking my cock. Well, technically, she banged me. Cowgirl-style.

Don't worry; I made sure she got hers too. I'm not a total asshole.

After we fucked, we put the clothes back on that we'd removed—well, I pulled my pants back up and zipped away the goods, and she put her panties back on and righted her tits back into her bra.

We left the dressing room and went back to the green room where the boys still were.

I remember Raze putting a beer in my hand. Cash put a shot in the other, and we started drinking.

The blonde …

Fuck, what was her name?

Mindy? Morgan?

Actually, it doesn't matter.

Whoever she was, she stuck around. Well, she stuck to me even though I'd been clear as day that it was one fuck and one fuck only.

Looks like I shook her off at some point in the night.

Slowly, I sit up. My head is pounding like a bitch.

I glance over at the brunette.

Ah. The blonde's here too. She's lying asleep on the other side of the unknown brunette.

Guess I didn't shake her off after all. I just upped my numbers.

I should feel good, waking up in bed with two women.

I don't.

I feel … nothing.

Empty.

Tired.

Bored of the same old shit.

Yet I keep doing it to myself.

Moving carefully so as not to wake my bed companions, I hold the duvet back and swing my legs over the edge of the bed.

The nightstand is littered with condom wrappers and a … dildo?

Where the fuck did the dildo come from?

Actually, I don't want to know.

My ass doesn't feel sore, so at least I know it wasn't used on me.

Hilarious, Slater.

My cell and wallet are among the condom wrappers. I grab my phone and check the screen.

Couple of texts. One from Tru to the family group.

One from Cash in our band group.

I slide my finger over it, opening it up.

Picture message.

What the hell is that?

Jesus Christ. It's my bare ass.

For fuck's sake, Cash.

I'm guessing the legs hooked over my bare ass belong to one of the women lying right behind me.

Not that you can see any faces.

Just my ass.

Where the fuck was this taken?

I scan the picture, zooming in on it.

I can't tell. It could be anywhere.

Maybe it was taken here, and the fuckers left after.

Well, wherever it was, Cash was there. Probably Raze and Levi too.

Not the first time I've banged a chick in front of one or all of them. Or shared a chick with one or all of them. Probably won't be the last.

I fire a text back to the group.

> *Me: Cash, delete the fucking picture.*

He texts back almost immediately.

> *Cash: Okay.*

Huh. That was easy.

Then, another text comes in.

> *Cash: Let me just send it to Tru-Mom before I do.*

For fuck's sake.

Tru-Mom is what the guys call my adoptive mom, Tru. Funny they call her that because I've only ever called her Tru.

I already had a mom, who I loved more than anyone else on this shit-for-fuck planet. Even if I did spend a lot of time being angry as hell with her before and after she died.

I guess I just feel it would be wrong of me to call anyone else Mom. And Tru's never seemed to have a problem with it.

Me: You're fucking hilarious. You send a picture of my bare ass to Tru, and Jake will kick yours.

It takes a minute for him to respond.

Then, a video drops in.

I turn the volume on my phone off. Then, I hit play.

Me: Jesus fucking Christ, Cash.

He videoed me fucking her too.

Although I'm not even surprised.

It's not like I haven't done similar kinds of shit to him or the other guys.

Me: Delete the fucking video, Cash.

Levi: Wait. Let me watch it first.

Great. Now, Levi's getting involved.

Me: Seriously, bro. You want to watch me bone some chick?

Levi: Porn is porn, man.

I actually start laughing at that. Quietly though. I don't want to wake my bed buddies.

I might be feeling off lately, but I can always rely on my boys to make me smile.

A reminder flashes up on my screen, covering up the sex tape.

Interview. Jasper Marsh, Amped magazine.
Brunch @ Republique, 11:00 a.m.

Ah shit, I forgot about that.

What time is it?

Swiping off the text app, I check the time on my phone. Just after ten a.m.

I've got less than an hour before I have to be there. Not that I'm looking forward to going.

I hate interviews. With a fiery passion.

They're a whole new level of hell.

Being Jonny Creed's kid saw to that.

I could skip the interview.

Nah, Zane would hang my ass out to dry if I did.

An hour should be plenty enough time for me to go home, shower, change, and get to the restaurant.

Considering we played the Microsoft Theater last night, I'm hoping this hotel is somewhere not too far from there. My place in Beverly Grove is only thirty minutes from there. Republique is fifteen minutes from home. Yeah, I'll do it, easy.

Shame.

Although, depending on where the hotel I am in right now actually is, there's still a possibility that I could be late.

Fingers crossed.

Or maybe I should just pray for a natural disaster to stop me from getting there.

Leaving my cell with my wallet, I push to my feet and quietly walk through the still-darkened suite, dodging the beer and wine bottles scattered on the floor—*how fucking much did I drink last night?*—as I locate the bathroom.

The light in here is bright as fuck. It makes me wince. I have to rapid-blink to get my eyes to adjust.

Hangovers suck ass.

Still squinting against the light, I take a piss.

While I'm washing my hands, I catch sight of myself in the mirror.

I look like shit.

I feel like shit.

Cupping cold water in my hands, I splash it over my face and run my wet hand through my hair. I dry my face and hands on a towel.

Turning off the light before exiting the bathroom so as not to wake anyone with the laser light, I crack the door open and poke my head out.

The suite is silent.

They're still sleeping.

I locate my clothes in a heap by the bottom of the bed. Clearly, I was in a hurry to strip because I dropped the lot there in a pile. That, or drunk me was readying myself for this morning's great escape. I get dressed in relative silence, which for a guy of my size is no mean feat.

I've gotten proficient at this shit. Sneaking out of hotel rooms.

Not something I'm wholly proud of, but obviously, I don't learn.

I tiptoe over to the nightstand and retrieve my cell and wallet.

My apartment keys are in my pants pocket, which is a relief. There have been a few instances when I lost the keys to my apartment when I got trashed. Meaning I either lost them or someone took them—quite possibly the someone I'd slept with. So, I've had to have my locks changed more times than I'm proud of.

I pocket my cell and wallet. Find my boots by the door and push my bare feet into them.

I glance back over at the still-sleeping forms.

The brunette has rolled over and is sleeping where I vacated.

Dark hair covers her face.

I don't even know what she looks like, let alone know her name.

And I barely remember what the blonde looks like even though I was pretty much sober when I met her.

I used to be proud of this shit when I was younger.

Younger … fuck, listen to me. I'm twenty-four years old and already jaded as hell.

And I know I should feel bad for skipping out on them, but I don't. I just want out of here and away from the reminder that I'm just rinsing and repeating the same old shit again.

All it serves to do is remind me of how very little I feel about this—or anything at the moment.

With a quick turn of the lock, handle down, I'm out of there. I quietly close the door behind me.

A glance around the hallway, and I spot the Exit sign and follow it to the elevator.

I press the call button. The elevator arrives almost immediately. When I reach the stylish lobby, I look around to see where the fuck I am.

The Ritz-Carlton.

Guess I was feeling plush last night.

Honestly, I'm surprised they even let me in. I was definitely trashed, clearly up for partying and not alone.

But then celebrity gives you all sorts of powers that non-celeb folk don't have. And being the only child of Jonny Creed and the adopted son of Jake Wethers has its pull and perks.

Honestly, I feel like a jackass, just thinking it.

I walk over to the reception desk and settle up my bill. I tell them to send breakfast up to the suite for my two remaining guests.

I might be a shit. But I'm not a total shit.

The polished thirty-something receptionist doesn't even flinch that I had two women up there with me for the night.

I guess they must see shit like this all the time, even in a nice establishment like this.

Money doesn't always buy class.

The doorman gets me a cab. I thank him and give the driver my address.

I moved in my place a year ago.

I was living with the guys in a rented house after moving out of Jake and Tru's.

I honestly loved living with Jake, Tru, and the kids. It wasn't my first home. It won't be my last. But I know it's a home that I will always be welcome back to.

But I was a twenty-year-old rock star still living at home. The band was taking off big time. It was time to move out, so me and the guys rented a house together in West Hollywood.

But recording and touring together and living together just got to be too much.

I love those guys, but not twenty-four/seven. I needed my own space, so I moved out a year ago to my place in Beverly Grove.

Raze moved out when I did. His apartment is two blocks from mine.

Cash and Levi still live together in our old apartment, which is ten blocks away.

Raze and I didn't go far.

And I didn't go far from Jake and Tru's either. I'm a ten-minute car ride away.

I might not want to live with any of them anymore, but I don't want to be too far from them either.

The cab pulls up outside my apartment building. I pay the guy and then head inside my building, saying morning to the doorman, Griffin.

I ride the elevator up to the tenth floor where my apartment is.

Letting myself in my apartment, I don't waste any time. I go straight to my bedroom. I kick off my boots and drop my cell, wallet, and keys on the bed.

I go into my bathroom and get two Advil from the cabinet and sink them with some water.

Teeth brushed, I strip off last night's clothes and climb in the shower, scrubbing the night off me.

Towel around my waist, I stand in front of the basin and wipe the steam from the mirror.

I stare at myself. I don't like what's staring back.

I look jaded.

My eyes are dark. Tired.

I look exactly like Jonny did in the months before he died.

Yes, I've analyzed photos of him.

And yes, I have major daddy issues—no fucking surprise there.

In the early photos of Jonny, when TMS had just started, he looked bright-eyed. Like the world was at his feet. I guess it was. Then, as time went on, the light in his eyes was replaced with a cynical look. A drugged-up look.

I wonder if there was a time in those final years of his life if he was ever actually clean.

You'd think that I would've learned from Jake and Jonny not to take drugs.

Not that I do it much now. But in the early days, I did.

Drugs are readily available to people like me, and back then, all I cared about was having a good time.

And unlike Jonny and Jake, I don't have an addictive personality. I can take them or leave them, so it's never been a concern for me.

But I don't so much bother with that shit now.

When something is readily available all the damn time, it loses its sheen. Its excitement.

It's the same with women.

I don't have to work for it. Any of it.

And it bores the shit out of me.

I know I sound like a whiny ass.

Poor little me, pussy at the ready, but I'm just … tired.

None of it makes me happy anymore.

Only the music.

But even that's clouded by the constant pressure of living up to the ghost of a man I never knew.

I guess I need to find something that makes me happy again.

Wherever or whatever the fuck that might be.

But for now, I have an interview to get to.

I dress in black jeans and my favorite vintage The Stooges white T-shirt.

I slip on my leather jacket, pocketing my cell, keys, and wallet. I push my feet in my boots, grab a pack of cigarettes from my stash in the kitchen, and leave my apartment.

3

STORM

I ride the elevator down to the parking garage, where my baby is waiting for me.

My girl.

My one and only.

She is the most beautiful thing I have ever seen.

I knew it the second I saw her that I had to have her.

It was love at first sight.

My gorgeous, sexy-as-sin Maserati GranTurismo Sport, custom-wrapped in black matte with a gold vinyl trim and gold alloys.

I love her like no other.

And I don't ever splurge on fancy things. Well, apart from hotel rooms when I'm wasted, apparently.

I grew up with very little money. My mom did the best she could for us, but she was never going to earn a lot while working at Marie's bakery. I went from living in a tiny apartment above the bakery to Jake and Tru's huge house in

Beverly Hills, gaining a trust fund with more zeros in it than I knew what to do with.

Going from nothing to that is hard to acclimatize to.

You either go one way or the other.

You spend it like your life depends on it, like Raze does now that he has money from the success of our band.

Or you hoard it, like I do.

Cash and Levi come from money, so they've never known anything different.

Although Cash burns through his money faster than Raze does. Levi is just fucking sensible—spends when necessary, indulges a little, and invests a lot.

I need to learn to be more like Levi, especially with my own money.

I've earned a hell of a lot from the band. But before that, until we established and started to take off, I had to live on Jonny's money, and that was hard to deal with.

So, spending excess amounts of Jonny's money wasn't high on my list. I would use only what I needed until I started earning real money.

Up until I bought my beauty, I was still driving around in the same shitty Chevy truck that was popular in the 1980s, which I'd bought with the money I'd earned working for Jake at his label, TMS Records.

The label he'd originally set up with Jonny.

After Jonny died, his half of TMS Records went to his parents—my grandparents. I never met my grandmother. She had died long before I found out that Jonny was my biological father. My blood relatives drop like flies. I'm the last of my kind. Maybe I should be worried.

Funny, Slater.

Anyway, Jake bought their half of TMS Records not long after Jonny died.

That's where the big chunk of the money I have sitting in the bank came from. The trust my grandpa set up for me. Jonny's half of TMS Records and his earnings from the band. Royalties still come in now from the music made before Jonny died.

It's my money, technically, but I've never felt comfortable with spending it.

And I didn't get it until I turned twenty-one anyway, so I had to earn my way, and I did that by working for the label—basically doing all the shitty jobs no one else wanted to do.

Brought coffee. Ran errands. Unblocked toilets.

All the awesome jobs.

Tru and Jake might be loaded, but they make their kids earn their money to learn the value of it, and because I was—*am*—legally one of their kids, the same applied to me.

I had to earn my way like everyone else.

Well, maybe except for my fourteen-year-old baby sister, Belle. She's got Jake wrapped around her finger. My brothers have part-time jobs like I did. JJ is seventeen and a star athlete. He's an amazing soccer player. Some European clubs are showing an interest in him. He has a part-time job at a local coffee shop. Billy is sixteen and massively into music. He does jobs around the label just like I did. Poor kid.

I go to the trunk and pop it open. Take my leather jacket off and put it in there. Shut down the trunk, round the car, and climb in my girl. Pressing the ignition button, I fire her up. She purrs to life.

I put my seat belt on.

Bluetooth hooks up my phone. I select Music and press Random Play.

A second later, Jimi Hendrix's "Purple Haze" hums out of the speakers.

Turning the volume up, my fingers strum against the steering wheel in time to the guitar riff.

Now, this here makes me happy.

My car and good music.

The simple things in life.

Maybe this is all I really need. Fuck all the other shit.

I slide her into drive and exit the parking garage, driving in the direction of Republique.

Can't say I'm looking forward to this interview.

I don't like interviews, period.

Journalists prying into my life? No, thanks.

People think because I'm a musician and my life is on the stage that I like being in the public eye.

I detest it.

For an intensely private person like me, it's difficult, being the focal point of people's interest.

What I wouldn't give to be able to just make music and live a media-free life.

But the world doesn't work that way, and to be able to do what I love, this is the way it has to be.

I have to share my life with the world.

And at this point, it's not like there's anything anyone doesn't know about my life already.

It's all there in large print on Wikipedia.

Raze might be our front man. But my biological father makes me press-worthy.

So, when a hugely popular magazine wants an interview with me, I go do it for the band.

Any press is good press, as Zane always tells us. Zane is the VP at TMS Records, which my band is signed to.

Yes, I know I'm signed to my adopted dad's label. I know how it looks, special treatment and all that, but Jake didn't sign us.

Zane did.

Jake has nothing to do with my band. Zane makes all the calls when it comes to us.

If Zane wanted to can us, Jake wouldn't stop him.

He doesn't play favorites in business.

We do what Zane says, and if Zane tells me I'm going to do an interview, then that's what I go do.

I should be thankful that people want to interview us.

When journalists are still asking for interviews, it means you're relevant, and if you're relevant, then you're selling records. And ultimately, that's all that matters—that people are still listening to our music.

That's why I do this.

Because, despite what people say about me, we are damn good fucking musicians.

I just wish the boys were here for this interview.

It's a million times easier for me when I have them with me at interviews. Raze is deft at deflecting questions aimed at me about Jonny.

Me, not so much.

I just answer the questions, like a good little robot. All the while, getting angry and pissed inside. Because if I don't answer their questions or give them the words they want, then I'm being disrespectful and ungrateful. I'm shitting on Jonny's memory and what he gave me, which is my talent, apparently—you know, the talent that doesn't measure up to his.

The thing these people forget is that I didn't know Jonny. Yes, he's my biological father, but I never met the man. Yet I'm expected to answer questions about him like I did.

People speak about Jonny with reverence. They love him, and that's great for them.

But for me, Jonny Creed is the black fucking cloud over my life.

I would never say this out loud, but I resent it.

I resent him—a dead man.

I'm angry with my mom for doing things the way she did back then. Keeping me from him.

I get her reasoning. I understand it more now that I'm older, but it doesn't change the way I feel.

And the way I feel is …

Trapped in my own life.

Do I say any of this out loud?

Nope.

I can never say what I really feel about his impact on my life. How hard it was—and still is—finding out that Jonny Creed was my father.

How being constantly compared to him on a daily basis is no picnic.

Hearing people say that my musical talent will never equal his.

But the thing is … I don't want to equal his talent.

I want my talent to stand on its own.

But it never will.

Because the moment the world found out that a living, breathing genetic piece of Jonny Creed was left behind, my life stopped being my own.

I knew all of this. I knew me going into music would give them an open pass to me.

I just didn't realize how hard it would be.

I guess the hollow feeling I have inside of me nowadays is all that's left after being chipped away at all these years.

If only I could stand up and say what I really feel.

But I can't.

I can speak my mind on anything. But Jonny Creed.

I swear though, one of these days, I'm gonna snap and go all Michael Douglas in *Falling Down* if I'm asked one more time if Jonny's musical influence is the reason why I became a guitarist.

I drive up to Republique twenty minutes later and get lucky, finding a parking spot that just opened close by.

I slide my baby into it and turn off the engine, leaving the music playing—Eminem's "The Monster."

I glance at the clock on the dash.

I'm a few minutes late.

How very rock 'n' roll of me.

Needing a nicotine fix to get me through the next hour, I light a cigarette up and inhale deeply, resting my head back on the headrest. I lower my window down a touch and blow the smoke outside.

Sometimes, I think life would be easier if I wasn't a musician. Well, I don't think it. I know it.

If I lived my life away from the music business, worked a nine-to-five job, life would be piss easy.

I close my eyes and imagine it.

No more press. No more social media. No one saying I'm not good enough.

Sounds like fucking heaven.

But then there'd be no more music. No more Slater Raze.

No more days and nights in the studio. No more writing sessions with the boys.

No more shows.

I know I feel off at the moment, but I also know without a doubt that I would miss being onstage. I would miss the sounds of thousands of people singing along to the words of the songs that I wrote.

There's nothing like that feeling that comes from hearing people sing your words back to you.

Sometimes, when something is embedded so deeply inside that it makes you who you are, you can't give it up, no matter the damage it does to you.

I do what I love; I pay the price. I give it up; I pay the price.

Sounds like a fucking winner to me.

Jake once said to me, "You wanna live your life the way you do, then you gotta listen to people's criticism. But that doesn't mean you have to hear it."

And I try not to hear it. I do. But it's hard.

At times, it's all I hear.

Sighing, I put my cigarette out, dumping it in the empty coffee cup I left in here yesterday.

Leaving my car, I take the cup with me and drop it in a nearby trash can.

Okay, let's get this shit done, and then I get back in the studio, where I belong.

I walk over to the restaurant, push open the door, and walk inside.

I've been here once before, years ago though.

I walk over to the hostess station.

The woman behind it looks up at me.

I'm hit with a moment of recognition.

I have a shit memory, and I forget faces easily, but I wouldn't forget her face anytime soon—or, well, ever.

She's the chick who screwed me 'cause I'm Jonny Creed's kid and had his posters all over her bedroom wall.

And this was where I met her all those years ago.

How am I only just remembering this now?

"Storm." She beams at me like we're old buddies.

We fucked once, lady, and you're as crazy as a box of frogs.

What do I do? Let her know that I remember her or feign ignorance?

Pretend I don't know who she is?

I'm totally going with the latter.

I smile my best *I don't know you, but I'm being polite and congenial* smile. I use it often. "Hi. I'm here to meet Jasper Marsh. The table's in his name."

Her gaze sharpens. "You don't remember me, do you?"

Oh boy.

I remember you all right, lady. I just wish I didn't.

"Sorry, have we met before?"

I'm a rock star. I meet loads of people. This should fly.

Or not.

She's looking at me like she wants to stab me with the pen she's holding. "Have we met before?" Her voice pitches high.

Abort! Abort!

"Oh, wait." I click my fingers, trying to rectify the crazy. "I do remember you."

Nothing. She doesn't even blink.

She's just staring at me, eyes scarily wide.

"Yeah … of course. You and me … yeah, I remember you."

Wow. Well done, Slater. Oscar-worthy performance there.

"What's my name?"

"Huh?"

"My name. If you remember me, you know my name."

Shit.

My eyes quickly scan her shirt, looking for a name badge.

And wouldn't you know it? She doesn't have one on.

See, this is why you should go to IHOP. The staff there wears fucking name badges.

I'm staring at her, trying to will her name from the deepest recesses of my mind, but it's pointless. Even if I had asked for her name all those years ago, I wouldn't have remembered it a second after she told me.

So, I do the only thing a guy can do in this situation.

Go for broke.

"Sarah, right?"

Her eyes narrow until they're like pissholes in snow.

"No. Right. Mandy then? Stephanie? Becky? Claire?"

I'm throwing names out there like they're a damn life raft.

She makes this noise in the back of her throat, cutting me off. It sounds like she just swallowed a rock.

I'm so dead.

"Asshole."

She turns away from me and picks up a menu from the shelf behind her. Turns back to me. Her face is a total mask. Not a shred of emotion on it.

She's going to kill me.

This is how I'll go.

Death by psycho.

"Your dad would never have treated a woman like this. He was a gentleman. You're an asshole," she hisses.

You couldn't be more wrong, lady. I didn't know Jonny because he did treat women exactly like this.

And I'm behaving just the same as him.

Well, if that isn't a sobering thought, nothing is.

"Let me show you to your table, Asshole." Her voice is scarily high. "Mr. Marsh is already here."

She storms off through the restaurant. Her heels click aggressively against the tiled floor.

I follow behind her. What else can I do?

I know for sure she's going to poison my food. Or at the very least, spit in my coffee.

This chick should be a warning to me to be more careful where I put my dick. Obviously, I didn't learn the first time, but I will now.

I swear, if I make it through this brunch, I'll stop screwing random women. Or at least, I'll write down their fucking names.

I approach the table, and the guy I figure to be Jasper Marsh rises from his seat. He looks to be in his mid- to late-forties. Shorter than me. Thickset around the middle. Thinning black hair.

"Storm, thanks for coming."

He puts his hand out, and I shake it, noting how clammy his palm is.

"No problem. Sorry I'm late," I tell him.

"You're hardly late." He waves me off before sitting back down.

I take my seat across from him and surreptitiously wipe my hand on my thigh.

The menu my new best friend was carrying is tossed on the table in front of me. "What do you want to drink?" she barks at me.

I see Jasper's eyes rise at the tone of her voice.

"Coffee. Black," I mutter. "Jasper?"

"I'm good." He picks up his coffee cup.

I can see his lips twitching a smile.

Great. He's figured it out that I banged her at some point. It wouldn't take a rocket scientist to figure it out by the tension radiating from her or from the holes I feel her eyes burning into the side of my head.

But if he didn't know, then the, "Asshole," she hisses at me before she departs confirms it.

The first thing he's going to write in his article is about how I previously screwed the hostess who served us. Never mind that she's crazy or slept with me because she's obsessed with Jonny. No, I'll be the bastard in the situation.

Fucking fabulous.

Zane's gonna love this.

"Is there a problem?" Jasper asks, his eyes moving between me and wherever my bad error in judgment has retreated to.

"She wasn't keen on our last song." I give him a smirk and pick up my menu. "So, what's good to eat here?" I go for a subject change.

But it's not always that easy with journalists.

So, I wait for him to probe some more. Thankfully, he doesn't.

"Well, if you're a pancake man—and who isn't, right?" He grins, showing me slightly yellow teeth. Odd to see that here in LA where everybody's smile is blinding white. "Then, the Austrian pancakes are top-notch. But the Maine Lobster omelet is sublime as well."

"Pancakes it is." I need the carbs after last night's escapade.

We make small talk until my coffee arrives, which is thankfully brought over by a waiter.

Still, I check it for signs of poison or floaters. Just because she didn't bring it doesn't mean she hadn't made it or dropped anything in it.

It looks okay. I gingerly give it a sip.

Tastes okay too.

We both place our orders with the waiter, who takes our menus away with him.

I relax back into my chair. I feel my cell vibrate in my pocket, but I ignore it. I never get my cell out during an interview. It's rude as fuck to do so. Honestly, I can't stand it when you see people sitting together at a table, eating or whatever, and they're on their phones, ignoring each other.

I guess I picked it up from Tru. She doesn't allow cell phones at the dinner table at home or when we eat out together.

I take another drink of my coffee. A bigger gulp now that I'm ninety percent sure it's not poisoned.

"I appreciate you coming down to talk with me today."

"Well, it's a free lunch. Of course I'm here," I quip, and he laughs.

"You mind if we start the interview now, or do you want to wait until after we eat?"

"Now's fine." Sooner we're done, the sooner I can leave.

"You don't have a problem if I record it?" he asks, reaching into his pocket, pulling out his cell phone. "Saves me from missing anything."

"Sure." I shrug.

Jasper taps the screen on his phone and then sets it on the table between us.

"Okay. Well, I'm just gonna start with a few basic questions, things the readers want to know. Like who your favorite bands are, what music is on your current playlist—the basic shit. What's next from you guys. What you're currently working on. Then, we'll move on to the night Jonny died."

I pause. My eyes snapping up to his. "What?"

"I want to talk about the night Jonny died and how you feel, knowing you were the reason he was in his car that night."

It's like water has gushed into my ears. All voices and chatter around me disappear. Time seems to slow to a stop.

"I … I …" I shake my head. "What?"

I don't miss the smile that appears in his eyes.

"The night Jonny died, he received a phone call from a"—he pulls a small notepad from his pants pocket and glances at it—"Marie Walker. She was your mother's employer and friend, correct?"

I don't answer. I can't.

"Marie called Jonny the night he died. She told him about you. That he had a son. Jonny got in his car—loaded to his eyeballs, enough drugs and booze in his system to take down a horse—because he was coming to see you. He was driving to the airport to catch a flight, which, of course, he never made. It wasn't suicide, like many have hypothesized. He didn't drive his car into that ravine that night on purpose."

Jonny knew …

He knew about me.

He was coming to see me.

The smile in Jasper's eyes turns to a smirk on his lips. "But, by the look on your face right now, I'm guessing you didn't know, did you? You had no idea that he knew of your existence. No clue that your father, one of the greatest musicians to have ever lived, died that night because he was coming to meet you."

4

STORM

The dirty bomb that was just dropped in front of me has fired off shrapnel straight into my chest.

I can't breathe.

Jonny knew.

He knew.

He was on his way to see me.

He died, coming to see me.

"Storm, do you have anything you'd like to say in response?"

Jasper's voice flickers me back to life. I drag my eyes up to his.

The smirk in them makes me want to wipe it off his face.

My hand twitches at my side.

My heart is pounding against my ribs. Adrenaline coursing through my veins. My mouth dry as fuck.

Standing, I shove my chair back, and it falls to the floor with a clatter.

I'm well aware of the silence that hits the restaurant, but I ignore it. Ignore everyone but the little prick across the table from me.

I grab my wallet from my pocket, pull some bills out, and toss them on the table.

"You're talking shit. And this interview is over."

Jasper stands, pushing his chair back. "I can assure you, I'm not. Everything I said is the truth."

"You're a fucking liar." I point a finger at him before I start to walk away.

My legs feel rubbery. I honestly don't know if they'll get me out of here.

"If you don't believe me, ask Jake."

That stops me dead.

"Or Tom, Denny … *Tru.*" His words hit my frozen back.

They knew?

Slowly, I turn to face him.

"They all know the truth. Marie told Jake years ago. When you first moved to LA. They've known for all this time, and they've never bothered to tell you. Left you thinking that Jonny never knew about you. Never cared. A whole decade of lies. Makes you wonder why they've never said anything to you, doesn't it? Makes you wonder what else they haven't told you."

I pin him with a stare. "You know fuck all."

"Actually, I know a lot. More than you, clearly."

"Fuck you."

The prick actually has the audacity to laugh.

I need to get the fuck out of here. As I move my stare away from him, my eyes catch on his phone sitting on the table.

The phone that has been recording this whole conversation.

My life on tape for the world to hear.

Whether what he's saying about Jonny is true or not, it'll make for one hell of a story.

My life up for debate again.

I can see the fucking headlines now.

Jonny Creed died because of his illegitimate son, Storm Slater.

It's irrational. But people aren't rational. Mob mentality rules.

I'll be crucified in the press and by social media, depending on the way the story is swung.

Jesus.

I don't want this to be true.

The people I call family. People I love and admire, keeping the truth from me.

The thought makes me feel sick.

But something deep in my gut tells me that Jasper's not lying. He's a cunt, but he's telling the truth.

Jonny knew about me. He got in his car and drove it straight into a ravine, coming to see me.

And this fucker is going to print the story for all the world to see.

And there's nothing I can do about it.

Unless …

For a big man, I can move fast.

I lunge forward and swipe his cell off the table before he even gets a chance to move. I drop it on the floor and stamp my boot on it, crushing it. The crack of glass beneath my foot is satisfying as fuck.

"You'll pay me for that."

It's my turn to laugh. I grab some more bills out of my wallet and throw them in his face. "This should cover it."

The money flutters to the floor. He makes no attempt to get it.

I watch as he puts his hand in his pants pocket and pulls out a small recording device. Holding it up, he curls his fingers around it. And my brief, momentary sense of relief is gone.

"I always have a backup." The smug cunt shrugs. "I enjoyed our chat today, Storm. I'll send the finished article over before it's published."

Motherfucker.

I grind my teeth so hard that I'm surprised I don't crack a tooth.

He walks around the table, coming toward me.

He's got some balls; I'll give him that.

I clench my hands at my sides.

Jasper stops directly in front of me.

I stare down at him. He's sweating. He's not as calm as he likes to make out he is.

"Jonny died in his prime," he says in a low voice. "Twenty-five years old, and he was already a musical genius. Just think what the music industry would've been like if he'd lived. He died because of *you*. You deprived the world of what could have been. And what were we left with? A once-great band that could never recover the loss of its main talent. And your shitty attempt at playing dress-up with your lame excuse for a band. You're a fucking insult to Jonny's memory."

My hand snaps out before I can stop it, and I grab the fucker by the throat, lifting him up onto his toes. I lean my face into his. "You sure have a hard-on for Jonny."

I hear someone shout something, but I ignore them.

My sole focus is on this prick.

"Nothing to say now, fucker? Or have you run out of shit to talk?"

I flex my fingers around his neck, applying more pressure.

"Nah," he croaks out, face red. "I just knew how to push your buttons. So predictable. Smile for the cameras, Storm."

Stone sinks into my stomach.

I don't even bother to look up.

A fucking setup. How could I have been so stupid?

This was about money.

Of course it was about money.

He wound me up to get me to react, and I played right into his hands.

I push him away from me, not even enjoying the satisfaction of hearing him hit the floor.

I push past the people who have gathered around to watch the show.

And I'm well aware of how many fucking phones are held up, recording this, even still now.

"My lawyer will be in touch!" Jasper calls after me as I weave my way through the restaurant. "Oh, and I wasn't lying about Jonny and why he was in his car that night! Just ask Jake!"

I slam out of the restaurant and get straight in my car.

I don't even bother putting on my seat belt before I'm pulling out into traffic, cutting cars up to get in the lane I need to be in.

I ignore the sounds of car horns blaring.

Ignore everything.

The thoughts swirling around my brain.

The crushing pain in my chest.

Because I'm focused on one thing only.

And that's the direction I'm heading in.

Straight to TMS Records.

5

STORM

I'm on autopilot when I pull up outside the building that houses TMS Records.

A place I love.

I wonder if I'll love it the same after this.

I leave my car in a no-parking zone outside the entrance.

I don't plan on staying here long. And if I get a ticket, so what?

Exiting my car, I lock it and stride up to the door. I push my way into the building. I barely even feel the cool of the AC hitting me. I'm running off pure anger.

I walk past security, barely acknowledging them, and go straight to the reception desk.

"Storm, hey." Patty, one of the receptionists, smiles at me, and then her brow furrows when she sees my expression. I must look like thunder. "You okay?"

Patty's worked here forever. She's part of the TMS family.

Wonder if Jake's lied to her too.

Not in the mood to answer, I just ask, "Is Jake here?" I can hear how stony my voice is.

If he isn't, I'll go wherever he is. I'm not sitting on this.

I want answers.

Patty gives me a concerned look and reaches for her desk phone. "He's here. Not sure where though. Let me call up to his office and check."

I wait a moment, my muscles locked up tight, rage swirling around my brain, while she speaks on the phone.

She puts the receiver back in the cradle. "He's in studio four."

I'm moving, heading for the stairs to take me up to the first floor, where Jake is.

I take the steps two at a time.

I turn left, ignoring everyone I pass, focused on my destination.

I stop outside the door. I can see Jake through the glass window on the door.

He's in the booth.

Tom and Denny are here too, sitting at the mixing desk with Noel, one of the producers.

Now that I'm here, I'm frozen, unable to go in.

I stare at the three of them through the glass.

I thought they were my family.

I trusted them.

They've been lying to me for years.

The betrayal cuts deep.

As if sensing I'm here, Jake's eyes flicker up to mine. Whatever he sees on my face has him stopping singing.

He speaks. Saying something to Tom and Denny through the mike because they both turn around to look at me.

The hurt and humiliation of what happened in the restaurant flares back up, and I shove the door open. So forcefully that it bounces off the drywall.

"Storm?"

That's Denny. He sounds worried. He should be.

"Take ten, Noel," Tom says.

Noel looks at Tom and then me. Nods and leaves. I move a fraction to let him pass me in the doorway.

Jake walks into the room, and then it's just the four of us.

One big, happy fucking family.

"What's going on?" Jake looks from me to Tom to Den and back to me again. "What's happened?"

I note the concern in his voice, and I don't care.

My heart is pounding. My fists clenched at my sides.

My anger is palpable.

"Storm?" Tom sounds annoyed now.

That pisses me off further.

"I know," I grind out.

"What?" Denny sounds confused. So much so that it'd be funny if it wasn't so fucking bad.

"Jonny. I know."

And that's all I have to say.

Like the dirty bomb that was dropped on me less than thirty minutes ago, I drop it right back on them.

It ricochets around the room, an explosion of silence.

And if there was any doubt in my mind that it wasn't true, I know for sure now that it is.

"Who told you?"

That's Jake. I've never heard him speak so quietly before.

My eyes laser onto him. "Does it matter?" I snap.

"It wasn't—" Jake takes a step toward me.

"Don't"—I point a finger at him—"fucking come near me."

He stops. He looks contrite. Guilty.

I hate him in this moment.

And Tom.

And Denny.

I hate all of them.

Mostly, I hate myself for being so fucking stupid.

"We should have told you," Tom speaks quietly, a voice I've never heard him use before. "You shouldn't have heard it from anyone else. That's on us. We fucked up."

I laugh. With zero humor. "How very fucking gracious of you."

"Storm …" Den says low and with warning. He always did have that parental tone down pat.

I slice my eyes to him. "Fuck you. I'm not a kid anymore. So, don't talk to me like one."

"Storm, just listen …"

My eyes whip to Jake. "Why the fuck should I? I was supposed to be able to trust you. You were supposed to be my family—"

"We are your family," Tom cuts me off, sounding pissed.

And that's like a hot poker to my rage.

"Like hell you are!" I roar. "Families don't fucking lie to each other! Keep important secrets from each other, like how Jonny knew I existed! That he was coming for me that night!" Grief catches in my throat. And I get annoyed that I'm fucking moments away from breaking down.

I suck in a harsh breath.

"Families don't keep important shit from each other, so you don't get to call yourselves that anymore."

"Storm, it wasn't … you were just a kid … when I found out the truth, your mom had just died, and I didn't want—"

"Fine," I cut Jake off. "You didn't want to tell me while I was going through shit. I get that. What about all the years after?"

The silence is deafening.

Jake's eyes sweep the ground before coming back to mine. He sighs, dragging a hand through his black hair. "There … was just never a right time."

I laugh a hollow sound. "Never a right time? Funny that. Because I was with you every fucking day! All of you! And not once did one of you think to say, *Oh, Storm, just so you know, the guy who knocked your mom up—you know, the guy you thought didn't know you existed—well, actually, he did! And he died, coming to see you!*" I'm yelling now, and I don't care.

"We fucked up. Okay?" Tom says quietly.

I round on him. "No! It's not fucking okay! And to hear it from a fucking journalist …" My hands go to my hips, and I look at the floor for a moment, gulping in some air.

I feel like my head's going to explode. I just can't believe this. Any of it.

They were like dads to me.

Jake actually adopted me, for fuck's sake.

I was supposed to be able to count on them. I thought I could trust them. Over anyone else in this shitty fucking world, I thought they had my back.

What a joke.

Slowly, I lift my head. "Would any of you have ever told me the truth?"

The silence in the room and the guilt in their eyes answer my question.

A laugh of disappointment escapes me. Lifting my hands, I say, "I'm done." I walk out of the studio.

They chase me out into the hall. Which is surprisingly empty. I'm guessing everyone heard us arguing. But then I wasn't exactly being quiet.

And at this point, it's the least of my fucking concerns.

"Storm, wait!" Jake calls after me.

A second later, his hand lands on my shoulder. I shove his hand off, rounding on him.

"Don't fucking touch me," I grind out.

He lifts his hands up in surrender. "Okay," he says, but he doesn't back off either.

He stands there right in front of me, staring me in the face.

"I screwed up. This is on me. Marie told me the day of your mom's funeral. She told me." He bangs a hand to his chest. "No one else."

"Jake, we all knew. This wasn't just you …" Denny steps forward, moving closer to him.

Jake lifts his hand, stopping him. "They only knew because I told them. It was me who said we shouldn't tell you. I also asked them not to. This is on me. Not them."

I know what he's doing—trying to take full blame. But it won't wash with me.

They were all Jonny's friends. All three of them.

They all knew.

They're all culpable.

"Who else knows?" I ask in a lowered voice.

"Lyla. Smith. Stuart," Tom is the first to say, naming his wife, the guitarist who took Jonny's place in the band after he died, and Jake's assistant.

"Simone," Denny adds, naming his wife.

And the betrayal just keeps cutting deeper.

"So, basically, everyone but me," I bite.

I love all of those people. And they all knew.

I stare at Jake. "Does Tru know?" my voice whispers down the hallway.

I already know the answer to this question. He wouldn't keep this from her. He doesn't keep anything from her.

But a stupid part of me is hoping Tru doesn't know. Because I don't want to have to be mad at her too. She matters as much as these three standing before me. She adopted me. Loved me. Held me when I cried after losing my mom.

Jake stares at me for what feels like forever. Then, he nods once.

Pain lances across my chest.

"But don't blame Tru," he's quick to say. "Like I said before, this is on me. She wanted to tell you. I wouldn't let her."

I stare at Jake.

The pain and anger and hurt are coursing through me. I can't feel anything but that.

I shut it all down, numbing myself to it. No longer allowing myself to feel anything.

When you've been hurt over the years, you get used to protecting yourself.

"I don't blame her. Or the others." My voice is arctic.

My eyes move over Tom and Denny and then rest on Jake.

"I blame the three of you. You were Jonny's family. You were my family." I let out a cold laugh. "And as of right now, we're done." I let my eyes flash over them all again, so they know that I'm serious. That I mean this. That I blame them all equally. "As far as I'm concerned, the three of you are as dead to me as Jonny is."

I don't miss the way they flinch.

And I don't fucking care either.

I turn on my heel and stride down the hall, getting the fuck out of there, ignoring the sound of them all calling my name.

6

STORM

I jog out of the building, shoving past some people coming in, ignoring their grunts of annoyance.

I don't care about anything but getting as far away from here as possible.

Anger is like my life force at the moment. It's what's keeping me going.

I'm at my car in seconds. Spotting a ticket on my windshield, I grab it and toss it onto the passenger seat as I get in my car.

I start my car and shove it into drive, and I take off with a screech of tires.

As I glance back in my rearview, I see Jake, Tom, and Denny come bursting out of the doors I just exited.

The sight of them enrages me further.

I raise my hand and lift my middle finger to them even though there's no way they'll see.

The pissed off, humiliated child in me feels marginally better for a moment.

A minute later, my cell starts vibrating in my pocket and ringing through the car system.

My eyes flash to the car's screen display.

Jake.

"Fuck off." I grit my teeth, my hands gripping the steering wheel. I press my foot down on the gas, propelling my car forward faster.

The ringing stops.

It starts up again.

Tom this time.

"FUCK OFF!" I yell at the display screen.

Punching the Ignore button, I cut off the call and switch off the system, leaving me in complete silence.

A text buzzes in a few seconds later.

I pull my cell out of my pocket, turn it off without looking at it, and toss it on the passenger seat alongside my parking ticket.

I come up to a red light, forcing me to stop.

Impatience has me rapping my fingers against the wheel. I just want to keep driving. I *need* to keep driving. Keep moving.

The light changes, and I'm pedal to the metal. But before I know it, I'm stopping at another set of traffic lights.

For fuck's sake.

My leg starts to jig restlessly.

He died because of me.

Jonny Creed died because of me.

He got in the car that night because he was coming to see me.

I scrub my hand over my face.

Sure, my rational mind tells me it's not my fault. But rationality means fuck all right now.

I'm feeling so far from rational; I might as well be on another planet.

One of the greatest guitarists who ever lived died because of me. And I can't even live up to his legacy.

It's almost fucking laughable.

My chest starts to tighten.

My breaths coming in short.

This used to happen a lot after Mom died.

What did Tru used to say to me?

"Nice and slow, Storm. Deep breaths. Slow everything down."

Tru.

Jake.

An ache lances across my chest.

I inhale a deep breath and slowly let it out. And repeat.

A horn beeping behind me shakes me out of my angst.

I lift my foot off the brake and let the car shoot forward.

I need to get out of the city. I need time to clear my mind. I just want to drive.

Dragging my hand through my hair, I catch sight of a sign for the highway. Cutting across lanes to the sounds of more blaring horns—and honestly not giving a shit right now—I take the turn to take me onto the highway.

It's the only place I can drive with no interruptions. I just want to put as much distance between them and me as humanly possible.

Me being in LA right now is not the best idea.

I take the exit ramp. Before I know it, I'm on the I-40, heading west, and I finally—*finally*—feel like I can relax.

Well, not relax.

I'm still mad as fuck.

But it's the best I'm going to get with my current frame of mind.

I maneuver my car over the lanes into the high-speed lane, and then I put my foot down, opening her up.

I switch the screen back on, needing to fill the silence in the car and cover the noise in my head.

Remembering I can't listen to the music on my phone through the Bluetooth because I turned my cell off, I opt for the radio. I search through the channels.

I need music to suit my mood.

The search stops on a station, and one of TMS's early songs blares out the speakers.

Seriously?

My eyes go skyward.

Are you fucking joking right now?

I glare at the stereo like it's personally fucked me over.

I hit the search button again. And when I say hit, I mean, punch.

The Killers' "Mr. Brightside" comes on, midway through the song.

Fucking love that song. But not in the mood right now.

I need loud guitars. And bass. And drums. I need something to feed my black soul.

Search stops on a heavy metal station, and the starting sounds of AC/DC's Thunderstruck" pour out of the speakers.

"Fucking finally," I mutter to myself.

Using the controls on my steering wheel, I turn the volume up to max.

Bass pounds inside my car, humming over my skin like electricity and settling inside of me like a drug.

A feeling close to peace settles over my barely hidden rage.

Only music can calm me in this way.

Driving fast and listening to loud music might be a fucked up way to relax when, internally, I feel like I could pummel someone to death, but it works for me.

But I know the moment I stop moving, it's going to hurt.

And I don't want to hurt.

"Thunderstruck" ends, and the haunting, humming sounds of Metallica's "Enter Sandman" fills my car.

I fish out a cigarette from my pack. Put it between my lips and spark it up. I lower the window down and let the speed of my car, the low hum of the engine, and the thumping music take me over.

7

STORM

I rub at my eyes and cast a glance at the clock on my dash.

Jesus. I've been driving for almost four hours.

Last time I checked the time, I'd been driving for just under an hour, and I wasn't ready to stop.

Clearly, I had a lot of driving left in me. I must've completely zoned out.

Lost in my head, on total autopilot.

I wouldn't say I've calmed down, but I'm not as mad as I was.

I just feel … like shit.

And I'm fucking tired of thinking about it.

I spot a sign for a gas station. The gas light on the dash has been on for a while, so I'd better fill my girl up. I could do with some fuel myself, and I need to take a piss.

And also figure out where the fuck I am.

I reckon I'm out of LA by now. I was heading east on the I-40, so I'm either in Nevada or Arizona. And I've done the Vegas route enough times to know, this place isn't Sin City.

I take the off-ramp and follow the signs to the gas station.

Yep, I'm in Arizona. The big-ass sign over there says, *Welcome to Lake Havasu City.*

I pull in the service station and stop at the pump. It's self-service.

I turn off the engine and glance over at my cell.

I wonder how many missed calls and texts I have.

They're probably worried about me. I know them.

Well, they should have thought about that before they decided to lie to me for the last eleven years.

Anger quickly coats any guilt I was feeling.

I grab my sunglasses from the glove compartment and slide them on. Using the little button on the inside of the door, I pop open the gas cap.

Buy an expensive car, you get some lazy-ass gadgets with it.

I climb out of my car. Yawning, I stretch. *Man, that feels good.* Pushing my glasses up my forehead, I rub my eyes again and then let the sunglasses drop back into place.

I grab the only gas nozzle on this pump and stick it in the gas cap. It's a tight fit. I have to give it a good shove to get it in.

Basically like when I'm fucking a woman with my big dick.

Child that I am, I chuckle to myself.

I fill her up and tug the nozzle back out, hanging it back up.

On another yawn, I go inside the gas station. Firstly, I use the restroom, and then I get a to-go coffee from the machine. Wandering around, I pick up a bag of Flamin' Hot Cheetos, M&M's—peanut, of course—and Twizzlers.

I go to the cashier and pay for my fuel and food, and then I head back to my car.

I unlock the doors as I approach. Using one arm, setting the coffee and all my shit against my chest, I open the door and climb inside.

"Ah fuck!"

I spilled the damn coffee all down my front.

"Fuck! Shit! That burns!"

Grabbing the coffee, I set it in the cupholder and toss all the other shit on the passenger side.

I jump back out of my car. Pulling my sunglasses off, I toss them in the car. I drag my coffee-soaked T-shirt off over my head.

Sighing, I dry my chest off with my T-shirt.

I drag my hands through my hair, looking up to see an older woman—looks to be in her late fifties, maybe early sixties—filling up her car at the next pump over, and she's blatantly ogling me.

Well, my chest.

She catches my eye and winks at me.

I suppress a laugh, my lips curling into a grin.

She's a total GILF. Not that I'm into fucking grannies. But she's a looker for her age, for sure.

I go over to the trunk of my car and pop it open. Get my leather jacket out and toss my wet shirt in. I pull on my jacket, not wanting to drive around shirtless.

I'm back in my car and driving out of there.

I'm not even five minutes out of the gas station, chewing on a Twizzler—*goddamn, I love these things*—and trying to figure out how to get back on the highway and maybe find a hotel for the night, when my car starts making this sputtering noise. Then, it starts to chug. Really fucking loudly. It sounds like a tank.

"What the hell, girl?"

I glance at my dash. There're no warning lights. Nothing telling me what's wrong with her.

A glance in my rearview, and that's when I see the black smoke pouring out the back of my car.

My heart sinks.

"What the actual fuck!"

Pulling my car to the roadside, I shut the engine off and jump out.

Jesus, it fucking stinks.

I go to the rear of my car and look down at the exhaust. There are still small trails of black smoke coming out.

Just great. This is just fucking great.

I pop the hood and have a look at the engine. Not that I know jack shit about cars, but nothing seems out of the ordinary. I mean, it's not on fire or anything.

Leaving the hood up, I try turning the engine back on.

Same again. Black smoke pouring out of the exhaust.

I walk back to the hood, staring down at the mechanics of my car.

An almost two-hundred-thousand-dollar car that I've had not even six months, and this happens.

Grumbling to myself, cursing Jake, Tom, Denny, and that fucking journalist Jasper—this is their fault; I wouldn't be out here if it wasn't for them—I drop the hood. Then, I reach back in my car and turn off the ignition.

I grab my cell and fire it to life.

I need to call AAA.

Do I even have AAA?

My cell starts to go crazy in my hand with incoming messages.

Growling with irritation, I ignore them all.

I pull up Google, search for AAA's number, and put a call into them.

Okay, so it turns out, I don't have AAA. And the woman on the phone wasn't exactly helpful.

For fuck's sake.

What do I do now?

I glance around like the answer is going to come walking over to me.

It doesn't.

Well, I ain't calling anyone for help.

I mean, I could call Raze, but I'm four hours out, and I'm not standing around here for that long.

Think, Slater. Think. I tap my cell against my head.

A garage. I need a garage.

I look around again, but nothing nearby looks like a garage.

I could go back to the gas station. Or …

Google one, ya dumb fuck.

I open up another Google search and type in *garages in my area.* God bless the internet and its location tracking shit.

Only one garage pops up. It's a mile away, according to Google. And it's open. Thank Christ for that.

I need something to go my way right now because, so far, my day has gone to complete and utter shit.

I press my thumb down on the number for the garage, select Call, and then put my cell to my ear as it starts to ring.

8

Stevie

I've got my hand down one of the guest bathroom toilets when Simple Minds' "Don't You (Forget About Me)" blares out of my cell, letting me know someone is calling.

Why do you have your hand down the toilet? you ask.

Because the last guest who stayed, who left this morning, decided it would be a good idea to flush baby wipes down the toilet.

It wasn't.

Firstly, gross.

And hello, pollution.

So, now, I have a blocked toilet.

And I'm the one who has to unblock it.

The downside of running a B&B.

A rubber glove on my hand and said hand in the toilet, I try to get all these frigging wipes out that have clogged up the toilet.

I glance over at my cell sitting on the bath edge, where I left it, and it tells me it's Beck, my annoying older brother.

Well, Beck can just wait. I'm busy right now. I'll call him back when I'm done unclogging this toilet.

Running a B&B is an easy job, said no one ever.

I love this place. I grew up here. It's the only home I've ever known. All my best memories are in this house.

I just don't love the shitty jobs. Pun intended.

I leave my cell ringing, so I can sing along with Jim Kerr.

I'm not the best singer. Actually, I'm the worst. Tone-deaf, as my best friend, Penny, tells me.

But this song is from one of the best movies ever, *The Breakfast Club*, so it would be sacrilegious not to sing along. And the house is empty of guests at the moment, so it's not like I'm scarring anyone's eardrums.

And the eighties were the best decade for films and music. Not that I was around to see them. I'm only twenty-four, but I grew up with a dad who loves the music and movies from that era, so Beck and I were raised on it. It's not that I don't like modern music. I just have zero interest in it.

Jim Kerr stops singing, cutting off my singing. But then, immediately, it starts up again.

I love this song, but sweet Jesus, Beck!

My hand still in the toilet, I reach over with my other hand and grab my phone off the bath edge, swiping the screen with my thumb, accepting the call.

"What?" I answer.

"Hello to you too, baby sister."

Twelve months older than me, but you'd think it was twelve years with the way he goes on.

"Beck, I've currently got my hand down the toilet, so can you get to the point?"

"I need a favor."

And there it is. Honestly, I love my brother, but I could drop-kick him at times. He always needs a favor.

I tuck the phone between my ear and shoulder and pull out a wipe I managed to dislodge, dropping it in the bucket. beside the toilet. "What's the favor?"

"I need you to go do a tow for me."

"Ah, why can't you or Dad go?" I sigh. I hate taking the pickup truck out.

"Because we're right in the middle of fitting that new engine on Peterson's truck."

I sigh again. "Fine, but you owe me."

It's his turn to sigh. "What?"

"You can finish off unblocking this toilet for me when you get home."

He makes a sound of disgust. Works with dirty cars all day long, but the thought of putting his hand down a toilet grosses him out.

I roll my eyes.

"Why can't Gran do it?" he asks.

I let out a laugh. "Did you seriously just ask why our sixty-six-year-old grandmother can't unblock the toilet?"

"Um … no …" he edges the words out, his voice lowering. "Stevie … is Gran there, listening right now?"

I laugh again.

It's not uncommon for Gran to listen in on a phone conversation.

What does she always say?

"If you want to know something, you ask. If they don't tell you, then you spy."

The woman is all-seeing, all-knowing. You want the local gossip, Gran is your woman.

Although even Gran had no clue that my fiancé, my boyfriend since high school, was cheating on me.

Nope. Not going there right now.

"Nah, she's not here." I chuckle. "It's Saturday. She went to get her hair done."

"Thank fuck," he breathes.

Gran would have totally kicked his ass if she'd heard him ask why she couldn't unblock the toilet.

Aside from being sixty-six, Gran is incredibly glamorous. She's a total knockout. I can only pray I look as good as she does at her age. Not that I'll ever reach her level of glamour.

Gran's hair, clothes, nails, and makeup are always on point. She would never be seen dead with her hand down a toilet.

She always says to me, "Stevie darling, you never know when it's your time to go, and I ain't turning up at the pearly gates of heaven in anything less than my best."

Me, I'll probably rock up at the gates of heaven, wearing bleach-stained ripped jeans and the white tank I've had since high school.

And yes, that's what I'm wearing right now.

I just don't see the point in getting dressed up when I'm working.

And it's not like I don't ever dress up or wear makeup. I get glammed up when I go out with Penny. But when I'm working at the B&B, which is pretty much all the time, I don't see the point.

I do most of the day-to-day work around here—cleaning, making beds, washing, vacuuming—and Gran does the food. We only serve breakfast and evening dinner, so she has her days to herself.

I've always helped out here, but I started working here full-time when I got out of high school. I could have gone to college—I think Dad would have preferred if I did—but honestly, I didn't want to leave home.

I love where I live. And I wanted to give something back to Gran by helping her here. It was the least I could do.

When our mom ran out on Beck and me when I was still a baby, leaving Dad to raise us alone, Gran stepped in. Moved us all into the B&B and helped Dad raise us.

Gran is the shit. She's the strongest woman I know.

Gran and Grandpa moved here when Dad was small. Grandpa had gotten a sizeable inheritance when his dad passed. Using the money, they bought this house, and Gran turned it into a B&B, keeping the back part of the building as a home for them, which is where Gran, Dad, Beck, and I all still live now.

With the rest of his inheritance, Grandpa bought a building five minutes from here and turned it into a garage. I think he wanted a business that he could one day hand over to his son.

Gran and Grandpa were the epitome of high school sweethearts. Together from the first year of high school. Married as soon as they graduated.

Grandpa passed before Beck and I were born, so we never knew him. Only the stories Dad and Gran have told us about him over the years, and he sounds like he was the best. I figure it's where Dad got his parenting skills because he's literally the coolest dad ever.

In all the time I've known Gran, she's never had another man in her life. Grandpa was her one and only.

I thought that was gonna be me and—

Nope, not thinking the jerk's name today.

"So, you doing this tow or not?" Beck grumbles, dragging my attention back to him.

"Are you unblocking this toilet for me?" I volley back.

"Fine." He sighs. "I'll sort it when I get back later."

I grin. I don't like doing pickups, but they're a hell of a lot better than unblocking a toilet.

"Where's the tow?"

"Main Street."

"Uh, where on Main Street?"

"No clue. All I got was Main Street. I was busy when I took the call."

I give a mental eye roll. "Well, what's wrong with the car?" I ask him, wanting to know what I'm gonna be rolling up to.

"Considering I haven't seen it, I'm gonna have to say, no fucking clue."

"You're hilarious," I say in a droll voice. "I *meant*, what did they say was wrong with it?"

"The dude said there was black smoke coming out of the exhaust, and it was making a clanging sound. It could be the air filter."

"Is this dude someone I know?"

"Didn't recognize the voice. So, I'd say no."

"And did you get a name?"

"Nope."

"Christ, Beck. You didn't get a name?"

"I. Was. Busy." He punctuates. "Still am."

"You're such a pain in the ass," I tell him. "You're sending me out to tow a total stranger, and you didn't even get his details. He could be a serial killer."

"Who gets his victims by ringing a garage," he says drily.

"Could be his MO."

"Drama queen."

"Buttmunch."

"If he is a killer, you'll probably talk him to death before he gets a chance to kill you. So, I wouldn't worry."

I flip the bird even though he can't see. "If I get murdered on the side of the road, I'm gonna haunt you for the rest of your life."

"So, no different to every day of my life for the past twenty-four years."

"Asswipe."

He laughs. "Go do the fucking tow, cry baby. Dad's waiting on me."

"Make sure you unblock—"

The fucker hangs up on me before I get a chance to finish my sentence.

"Ugh!" I grumble, getting to my feet.

Then, I realize that he never told me what make the car I'm going to collect is.

Christ almighty, Beck.

All I have is a guy with a car somewhere on Main Street.

As Gran would say, he's about as useful as a fork in a sugar bowl.

I yank my rubber glove off, leaving it in the sink, and I wash my hands.

Scooping up my phone, I jog downstairs.

After I slip on my canvas flats, I write a quick note, telling Gran where I've gone, and leave it on the reception desk for her to see when she gets home.

Leaving the B&B, I don't lock the front door because I know Gran didn't take her keys with her. The town we live in is a safe place. It has a low crime rate. It's the kind of place where you can leave your doors unlocked.

I walk the ten minutes to Dad's garage. The tow truck is in the forecourt where it always sits.

I pop my head inside the door and grab the keys off the hook on the wall by the door.

"It's me, just getting the tow truck keys," I call out.

Dad's legs are poking out from underneath Mr. Peterson's truck. Beck's under the hood.

"Okay, baby girl." Dad's voice echoes out from under the truck. "Be careful."

"Will do."

"You got your cell with you?"

"Yep."

"Pepper spray's in the glove compartment. Put it in your pocket."

At least my dad cares about safety. Can't say the same for my brother. Which reminds me …

"Beck, any clue on what the car I'm towing looks like?"

"Uh …"

"Christ's sake, Beck!"

"I'm kidding!" He laughs. "Dude said it's a Maserati. Said you'll spot it, no problem."

That stops me. Maserati. "Bit fancy for round here, isn't it?"

Not that we live in a shithole. But not many people, if any, around here would drive a car like that.

"Probably just passing through," Beck says.

"Yeah," I muse. "Okay, back soon."

"Pepper spray!" Dad hollers.

"Okay, Dad." I chuckle.

I head to the tow truck. Climb up inside and turn the engine on, letting it rumble to life.

While the engine's warming up, I get the pepper spray out, shove it in my pocket, and rifle through the CDs in there.

I pull out Fleetwood Mac's *Rumours* album and pop the CD in the stereo. I skip to track two, and "Dreams" starts to play.

Dad's a big Fleetwood Mac and Stevie Nicks fan. It's where my name came from. Dad chose my name. Apparently, Mom picked Beck's name—not that she stuck around long enough to tell us that.

Beck's just lucky Dad didn't get to name him, or he could have ended up being called Mick … or even better, Lindsey.

Man, I would've loved if he'd been called Lindsey. I would have tortured him for his entire existence with a name like that.

Chuckling to myself, I pull the truck off the garage forecourt and drive in the direction of Main Street to go collect the mystery man waiting to be towed.

Driving down Main Street, I keep my eyes peeled for a Maserati.

I spot it halfway down by the small stretch of industrial space.

He wasn't kidding when he told Beck I'd easily spot it. It's not a car you could miss. I'm not a gearhead, but I've been around enough cars in my life to know that's a shit-hot car. A Maserati GranTurismo.

A couple of hundred thousand dollars' worth of a car.

Matte black with a gold "go-faster" stripe, as my dad calls them, running over the trunk, roof, and hood of the car.

I spot a tall dude leaning up against the hood, faced away from me.

Flicking on my blinker, I pull the tow truck up in front of the Maserati.

Turning off the engine, I open the door, jump out of the truck, and head over to the guy.

Lifting his ass off the hood, he straightens up, and—

Well.

Oh.

Wow.

He's tall. A lot taller than me. I come in at an average five feet four. This guy must be six-two, six-three at least. About the same height as Dad and Beck.

And he's hot.

Super hot.

Like if his hotness were a temperature right now, we'd be in the upper kelvins.

Dude is sun hot.

I have honestly never in all my life seen a guy who looks like him before.

Of course I've seen hot guys before.

But this guy, he's on a whole other level, all his own.

Dirty-blond hair that looks like someone spent the whole night running their hands through it. Leather jacket. No shirt—yep, no frigging shirt. Who even does that? Hot kelvin-temperature guys do, apparently. His bare chest has some serious ink on it, and just beneath the ink are abs that I didn't even know existed outside of Marvel movies.

And following down from those superhero abs is a happy trail disappearing into those fitted black jeans.

My eyes briefly drift skyward.

Seriously, God, you couldn't have at least given me a heads-up that I was coming to tow a car that belongs to Thor and Captain Marvel's love child.

I never feel conscious of my appearance. I'm happy with the way I look. But in this moment, I find myself feeling inadequate in my ripped jeans, tank top, and sneakers. Face clean of makeup and my hair in a messy bun.

Not that I'm out to attract any man. I was done with men when I found my ex with his dick in another woman.

And this dude here has got heartbreak written all over him in capital letters in bold, italicized ink. Probably put there by the trail of broken hearts he's left in his wake.

Not that I'd even register on leather-jacket hottie's radar.

Cleaned-up Stevie? Maybe.

Hobo Stevie? Not a chance.

Basically, if hotness had a smell, his would be Chanel No. 5.

Mine would be store-bought body spray. The dollar-store kind.

I was not expecting a guy like this. I figured a suit when Beck said Maserati. This guy looks like he just stepped out for a break from shooting a movie, in which his hotness smoldered his shirt right off his back.

It's then I register that he's got a cigarette in his hand. He's holding it between his thumb and index finger. Which would be cool if smoking wasn't responsible for half a million deaths in the US alone each year. A good forty thousand of them from passive smoking.

The thought makes me lean back a touch.

I watch him put it between his lips and inhale. The smoke drifts out between his lips, curling up into the air, polluting my oxygen.

Even though he looks seriously sexy doing it, old-movie-star sexy, it's still gross. Cigarettes are bad for people. Terrible for marine life.

He might want to kill himself slowly.

But our marine life didn't ask to die.

Hotness point deducted for a lack of care about the environment.

He drops the cigarette butt to the floor as I approach, putting it out with his boot. Christ, his feet are big.

Big feet, big … shoes.

Funny, Stevie.

I stop before him and wait for him to pick the butt off the ground. He doesn't.

Environmental issues aside, littering is my bugbear.

"That's littering." I point at the butt on the floor by his feet.

His eyes follow my finger down and then come back up to my face, staring straight into mine.

I feel a jolt in my stomach. A tightening in my chest. His eyes are intense. Bright blue. Stunning.

Christ almighty.

It takes me a good few seconds to regulate my breathing.

He's watching me like he's waiting for something.

Not sure what.

But I do know that I'm waiting for him to pick up that damn cigarette butt.

I watch confusion flicker over his face, drawing his brows in and tightening his lips.

His head tips to the side. Then, his expression relaxes, and something close to amusement fills his gaze.

Does he think this is funny? Because littering is no joke.

My hands find my hips. Those striking eyes follow the movement down. "Did you know that cigarette butts are the single biggest polluter of the ocean?"

He moistens his lips. It's insanely distracting. "I thought it was plastic," he speaks before bringing his shocking gaze back to my face.

And his voice is … yum.

Deep. Husky.

Like molten molasses. The kind of voice that whispers dirty words into your ear in the dark of night while he fucks you good and proper.

Sweet Lawd.

My nipples have hardened, and there's definitely no cool breeze at the moment that I can blame it on.

I cross my arms over my chest and clear my throat. "Nope. Cigarette butts. I read an article on it last year. They're the forgotten plastic pollution. Butts or filters are the most littered item on the planet. We focus on straws, plastic bags, disposable coffee cups, but cigarette butts are just as bad. Well, worse. Did you know people like you burn through five trillion cigarettes a year, and two-thirds end up littering our world? And also"—*I'm on a roll, and I cannot stop. Why can't I stop?*—"did you know that it's been scientifically proven that cigarette butts provide no health benefit at all? They're just a marketing tool. They make it easier for a person to smoke."

He's staring at me like I just landed in from another planet.

To be fair, I did go off on him about the damaging effects of cigarette butts on the environment.

Why do I know such random shit?

I really need to stop watching nature shows and reading the news. I'm such a dork.

"I did not know that." His tone is dry.

And now, I feel like a total dick. "If you don't believe me, Google it." I shrug like I didn't just lecture the hell out of him.

"No. I'm sure you know what you're talking about."

Yep, that was definitely mocking I detected in his voice.

I don't know why, but it instantly annoys me. Like a cattle prod to the spine.

Maybe it's because he's hotter than any man legally should be.

But it just sets me off again.

"You really should stop smoking. Not only is it bad for your health and those around you, but it's also bad for marine life."

Please stop talking.

Another pause.

His brow lifts. I hate it when people do that. Only because I can't. There's seriously no single movement up there. It's both or nothing at all. And if both go up, I either look surprised or confused. Neither is a good look on me.

"I'll take it into consideration," he says slowly.

"And you should also pick that butt up and dispose of it responsibly."

Now, he's looking at me like I've lost my damn mind.

I think I might have. Horny brain cells killed my good ones.

I don't break eye contact with him even though I really want to.

His eyes really are something else. Intimidating and exciting, all at the same time.

I watch his lips lift at the corner. He's got nice lips. Kissable lips. They're surrounded by a good week's worth of stubble. Defined cupid's bow, lower lip slightly fuller than the upper. I could imagine sinking my teeth into that bottom lip.

And clearly, I need to get laid.

For a moment, I don't think he'll pick the butt up.

But then he does. He bends that ripped chest forward and leans down and picks it up.

I feel a flash of heat between my legs at the sight of him down there.

Yep. Definitely need some sex. Or alone time with my vibrator.

Straightening up, Hottie holds the butt between his thumb and finger. "So, what's the responsible way to dispose of it?" he asks, that damn eyebrow quirked up again.

And shit.

I don't remember that part of the article. I can remember statistics and figures. But not how to deal with the actual problem.

This is me all over.

And now, I have to come up with something at least believable; otherwise, I'm going to look like a dick.

"Well, um …" I unfold my arms and then don't know what to do with them, so I place my hands back on my hips. "I'm … not one hundred percent sure, but I'd say putting it in the trash rather than on the ground would be a good way to start."

There, that'll do. It was a good solution.

He glances around. "There are no trash cans around here."

Oh. For fuck's sake.

"Give it to me." I stick my hand out, palm up.

Hottie glances down at my hand. Then, he smiles. For real. Teeth and all.

And of course, he has a set of straight, well-proportioned, perfectly white teeth.

My teeth are straight, but I had to wear braces for years to get them like this. He probably came out of the womb with those teeth. Which would be weird.

I'm weird.

I just asked this guy to put his used cigarette butt in my hand. What was I thinking? Then again, I did have the same hand down a toilet only half an hour ago.

How was I raised by such a classy, stylish woman as Gran?

"You sure?" he asks, still smiling, a look of *is this chick for real* on his face.

I want to say no, but I can't exactly back out now after the fuss I made.

No matter how gross this is.

And it is gross. So fucking gross.

I wiggle my fingers at him, hurrying him to get this over and done with.

He places the butt in the center of my palm.

Ew.

I'm gonna vom.

I have nicotine, God knows what other chemicals, and a complete stranger's saliva on my hand.

A hot stranger.

But still …

Ewww!

And now, what the heck am I going to do with it?

I turn around and march back to the truck, knowing full well there is something in there I can put it in. My brother is a slob.

I yank open the driver's door, and yep, in the pocket of the door is an empty bag of chips.

Gross, Beck.

I deposit the butt in the empty chip bag and fold it over to contain the smell, tucking it back in the pocket. I'll get rid of it in the trash when I get back to the garage.

I grab the small bottle of sanitizer we keep in the truck and lather my hands and arms with it.

Marginally better.

When I turn back to Hottie, he's still standing there, looking at me with amusement and something else that I can't quite place. If I didn't know better, I'd say interest.

I walk back over to him. "Right, let's get this show on the road. Or car on the truck …" I trail off, wanting to slap myself in the face.

Why can't I be cool, just once?

"You need me to do anything?" Hottie asks.

"Nah, I've got it. But thanks." I've done this a hundred times. I'm a pro.

I go back to the truck, fire her up, and set to getting his car on the truck, so I can get it back to the garage while Hottie watches on.

I'm totally aware of his eyes on me the whole time.

It's disconcerting to say the least.

"You can wait in the truck if you want," I offer.

He gives me an easy smile. "I'm good here."

You might be good. I'm not.

I force myself to pay attention to the task at hand before I lose focus and possibly a finger.

10

Stevie

When Hottie's supercar is secured up on the bed of the truck, we both climb in the cab.

I pull my seat belt on and start the engine. While I wait for him to secure his seat belt, I switch over to the radio, putting on my favorite eighties station.

The B-52s' "Love Shack" comes on, loud and proud.

I do a little jig in my seat. This is my and Penny's party anthem. I don't care who you are. You can't *not* dance to this song. It's awesome.

I hear a low chuckle from beside me.

"You like this song?" Hottie asks.

Negative connotation I'm getting there.

Oh no.

I slide my eyes to him. "Um, you don't?"

A slow grin and a shake of his head. "Not my kind of music."

Oh dear. Another hot point gone. Shame 'cause he's so pretty.

"Dude. It's The B-52s! Come on! 'Love Shack'? Really?"

Amusement fills his eyes. "Nope. Definitely not my kind of music."

"Fun music isn't your kind of music? Shame. Your life must be so dull."

He chuckles. "It's gimmicky crap."

"Oh no." I wrinkle my nose at him. "You're one of *those*."

He frowns, a line drawing between his brows. "One of what?"

"A music snob. You're all hoity-toity about songs. Like those people who sip wine and then spit it out to experience the flavor or some shit when, really, they should be swallowing."

He chokes out a laugh, but I keep going.

"Music snobs think they have a far more refined taste in music than us mere mortals. Never would they be heard rocking out to 'Wake Me Up Before You Go-Go.' "

"To be fair, it is a shit song."

My mouth pops into an O. "Sacrilege! How dare you bad-mouth Wham! Get out of my truck!" I joke, pointing at the door beside him.

"Come on, it's absolute shit. Total novelty song. Just like this one is." He gestures to the radio, which is still playing The B-52s.

"Music snob." I shake my head in mock disgust. "What is this fun music I'm hearing?" I put on my best snooty voice, pressing my hand to my chest in dramatic flair. "Music should be depressing. About love gone wrong. This is not music. Don't even get me started on those happy lyrics!" I give a sardonic eye roll.

He's laughing properly now. A full-on belly laugh.

Weirdly, I feel like I've won something in this moment. I smile wider than I have in ages.

"A song should make sense," he says, his laughter slowing. " 'Love Shack' does not make sense."

"Hey! It makes total sense."

"Really?" His damn brow goes up again, and he angles his body my way. "What's it about then?"

"Um … a love shack. A place where people go to get together. And dance." I give a cheesy grin.

He chuckles, shaking his head.

"And the tin roof is rusted."

His laugh intensifies.

"It's about sex."

That shuts him up.

And I can't believe I just said that. If Pen could hear me now, she'd be high-fiving the hell out of me. I'm talking about sex with a guy I've known barely fifteen minutes.

Me, I'm about to stroke out.

I know my chest has gone red. It's always my tell when I'm embarrassed. Or turned on.

I risk a look at him. He's watching me with those intense eyes of his. Then, that deep voice of his says, "That's exactly what it's about."

I gulp. Then, I force my shoulder back and fake confidence. "See, I told you it had meaning," I toss the words at him. Flick on the indicator, check the road, and pull out onto the street.

Whitney Houston follows The B-52s, and I give an excited little squeal, my embarrassment quickly fading. I'm not one to dwell. Especially when a diamond like this is playing. I flipping love this song!

I hear a groan come from beside me.

I slide my eyes to him. "Aw, come on, don't tell me you don't like Whitney?"

A curl of his upper lip and a shrug. "She was okay, I guess."

Okay. He guesses?

Sweet Lawd.

Come on, who doesn't "Wanna Dance with Somebody (Who Loves Me)"?

Apparently, this dude.

The rate he's dropping hot points, he'll have none left. Which is probably a good thing for me.

"Do you want me to change the station or turn it off?" I reach for the dial.

"No. It's okay."

I catch his eyes. He gives me a soft smile. I feel this odd flutter in my stomach. Probably indigestion.

It hits me then that I still haven't gotten his name.

I gave Beck shit for not getting his name, and I still haven't gotten it either.

I take a right turn off Main Street, heading in the direction of Dad's garage. "So, I probably should have introduced myself before now." *Before I lectured you about the effects of smoking on marine life and your terrible music choices in life.* I laugh. It sounds as awkward as I am. "I'm Stevie Cavalli. My dad owns the garage that I'm taking you to."

He doesn't say anything. I take my eyes off the road for a moment to look at him.

He's looking at me. But not at me. Like he's somewhere else in his mind.

"Um … usually, at this point, you would tell me your name. I do kind of need it for the paperwork back at the garage." Well, my dad does.

"Oh. Yeah. It's … Nick."

Then, I register his name together with mine, and I laugh.

"What's funny?" He sounds actually defensive. It surprises me.

I flicker a look at him. His brow is furrowed. Jaw tight.

Huh.

"Stevie." I point at myself. "Nick." I use the same finger to point at him.

He's staring at me in that *you're an alien that's just landed* way.

"Stevie Nicks. Fleetwood Mac. You've heard of her, right?"

If he hasn't, he'll lose another hotness point.

I flick my eyes his way again.

The tension in his face has gone. His lips have actually quirked into a smile.

Mood swing much?

"Yeah, I've heard of her."

"Thank God. I was gonna have to push you out of my truck if you hadn't."

He laughs at that.

"So, do you have a surname, Nick? Or are you one of those special people who only has one name? Like Cher. Or Madonna."

He chuckles again. "Slater."

"Nick Slater," I repeat. "Well, it's cool to meet you, Nick Slater."

I reach my hand over. He takes it and shakes it.

And I totally do not get any strange tingles in my hand at touching him.

Okay, I do.

What's that all about?

I pull back and wrap my hand around the steering wheel.

"So, did you lose your shirt?" *Or did someone rip it off your hot body?* I thumb at his bare chest. The one I've been desperately trying—and failing—not to stare at since I laid eyes on him. "Or do you just have something against shirts as a whole?"

There's a pause. I quickly look at him again. He's watching me again. This time, there's a smile in his eyes.

"I spilled coffee on it."

"Ah, well, that's gonna do it. I'd probably take my shirt off if I spilled coffee on it as well. To be fair, I'd also probably get charged with indecent exposure. You guys have it way too easy."

I hear a chuckle from his side of the truck. I honestly don't know if he's laughing at me or with me.

Probably at me.

Can't blame him. I do talk shit ninety-nine percent of the time.

We lull into silence.

I'm usually great with silences, but something about this guy has me sitting on all kinds of edges. I feel nervous. And not in the scared way.

More in the exhilarated, *I want to rip his clothes off* way.

Which is not good.

And causes verbal diarrhea to continue to pour from my mouth.

"Okay, so I know you don't like The B-52s or Whitney. Do you like Pat Benatar?"

Pat is queen. I love her like no other.

His remaining hotness points exist on his answer.

"In the biblical sense?"

I snort out a laugh. "She was definitely a total babe in her day." I nod. "But I did mean, musically."

"Why do I feel like my entire existence depends on this answer?"

"It does." *Well, your hotness points anyway.* Not that I'm sharing that fact with him.

I smirk, earning me a chuckle from him.

"Well … I don't hate her music, if that helps."

I look at him, and he's smiling. Showing me a hint of those white teeth again.

"But if we're going back to the eighties, I'm more of a Metallica, Iron Maiden kind of guy."

I look at his leather jacket and tattoos. Makes sense.

"Fair enough. I can accept that. They had some good songs."

He splutters out a choked sound. "I'm sorry, what? I think you're mistaken. Pretty sure you meant, they had a shit-ton of *great* songs. Or do I need to start naming them?"

I laugh despite myself. "Calm down, heavy metal boy. I like Guns N' Roses, if that helps."

A grunt. "I suppose." A pause then. "So, you really like the eighties cheese music then?"

"If by cheese, you mean, musical awesomeness, then yes."

There's another pause, but this one feels tangible. I can almost feel it in the air. I'm just not sure why.

"And what about recent music?" His voice sounds quieter than just before, and there's a difference to his tone.

"What about it?"

"Do you like it?"

When I glance at him, he's looking straight ahead, out of the window.

I shrug and answer, "I'm not really into modern music. Weird, I know, because I probably should be. But my dad loves the eighties, and I grew up listening to it. I only listen to the newer stuff when I'm in my best friend, Penny's, car because she has law over the stereo."

"What kind of music is your friend into?"

I slide him a look. "Uh … mostly Bieber."

He laughs. There's almost a hint of relief in it, which is strange.

"Dude, she's obsessed. It's his abs. They've got her mind all befuddled."

Like yours have mine.

"He does have good abs, to be fair." He shrugs.

Not as good as yours. "Yep," I agree with a nod. "So, I know you like heavy metal music from the eighties. What about movies?"

He thinks about this a moment. "*Terminator* is my favorite film."

"What? No way! Come on! *Terminator 2* was far superior!"

"Didn't that come out in the nineties?"

Huh. "Possibly. Maybe. Okay. Early nineties," I admit, and he laughs. "But it was way better. The only movie where the sequel trumped the first movie."

"Disagree. The first movie was better. I can't believe you're cheating on the eighties with the nineties."

My face heats. "Am not!" I exclaim. "It was just better! Linda Hamilton in T-1 was all meek and wimpy. Completely useless. T-2—total badass!"

"True." He nods. "But that was just character evolution. She saw a lot of shit after T-1. She had no choice but to be badass after that."

"No way!" I toss my hand in the air. "She should have been badass Sarah Connor from the word *go*. You bet your ass, if a terminator pulls a gun out on me, I ain't running, crying to the cops or Kyle Reese to save me—even though Kyle was hot as fire. Nope. I'm getting a grenade launcher and blowing that fucker's head off."

He laughs. A deep sound that rumbles out of his chest.

It makes my chest fill with this strange sense of warmth.

An awareness settles over my skin. Like electricity and fire. Calm and peace. It's … different.

I've known this guy not even half an hour. Yet we're talking like we've been friends for years.

"And to finish off—"

"There's more?"

I slide him a look. He's grinning, amused.

"There's always more when discussing the finer points of *Terminator 2*."

"I'm all ears."

"First off, T-2 had way better one-liners." I recite a couple of the well-known lines from the movie, doing my best Arnie impression, which earns me a laugh. "And secondly, T-2 has the better ending. The best ending of any movie ever."

"Okay." He nods. "I'll give you that."

"Right? When Arnie sacrifices himself for John"—I slap a hand to my chest—"gets me every time."

"You totally cried, didn't you?"

I frown in his direction. "Eh … no. Maybe. Okay … a little."

He chuckles.

"Come on!" I toss a hand into the air. "It was sad as all hell! When Arnie lowers himself into that vat of liquid steel … you can't tell me you didn't tear up a little at that." Even Beck did.

"Nope."

I give him a look of disappointment. "Cold, dude. Stone-cold." I shake my head, teasing.

He laughs again.

I'm finding I enjoy making him laugh.

Dad always says, "If you can make others smile, then why wouldn't you?"

"So, Stevie …" His voice sounds good, saying my name. Like Nutella sliding onto bread. "Anybody ever tell you that you're—"

"Weird?" I cut him off, beating him to the punch.

It's not the first time someone's said that to me. Won't be the last.

My ex used to tell me all the time that I was weird. He never meant it as a compliment.

I accepted my weirdness years ago. I wear my weirdo ways with pride.

"I was going to say, *different*."

Oh.

Well, I guess that's a kinder version of weird. But still weird.

"In high school, I was voted Most Likely to Do Weird Things in Public."

Beck got voted Most Likely to Always Be the Heartbreaker in his year. My brother's a pain in the ass. But he's a good-looking pain, and he knows it.

Penny got voted Most Likely to Go to a Justin Bieber Concert.

And they weren't wrong. And she made me go too.

As concerts go, it wasn't the worst. But Bieber's no Rick Astley.

Nick chuckles a low, sexy sound. "I was voted Most Likely to Have Sex in Public."

I nearly swallow my tongue. I have nothing. For once, literally nothing.

I cough.

Then, I clear my throat.

"Well … if you're gonna go around shirtless all the time, people are gonna get that impression," I finally manage to say with a shrug.

He grins.

It's panty-melting.

"I don't go shirtless all the time. Only when I know I'm about to meet a cute girl."

I slide a glance at him. Then, I roll my eyes. "Oh, very smooth."

"I do try."

We lull into a silence.

Then, he speaks, "If I'd have voted for you in high school, I would have voted you Most Intriguing."

Intriguing?

My eyes zipline to his. He's watching me with that thing in his eyes I saw earlier. It looks like interest. Yep, it's definitely interest. I momentarily freeze in his blue gaze. Well, I freeze as long as one can when driving a truck.

I force my eyes back to the road. Ignoring the thrum in my chest. I lick my dry lips. "Intriguing? Didn't you say a minute ago that I was weird?"

"No." He sounds affronted. "I said you were different."

A pause.

Then …

"Different … and intriguing."

11

Stevie

"D*ifferent … and intriguing.*"

What the heck is that supposed to mean?

I guess it's a compliment, right?

That he finds me intriguing.

Well, he's definitely smooth. I'll give him that.

But I'm not going to go gaga over it.

I'm not interested in him.

Sure, you're not.

Okay, he's hot. The hottest of the hot. But he's got *player* written all over him. And I'm not a one-night kind of girl.

I'm a relationship girl.

My ex was the only guy I've ever been with. We'd been together since high school. Hell, I thought I was going to marry the guy. And look how that turned out.

I'm a shitty judge of character when it comes to men.

And I'm really not interested in having my heart broken again, thank you very much.

Once was enough for me.

I'm as single as a Pringle. This girl definitely does not need to mingle.

"So, how long have you been towing cars for?" Nick asks, breaking my thoughts.

"Oh, this isn't my job. I'm just doing a favor for my dad and brother. It's their garage. Well, it's my dad's. Beck works for him, but it'll be his one day when Dad retires, I guess."

"Beck's your brother?"

"Yep. That's who you spoke to on the phone when you called for the tow. You got any siblings?" I ask him.

There's a brief pause. Then, he says, "Three."

"Three? That's a lot of people to share a bathroom with." It was bad enough, having to share a bathroom with Beck, growing up. Still is, considering he won't move his ass out of the B&B. I can't imagine having another two of Beck to deal with.

He laughs softly. "I had my own bathroom."

Of course he did. I knew from the car that he was loaded.

"Well, from thirteen I did."

"Why at thirteen?" I glance at him again, enough to see him shift in his seat. He suddenly looks uncomfortable.

"I … was, um … I was adopted when I was thirteen. My family … they have … a big house."

Oh. Wow.

Well, what do I say to that?

"At least you got your own bathroom, right?" I shrug, going for light humor, smiling at him.

He briefly meets my eyes. They don't look as happy as they did before. "Right."

After that, the mood in the car seems to lower. Nick doesn't say anything more. Even my innate urge to want to fill the silence has nothing. So, I'm a little relieved when I pull onto the forecourt of the garage. But, weirdly, I'm also a little disappointed that my time with Nick is over.

His hotness aside, I enjoyed bantering with him. Dude is fun to talk to.

There's no sign of Beck or Dad, so I press the horn to let them know we're here. Then, I climb out of the truck. Nick follows suit.

Beck comes sauntering out of the door that leads to the office.

"Where's Dad?" I ask him.

"On the phone with a supplier. He'll be out in a minute."

"Beck, this is Nick Slater." I thumb in Nick's direction, who's standing just to my right.

"Black smoke coming out of the exhaust?" Beck says to him, getting straight to the point, moving toward the back of the pickup where Nick's car is.

I follow them too.

"Yeah, that's right. She was fine. Then, she just started chugging, and black smoke started pouring out of the exhaust," Nick tells Beck.

Beck's got his head under the back end of the car, inspecting the exhaust.

"Any problems like this before?" Beck asks him.

"Nope. I've only had her six months."

Why do men always refer to cars as *her* and *she*? I've grown up around cars all my life, and I still don't get it.

Dad says it's because cars carry life. And women carry life.

But not all women carry life. Some women don't have children, so his point is moot in my opinion.

Beck runs his index finger around the inside of the exhaust. His finger comes out black. He puts it to his nose and sniffs his finger.

"Diesel," Beck says.

"What?" is Nick's reply.

"Diesel." Beck wipes his finger on a rag he got out of his coverall pocket. "She's a gas car, right?"

There's a pause.

Then, Nick glances at his car and then back to Beck. "Yeah." His word comes out slowly.

"You filled her up just before she started acting up, right?"

I can see the color start to drain from Nick's face. Even I know where this is going. He put the wrong fuel in his car.

Uh-oh.

"Uh-huh." Nick nods.

"Sorry to say this, man. But you put diesel in her. I can smell it."

"What?" Another glance to his car. "No. I've filled her up a hundred times. I've never …" He drifts off, eyes going to his car again. "Fucking hell." He sighs. "I'd been driving for a while. I was tired." He drags his hands through his hair. "I can't believe I did that."

"Happens to the best of us, man. Don't sweat it," Beck says kindly.

"Is she fucked?" Nick asks.

"I can't say without looking at her. But I'd be surprised if she was. You pulled over as soon as the smoke started kicking out, right?"

"Yeah."

"I can't promise anything. But worst-case scenario, she'll need a new fuel system. That's worst case. Just let me take a look at her, and I can tell you better."

"How long will it take?"

"You ain't going anywhere today," Beck tells him. "After that, hard to say 'til I've looked at her."

Nick sighs, dragging a hand through his hair again.

"I'll check her over and give you an estimate."

Nick waves a hand. "Whatever it costs is fine. Just fix her."

Beck pauses and glances at me. I shrug my shoulders.

"Well, let me price her up, and you can make your mind up from there."

Nick stares at Beck. "She needs fixing. I ain't taking her anywhere else." He glances at me before looking back to Nick. "You seem like trustworthy people. So, I'm happy with whatever you say."

"Uh …" Beck looks a little stunned. Customers are never that easy. Usually, they argue about the price or even try to haggle it down. "Okay. If you're sure."

"I'm sure."

Hate to say it, but Nick's confidence is super sexy. It's just ramped back up the points that he lost earlier.

Imagine if he's that confident and take-charge in the bedroom. It'd definitely be an experience; that's for sure.

I start to feel a little knock-kneed.

"Well, at least let us hook you up with a car to use in the meantime. We have a loaner here, but you can use it free of charge. Just put back in the fuel you use—but not diesel." Beck laughs. So do I. Nick not so much.

"It's no Maserati, but it'll get you where you need to be," I say.

Nick looks at me. "Not necessary. I ain't going anywhere."

Oh.

Are those flutters in my stomach I feel or indigestion?

Indigestion. Definitely.

The air suddenly feels thick. I want to look away from him, but I can't seem to will my eyes to move.

"How's it looking?" Dad appears, his voice breaking the moment.

Thank God.

I glance at Beck, and he's grinning at me.

I stick my tongue out at him.

Grinning, Beck turns his head to Dad. "Wrong fuel input."

Dad puts his hand out to Nick, introducing himself, "Bryan Cavalli."

Nick takes his hand and shakes it. "Nick Slater."

Dad turns to the car. "Diesel?" Dad asks Beck.

"Yep. It didn't run through the system too long, from what Nick said. So, the damage shouldn't be extensive. Won't know until I get under her and have a look. I've offered Nick the loaner until we have a better idea of how long it'll take to fix her."

"Like I said, not necessary," Nick says.

I refuse to look at Nick again, so I keep my eyes fixed on my dad.

"You local?" Dad asks. "Stevie can give you a ride to where you need to go."

"I'm not local," Nick answers. "I'm from LA."

That brings my eyes to him. He's not looking at me now.

He's from LA. What's he doing here in Lake Havasu?

"You here on vacation?" Dad asks, saying the next thought in my head.

We get a lot of tourists through here. A lot of boaters from March to September. Students come here in droves for spring break.

Spring break was when my ex's dick decided to take a detour into another vagina.

Not that he's ever admitted it, but I figure it wasn't his first detour into unknown territory.

Just the one that I caught him doing.

"Something like that," Nick answers vaguely.

"So, you got somewhere to stay then?" Dad probes, and I know where this is going. "'Cause no saying how long it'll take to fix her." Dad pats a hand to the rear bumper of Nick's car. "Not until we've looked her over. We've got a couple of jobs to finish today. We'll try to look at her tonight before we close, but if not, definitely first thing in the morning."

Nick's eyes come to me again. "No problem."

Why does he keep looking at me?

"And to answer your question," Nick continues, "no, I don't have a place to stay, so if you could point me in the direction of a hotel, I'd really appreciate it."

Dad beams. "Ah, great." He claps his hands together. "Well, Stevie is your woman if you're looking for a bed for the night."

There are a few things that happen in this moment.

I get whiplash from moving my head so quickly to look at Dad.

Nick makes a choking sound.

And Beck bursts out laughing.

"Dad!" I exclaim. I rub a hand to the back of my now-sore neck.

I can feel my chest going hot. It's going to be all red and blotchy; I just know it. It always happens when I'm embarrassed.

Dad looks back at me, confused. Then, dawning happens as he hears the words back in his head. His mouth drops open. His eyes dart from me to Nick and back to me, finally resting on Nick.

It'd be comical if it wasn't so embarrassing.

"God! No!" he says to Nick. "I didn't mean that how it sounded. Christ, no! Stevie runs the B&B with my mother. I meant, you can stay there. Not in Stevie's bed!"

I don't think I've ever heard my dad speak so quickly. Or seen his face go quite so red.

Beck's still laughing. He's almost doubled over from it.

I'm dying a silent, quiet death.

I daren't even look at Nick.

"Jesus, Dad," I groan.

Dad ignores me and just keeps on talking, "We all live there. At the B&B. Our part of the house is at the back. So, it won't just be Stevie there. We'll all be there."

I'm just waiting for the ground to open up and swallow me whole.

"He gets it, Dad." Beck laughs, patting Dad on the back. "A bed at the B&B. Not actually Stevie's bed."

"Uh …" Nick says, sounding as uncomfortable as I feel. "Sure. B&B. That sounds great."

Beck is still laughing as he walks toward the front of the truck. He's such a tool.

"I swear, that might be the funniest thing that Dad has ever said." Beck chuckles. "I can't wait to tell Gran."

"You shut your face!" I call after Beck.

But he just laughs again.

Asswipe.

"Well, I'm gonna go … help Beck … unload your car off the truck." Dad steps away. "Stevie, you'll get Nick sorted with a room of his *own*, right?"

I hold back a groan and the urge to run far from here. "Sure."

I force myself to turn to Nick. He's so damn tall. I have to crane my neck to look up at him.

There's a glimmer of amusement in his eyes.

"So, you run a B&B?" he says.

"Yep." I let the *P* pop. "Me and my gran." I take a small step toward him and lower my voice. "Uh … look, Nick … don't feel like you have to stay at the B&B, if you don't want to." I give his car a glance before looking back at him. "There are some nice hotels in town if you want to stay at one of those. No five stars, but decent places. The Nautical overlooks the bay, and it has a pool. I can give them a call for you. I'm sure they'll have availability."

It's only early February, so the season hasn't begun yet. It's still fairly quiet around here. That's why the B&B is quiet. This is our downtime before the crowds of tourists start to come.

And it's not that our B&B isn't the shiz. 'Cause it is. It's gorgeous. I love it. But the closest we have to a swimming pool is when I turn on the sprinkler to water the little grass we have.

Nick is clearly loaded, and rich people like nice hotels with swimming pools. Not B&Bs with a sprinkler.

Nick's brow furrows. He looks at his car and then back to me. The frown deepens. His arms fold over his chest. "Your B&B will do just fine. I'm actually looking forward to seeing it."

Oh. Right. Okay then.

I guess my time with Nick isn't coming to an end just yet.

And I'm honestly not sure how I feel about that.

12

STORM

Stevie thinks I'm some jacked-up rich boy who has to have expensive things.

Little does she know, that car is my only real indulgence. An indulgence which I've screwed up by putting the wrong fuel in her.

What kind of idiot puts the wrong fuel in his car? This kind of fucking idiot—that's who.

It bothers me that Stevie has that impression of me. Money doesn't matter to me. Don't get me wrong. It's nice to have. It makes some things in life easy. But I've lived without it. I could live without it again.

Why do I care so much about what she thinks?

Because I like her.

I can honestly say I have never met a girl like Stevie before.

So confident in who she is. She literally gives zero fucks.

She likes what she likes. And she likes who she is.

If only everyone could be like that, the world would be a much better place.

There is nothing fake about Stevie. She's as real as it gets.

Some women think that men want the fantasy when all we really want is reality.

An honest-to-God real woman.

And Stevie is reality. She's quirky. She's fun. She's a breath of fresh fucking air.

And the fact that she's hot as fuck is an absolute bonus.

I could not only stare at her all day, but I could spend my day talking to her too.

I've never experienced that really with anyone before. And I ain't sad that I'm going to have to hang around here while my baby gets fixed because it means I get to spend more time around Stevie. And feel this sense of freedom I've felt since the moment I met her, realizing that she has no clue who I am.

When she got out of that truck and walked over to me, I braced myself for it. The recognition. The excited giggle. Asking for a selfie with me. Probably asking me to sign her tits. And then she would subsequently hit on me.

That's the way it always happens.

But when Stevie looked at me, there was no recognition. She definitely liked what she was looking at. I saw the flicker of interest in her eyes before she quickly squashed it. But the interest wasn't because I was Storm Slater.

It was because she genuinely liked the way I looked.

Can't blame the girl.

But in that moment of realization where she had no clue who I was, I felt this weight leave my shoulders.

I felt light.

And when she started giving me shit about the cigarette butt, I'd never had that much fun in ages.

How fucking pathetic is that?

A pretty girl giving me a hard time is fun.

But she wasn't making it easy for me.

When you live your life around easy girls, willing to give you anything, meeting one who doesn't is refreshing.

I just didn't want that to change. So, when she asked my name, I lied.

Well, it's not a total lie. My middle name is Nicholas.

When I was younger, around six or seven, a kid from school made fun of my name. Said it was stupid. So, I went home and told my mom I was changing my name to Nick. I made her call me it for a month solid.

Until I realized that kid from school was a little prick and I didn't actually care what he thought of my name.

The likelihood of Stevie even knowing who I am or even caring who I am seems small. The girl said herself she isn't interested in music outside of the eighties.

But I just didn't want to take that chance.

I just don't want the way she treats me to change.

People have a tendency to act differently around *celebrities*. If someone finds out that you're famous, they treat you differently. It's just a fact.

It's the disease of the modern human condition called celebrity.

When she mentioned having a brother, I did worry he might know who I was and call me out on it, but he didn't seem to know me either.

Clearly, he's not into our music.

And that suits me just fine.

They seem like good people. Normal people.

And her dad is just as funny as fuck. When he said that thing about Stevie's bed, I nearly swallowed my tongue.

It was like he'd read all the dirty thoughts in my mind that I'd been having about his daughter since I met her not even an hour before.

It feels weird that I've only known her an hour.

I feel like I've known her way longer.

"Do you need to get anything from your car before we go to the B&B?" Stevie asks me.

"No, I'm good." I've got my cell, wallet, smokes, and sunglasses in my jacket pockets. I'm good to go.

She gives me a curious look. "You don't have a bag with you?"

Why would I have a bag? I'm not a chick.

"Nope."

Her head tips to the side, exposing her neck. I have the sudden urge to lick the skin there. Heat flashes in my groin.

A smile tilts the corner of her lips. "I know you're not keen on wearing clothes." She gestures a hand to my chest. "But do you always travel without clothes?"

Shit, yeah. When her dad asked if I was on vacation. I said, "Something like that," basically giving the impression that I was. And when people go on vacation, they take clothes with them.

I stare at her, unsure of what to say.

I've said enough already. Telling her I was adopted. What the fuck was I thinking? I lied about my name, but I tell her private details about my life? Well, not that I have any privacy in my life. But if I don't want her to know who I am, I need to stop flapping my lips.

"It was an … unplanned trip." That's the best I can come up with.

Her smile goes wider. Her eyes beaming.

God, she's fucking pretty.

"They're usually the best kinds of trips. I loves me an impromptu trip. Well, unless I'm stuck in a car, listening to shitty music. Then, it's not so fun. So, your trip must have sucked big time. Sorry about that."

The smile becomes a grin, and I laugh.

"I'll have you know, my taste in music is fucking awesome."

"Sure it is, Mr. I Don't Like Fun Music. Well, we can't have you walking around naked, so you can borrow one of

Beck's shirts if you want until you get some clothes. Stop you from scaring the locals with your naked skin."

"Scaring?" I chuckle, falling into step with her as she starts to walk toward the way we came in, exiting the garage forecourt. I pull my sunglasses from my pocket and slip them on. It's not exceptionally sunny today, but they help conceal my face a little. Help stop me from being recognized.

"Uh-huh," she answers.

"You not used to nudity in these parts?"

"Nudity, yes. Abs, no. Well, except for my brother, but he doesn't count because gross." She shudders, and I laugh.

"So … abs, huh?"

"Oh, come on! You know you've got abs. Eight of them at my last count."

She counted my abs? Multiple times.

Nice.

I have to stop myself from flexing them.

"Our neighbor, ninety-year-old Mrs. Hindley, sees your abs, and she'll have a stroke. And you don't want to be responsible for the death of a sweet old lady, do you?"

Well, I'm already responsible for the death of my father. So, what's one more?

I realize I've gone quiet.

I force myself to speak, "Yeah, no. Sure. I'll borrow a shirt, if that's okay."

She's watching me. I can feel her stare. But I don't look. I don't want her to see the shit going on in my head that I know will show in my eyes.

"Of course. I'll grab one when we get to the B&B. It's not far. Just a five-minute walk."

We walk side by side in relative silence. Aside from the shit going on inside my head, it's actually a nice walk.

We pass a couple of people. One walking a dog, which Stevie stops to pet, and a jogger. They both greet Stevie by name.

She's clearly liked by people in this town.

And who wouldn't like her? She's awesome.

I get a couple of looks from people, but I think it's more because I'm a stranger. Well, that or because I'm currently shirtless, wearing only a leather jacket.

I have the urge to smoke. My fingers twitch around the pack in my pocket. But I don't want to piss her off.

Although pissing her off does sound quite entertaining.

"You mind if I smoke?" I ask.

"I don't mind. But the months of life you'll take off my lungs will. And the fish that your cigarette butt will kill does too. He minds a lot. But by all means, smoke."

I grin.

Is it weird that I get off on her chiding me?

I have issues. I know.

"How do you know it'd be a he?"

"Who?"

"The fish. It could be a she," I tease.

"Even worse then because she might be pregnant with fish babies, and you'd murder all those innocent babies too. How do you sleep at night?"

I glance down at her, and the mirth in her eyes is everything I need to see right now.

Well, apart from her naked body writhing beneath mine, that is.

"Usually naked," I tell her, wanting to shock and humor her.

And I do both.

Laughter bursts from her, but her chest goes red. Not that I've spent time staring at her chest. Who am I kidding? Of course I have. She has great tits. And while I was staring at her tits, I noticed her chest goes red when she's embarrassed.

I'm just wondering if it does the same when she orgasms.

"Just so you know," she says, cutting into my awesomely pervy thoughts of her, "there's no smoking in the B&B. If that's a problem—"

"It's not a problem," I cut her off. I look down at her, and she's staring up at me. "Honestly," I assure her.

We lull into silence, and I don't like it. I want to keep talking to her.

"So, you've lived here your whole life?" I ask.

"Yep. My whole twenty-four years have been spent here."

"You're twenty-four? So am I."

"No way. I thought you were older."

I laugh. "I don't know whether to take that as a compliment or not."

"Is it ever a compliment when someone says you look older than you are?" At my outraged look, she laughs. "I'm kidding! It's not because of your face. It's just because you're so damn big."

"I am big." I puff my chest out.

"And when someone drives a car like yours, to have that kind of money, I guess I just expect them to be older. Which is crazy really because a baby can be rich, born to the right parents."

"You know many rich babies?" I ask her, teasing.

She screws her nose up in thought, and it's fucking adorable. She's adorable.

And since when did I start thinking women were adorable?

Since her, clearly.

"Nope. Only rich, shirtless dudes who have terrible taste in music."

"You don't even know what music I like." I laugh. "So, how do you know it's terrible?"

"Not true. I know you like heavy metal from the eighties."

"True." I nod.

"So, what else do you like?"

You. The thought surprises me.

"I like … Justin Bieber."

I grin at her, and she snorts out a laugh.

Again, fucking adorable.

"But, seriously, I do like metal," I tell her as I try to think of other bands she might know. "Led Zeppelin, Black Sabbath, AC/DC—you've heard of them, right? They graced the eighties."

She gives me a look. "I've heard of them."

I think of more modern-ish bands. Well, ones past the decade that she loves. "Avenged Sevenfold, Slipknot, Five Finger Death Punch."

She's shaking her head.

"You really listen to nothing outside of the eighties?"

She gives me a look. "There's really a band called Five Finger Death Punch?"

I laugh. "Yep. Terrible name, great fucking music. I'll play them for you sometime."

"You want to listen to Madonna with me?"

"I don't actually mind Madonna."

"Really?" Her whole face lights up.

"Just FYI, you do know that Madonna has made a shit-ton of music outside of the eighties?"

"I'm aware," she says primly. "I just like her early stuff."

"I really liked her erotica phase."

"Course you did." She rolls her eyes, and I laugh.

"So, you admit that you do know some music outside of the eighties?"

"Never said I didn't. I just choose not to listen to it."

And if I ain't thankful for that because it means she has no clue who I really am.

"So, you're from LA?" she asks me a moment later.

Oh, yeah, I said that when we were back at the garage.

"Yeah." I could stop at that, but my lips keep moving. "I was born in Queens though. Moved to LA when I was thirteen."

"When you were adopted?" she asks, her voice a touch quieter.

I nod. And she doesn't ask any more details, and I'm glad for it.

Stevie seems to know when I'm done talking. It's a trait I appreciate. Especially when everyone is always up in my business, asking me questions about my life all the time.

"This is us," she says a few moments later.

I follow her up the steps toward a big split-level house with gray bricks and blue paneling. The upstairs has a balcony over the entryway to the house.

It reminds me of a house you'd see in one of those Hallmark movies. You know the type, where the big-city guy shows up to try to buy the house, so he can flatten it and build offices there and ends up falling in love with the hot female owner.

And no, I don't spend all my time watching Hallmark movies. But Tru watches them, and sometimes, it's hard not to get drawn in.

Those shitty movies are as addictive as crack.

Not that I'd ever admit that out loud.

I ignore the pang I feel in the center of my chest when I think about Tru.

I'm not going there right now. I'm not losing this good feeling I have from being around Stevie.

She lets us in the front door, closing it behind us.

"Gran," she calls out, walking toward the reception desk in the hallway. She picks up a piece of paper off the desk. "I left her this note before I went out. She's probably not home yet." She rounds the desk and drops the paper into a waste bin behind there.

I lean my hip against the desk.

"I'll just quickly check you in. Grab that shirt I promised you. And then I'll show you to your room. Any preference to which room? You have your pick. Our last guest left this morning, and no one else is due for a couple of days."

I shrug. "As long as there's running water and a comfortable bed, I'm happy."

She laughs. "Easy to please."

I rest on my elbows and lean closer. I get a hint of cherries coming off her skin. I smelled it when I was in the truck cab with her earlier. "Some of the time. But definitely not all the time." I suggestively lift my brow, flirting with her.

Her cheeks go pink, and she looks down at the check-in book. My eyes go to her chest. It's blushing too.

"I'll put you in Bayview," she says without looking at me. "It has the nicest view. Hence the name. Bayview. Obvs."

I've noticed she also rambles when she's nervous. It's cute as fuck.

"Sounds good to me." I straighten up off the desk, giving her space.

"Let me just go get that shirt for you. Give me five minutes." She disappears off down the hall, and I hear a door open and close.

I wait in the peace, just enjoying it. This place is nice. Homely.

Has the same feel to it as Tru and Jake's house.

Nope, not going there.

Stevie appears a few minutes later, a black T-shirt in hand.

"I hope this is okay. It was all I could find in Beck's closet that didn't have oil stains on it. Although it might, and I just can't see them."

I take the shirt from her. "It's great. Thanks."

"Let me just grab your room key." She's back behind the desk, crouching down behind it. She reappears a moment later with a key in hand. "I'll show you up to your room."

I follow her up wide oak stairs, totally staring at her ass. Curvy, grabbable, and absolutely fuckable.

We go up another flight of stairs and down a hallway to a door at the end. She puts the key in and unlocks the door, opening it and letting us in.

I follow her inside.

It's a nice room. Big, spacey, a lot of light. Huge window. You can see the water from here. There's a big wooden-framed king-size bed. Looks comfy as hell.

I stifle a yawn at the sight of it.

"Bathroom's attached," Stevie says, opening a door, revealing a small bathroom. "Shower, toilet, but no bath."

"Works for me. I'm not a bath kind of guy." I drop the shirt on the bed and walk over to the window, looking out.

"Same. I don't get why people want to lie around in their own filth." She pulls a disgusted face.

"How dirty are the people you know?" I chuckle.

"I live with two stinky mechanics. What do you think?"

"Good call."

"So, is the room okay for you? There are others if it's not."

I turn to face her, looking away from the view. "It's perfect." *You're perfect.*

She smiles shyly. Almost like she can read the thoughts in my mind.

"Okay, good. Well, I'll leave you to get settled."

"Before you go," I say, stopping her, not ready for her to go just yet, "would you be able to point me in the direction of a clothes store and a drugstore? I'm going to need some stuff for while I'm here."

"Oh, sure. I mean, I can do one better if you want. I can take you. There's a department store in town. Sells everything. It's a thirty-minute walk from here. Which isn't bad. But I can drive you, if you want? I need to pick up a few things from town myself."

"If you don't mind?"

She gives a soft shake of her head. "I don't mind at all. When do you want to go? The store closes at nine, so we can go whenever."

I could probably do with a shower and sleep right now, but the thought of spending more time with her is too appealing. "Is now okay?"

"Sure." She smiles.

"Cool. Just let me put this shirt on, and I'm good to go."

I take my jacket off, not even thinking about her being in the room with me.

Whether this is because I feel comfortable around her or I'm just used to getting naked around woman, I'm not sure.

But she's not so comfortable.

She lets out a little squeak, covers her eyes, and spins on the spot, turning away from me.

I let out a low laugh. "You're not shy, are you?"

"Of course not!" Her voice is pitched high, making me smile. "Just giving you privacy."

"You've already seen my bare chest."

"Only part of it. And not by choice!"

I laugh at her awkwardness as I pull the T-shirt over my head.

"I'm covered," I tell her as I pull the shirt down and reach for my jacket.

"Good. Okay then." She pulls her hands from her face but doesn't turn around. "Shall we go?"

She's out of the door before I get to answer.

Laughing to myself, I put my jacket on and follow her out.

Stevie locks the door and hands me the key without once looking at me.

I follow her down the stairs. Her back is ramrod straight.

She clearly felt uncomfortable. It makes me feel like a dick.

"I'm sorry if I made you feel uncomfortable just then."

"You didn't."

She still isn't looking at me.

I stop her with a hand on her arm. Aside from shaking her hand in the truck earlier, it's the only other time I've touched her. And I get the same exact feeling as I did that first time. Like my nerve endings are all coming alive, chasing their way down my arm, racing all over my body, bringing me to life.

Stevie glances down at my hand and then up at my face.

"I'm sorry," I say the words firmly, so she knows I mean them. "I'm just used to undressing around people. I didn't think."

"You're a stripper?" she jokes.

Just like that, the mood is lightened, and we're back to before.

"Wouldn't you like to know?" I grin, removing my hand from her arm.

"No way! You're a stripper! Just to be clear, it's a profession I wholeheartedly approve of."

"Hold on. You'll pay to see a stripper but blush when I get shirtless in front of you?"

Her chest goes red. "Well, yeah … but I know what I'm getting when I go to see a stripper. You just took me off guard. We were in a bedroom, alone. With a bed. And you were"—she gestures at me with her hand—"shirtless. And tattooed. And muscly."

Ah. So, I didn't upset her. I turned her on. And that freaked her out.

Interesting.

"You know strippers are usually shirtless, tattooed, and muscly, right?"

She looks up into my eyes. They look so wide and innocent. Makes me want to dirty her right up.

"Of course I know. But I wouldn't be alone in a room with a stripper, would I?"

Her voice is softer now.

Just a touch.

If I had any doubt in my mind that she's attracted to me, I don't anymore.

But she's definitely guy-shy for such a confident girl.

Makes me wonder why.

"I'm sure you must have guys trying to get shirtless around you all the time." My voice is lowered now.

And is it just me, or are we closer than we were a second ago?

Her throat moves on a swallow, and I have the sudden urge to follow the movement with my tongue, heading downward.

She shakes her head.

"I find that hard to believe." My voice sounds hoarse.

Her tongue darts out, wetting her lips.

I don't think she even realizes she did it.

She wants me to kiss her.

"Stevie? That you up there, honey?" a female voice calls from below, breaking whatever was just happening between us.

Well, I'm pretty sure something fan-fucking-tastic was about to happen between us. But that's over now.

Stevie moves so quick that I'm surprised she doesn't break something.

"Yeah, Gran. It's me. I'm coming down."

She hightails it down the stairs like her ass is on fire. I follow behind in relaxed amusement.

She totally would have let me kiss her then. She wanted me to kiss her.

Just a damn shame I didn't get the chance. But it's good to know I might get another.

She likes me.

I can't believe how fucking jacked up that makes me feel.

Even drugs haven't gotten me this high before.

I reach the bottom step to see Stevie talking to a familiar-looking woman. Older and glamorous in a pantsuit, pearls, perfectly styled blonde hair.

The woman looks at me, and recognition sparks in her eyes. "I know you." She points a polished fingernail at me. "Shirtless boy from the gas station." She clicks her finger against her thumb.

A grin takes over my face, and I point a finger back at her. "Winking lady who ogled me in the gas station."

She laughs. "Guilty as charged."

"You've already met?" Stevie asks, sounding bemused at our exchange.

"Not officially," the woman says, turning to Stevie. "I was filling up my car when this young man decided to do a striptease at the gas station. Of course, I had to watch the show. Would have been rude not to."

I have to stop myself from laughing at her word choice, considering, not a minute ago, Stevie thought I was a stripper.

"Oh, that's when you spilled coffee on yourself," Stevie says to me, connecting the dots. "Well, Nick Slater, coffee-spiller and shirt-remover, meet my gran, Stella Cavalli, bare-chest-ogler and serial-winker and the owner of this fine establishment."

Stevie's introduction makes me smile. She's so damn goofy. And I like it so damn much.

"Nice to officially meet you, Mrs. Cavalli," I say, reaching out to shake her hand.

"Call me Stella. I hear Mrs. Cavalli, and I think of my late-husband's mother. That woman was a dragon. God rest her soul."

I chuckle. Stella is quite the character, this one. It's clear where Stevie gets it from.

"Gran, Nick is going to be staying with us until his car is fixed. I put him in Bayview."

"My car broke down after I saw you at the garage," I explain.

"He put the wrong fuel in," Stevie helpfully tells her. "Beck asked me to go tow him."

"Ooh, rookie error." Stella laughs. "Well, your car is in good hands with my son and grandson. So, what are you both up to now?"

"I offered to take Nick to the store," Stevie explains to her. "He needs some essentials."

"Oh, will you get me some hairspray while you're there?" Stella asks her.

"Of course. The usual brand?"

"Yes."

"Let me get my purse."

She reaches for her bag, hanging on her arm.

"Don't worry, Gran. I got it," Stevie says, stopping her.

"You sure?"

"I'm sure."

"You're a good girl," Stella says to Stevie, tucking a stray lock of Stevie's blonde hair behind her ear.

I see in this moment how much Stevie looks like her grandmother.

Stevie might be messy bun, no makeup, tank top and jeans, and her grandmother is the complete opposite. But the similarity between the two is uncanny.

I really like Stevie's laid-back approach to how she dresses. She doesn't give a shit.

And she doesn't need to.

Because she's fuck hot without all the extras.

"You'll be back for dinner? Both of you?" Stella asks.

"Dinner is part of the room rate," Stevie explains to me. "So is breakfast. And Gran is one hell of a cook."

"Well, in that case, I'll definitely be here."

"Good." Stella smiles, clapping her hands together. "You both go have fun at the store, and I'll see you later."

I was totally going to let Nick kiss me.

Well, I think he wanted to kiss me. I mean, I'm dumb when it comes to men, but the signals he was firing off sure seemed like he wanted to.

I know this because I was firing off the same damn signals.

Hell, what am I even doing? I can't be getting tangled up with a guy like Nick.

He's dangerous with a capital D.

Is it ego-boosting that a guy like him might be interested in a girl like me? And when I say a girl like me, I mean, hobo-looking Stevie, who hasn't showered since having her arm down a blocked toilet.

Of course it is. It's a massive ego boost.

But I like my heart.

I'm quite attached to her.

It took me a long time to heal her after my ex cracked her down the middle.

That crack is healed, but once something has had a fracture, it will always be weaker.

And I know that a guy like Nick Slater wouldn't just re-break my heart.

He'd obliterate it.

I don't need to know a guy long to know what type of man he is.

And Nick is a good guy. A fun guy. A flirty guy.

But a keeper he isn't.

We've just gotten in the car and buckled up when Nick says to me, "So, I've met your dad, brother, and now your grandmother. When do I get to meet your mom?"

I pull the car off the drive before I speak, "Um … probably never. She skipped out on us when I was a baby."

"Shit." I catch his wince. "Sorry."

"Don't be," I tell him, meaning it. "The only person who should be sorry is my mother. And, honestly, I'd rather have no mom than a shitty mom. I have my dad, Beck, and Gran. I'm lucky 'cause they're the absolute shit. Although don't tell Beck that. His ego is big enough as it is."

I turn onto the street, my Bluetooth connecting to the stereo, and my music plays.

James Cagney's voice echoes through my car speakers. The opening to Madonna's "White Heat" is a scene from an old black-and-white movie, titled the same. I tap my fingers in time to the music. I know this song by heart. I've listened to it enough times. It literally gives me goose bumps. Totally underrated in my opinion.

When the words kick in, I'm right there with Madonna, singing along.

"Okay, I give in," Nick says, pulling my attention to him. "I know this is Madonna from her voice. But I can honestly say I've never heard this song before in my life."

My eyes zip to his. "And you say you have good taste in music. You should be ashamed, Slater. Ashamed," I tease.

His lips curve into a smile.

It's panty-melting hot.

I have the sudden urge to turn on the air-con.

"It's from the *True Blue* album," I tell him. "But it was never released as a single. Should've been in my opinion." I continue to sing along.

"It's okay …" he starts, and I give him a look of playful disappointment. "For a fucking awesome song."

"Better," I tell him, grinning.

"Actually, the more I hear … it's the best song I've ever heard."

"Okay, too much." I laugh, and so does he. "And I'd apologize for my terrible singing voice. But I honestly don't care enough to. When a good song comes on, you just gotta sing." I shrug.

"True. And you are right; you're an awful fucking singer."

I look at him and laugh. "I know, right? Totally robbed of the vocal gift I could've given to the world. What about you?"

"What about me, what?"

"Can you sing?"

He's staring at me. This hidden expression in his eyes that I can't figure out.

"Can I sing?" he repeats my question.

"That's what I asked." I turn on my blinker and take the upcoming turn.

"Well … I guess I can hold a tune," he finally answers.

"Okay, so come on then. Let me hear this tune-holding voice of yours." I gesture to him with my hand.

There's a pause and then, "Okay. But I'm gonna need a song I know the words to."

I pick my cell up out of the cupholder sitting between us and hand it to him. "The passcode is one, two, three, four."

He chokes out a laugh. "Your passcode is one, two, three, four? Seriously, Stevie, you do realize it wouldn't take a genius to crack that code?"

"I know." I sigh. "But when you've locked yourself out of five different phones, it's time to accept that you're shit at remembering passcodes and just go with the easiest one there is."

"Or you could just have no passcode."

"But then people would be able to break into my phone. Duh." I grin at him.

He's laughing at me, shaking his head. "But you just gave me it. Not worried I'm gonna steal your phone at all?"

I slide a look at him. "Dude, you drive a Maserati. You're not gonna steal my four-year-old iPhone. Unless you have kleptomania. Do you?"

"Nope. Definitely no kleptomania here. But I could send a really bad sex joke to everyone in your Contacts."

"Oh my God! Do it! It'll be the most interesting thing to happen to most of them in a long while. Although you might give my dad a coronary."

He's cracking up laughing now, and I'm smiling.

I really like making him laugh. I feel like I've won the damn lottery every time I do.

"You're nuts," he tells me.

"A good nuts though, right?"

He catches my eye. "The best kind of nuts."

There's a dirty joke right on the tip of my tongue, but I hold it back. I'm feeling flustered from the way he's looking at me right now. Like he wants to devour me whole.

And I'm ignoring it because I think I want him to.

Throwing a sex joke into the mix will just push me over the edge, and then I'll let him do whatever he wants to me.

I look back out the windshield.

What the hell is wrong with me?

I've known this guy literally a handful of hours, and I'm ready to roll over and toss my panties into the wind.

It's crazy.

And a lot scary.

And not something I'm wholly ready to address with myself right now.

I'm just happy to keep having fun and laugh with him.

Nick is scrolling through my phone's playlist. I use the quiet time to get my shit together.

The guitar intro to Guns N' Roses' "Paradise City" starts to strum out of my speakers.

"Yes! I love this song!" I start seat-dancing, singing along with the opening words, throwing a quick glance Nick's way before looking back to the road ahead.

I realize that I was on my own singing just then. "Hey! Come on, it's your turn to sing, big man. After this instrumental, I want to hear you."

Axl starts singing, and Nick laughs. "Shit. Maybe I didn't think this through enough. I forgot how damn fast Axl sings the fucking verses in this song."

"Come on!" I bang my palm on the steering wheel. "You got this. I wanna hear you sing!"

And sing he does.

And he's really fucking good.

Like surprisingly good.

He's singing at the top of his lungs, and I'm catcalling and cheering him on. I even join in on the chorus even though I'm killing the song.

But isn't that what music is about? Enjoying the hell out of it.

I realize in this moment that this time I've spent with Nick today is the most fun I've had with any man, who is not my dad or brother, in a really long time.

The song eventually comes to an end, and I slap my hand against my leg, clapping and whistling. "Fuck, dude! You're a great singer! Ever think about giving up stripping and becoming a singer?" I half-joke the last part. Only half-joking because I know he isn't a stripper, but damn, he really should consider taking up singing.

His lips are still smiling at me, but his eyes are telling me a different story. "I enjoyed that," he says like it's something he's admitting out loud.

I think that's his way of telling me that it's been a while since he's enjoyed anything.

Honestly, just never know what kind of shit is going on in people's lives, do you?

So, I tell him a truth of mine, echoing the words I was just thinking before. "Same. I was literally just thinking that it's been a long time since I've had fun with a man who isn't my dad or Beck." I cast a smile his way.

"Can I ask why?"

Opened myself up to that one, didn't I?

"You don't have to tell me," he adds. "I totally get it."

I sigh. "No, it's fine. It's just boring, to be honest. The old cliché story. Girl is with the same boy through the latter part of high school. They stay together while he goes to college, and she stays home and waits dutifully for him to return. Girl thinks her and boy will be together forever. Boy finishes college, comes home, and takes a job, working for his dad at his family-owned golf club. Boy asks girl to marry him right there on the grounds of the golf club. Girl is over the moon. A month later, girl finds boy dick deep in a college student who was hired to work there over the summer. He's screwing her, on his office desk, at the very place he asked the stupid girl to marry him."

"Shit, Stevie," Nick whispers.

"Don't feel bad for me." I give a wave of my hand, brushing my words away. "It's been over a year. I'm past it."

"I don't feel bad for you," he tells me. "I'm just trying to figure out what kind of fucking dipshit has a girl like you and then cheats on her. He must be fifty fucking shades of stupid."

My throat tightens with … *something*.

I swallow back my feelings. “He did me a favor really. Better I found out who he really was before I married the jerk.”

“Well, he did all the men in the world a favor, setting you back free into it, if you ask me.”

Even though hearing those words makes me feel amazing, my inner cynic—the one who appeared when my ex cheated on me, zapping my ability to trust my own judgment and the words of a man—has my natural jokey instinct rising to protect my fragile heart at all costs.

“Dude, that was terrible as far as lines go.” I grin.

He smiles wide, his lips lifting at the corner, showing those gorgeous teeth of his. “Okay. Wait, I can do better,” he says. “Give me a minute …” He puts fingers to his forehead, tapping them in thought.

I intermittently watch him between watching the road, thoroughly interested and amused at what he’s going to say. My heart only still mildly hammering against my rib cage from Nick’s previous words.

“Okay, I’ve got one.” He clicks his fingers, turning in his seat to face me. “You’re gonna love this. You ready?”

“Hit me with it.”

“Are you from Tennessee? Because you are the only *ten* I *see*.”

“Ah, dude, no.” I chuckle.

“No? Okay, this one will get you for sure. Feel my jacket. It’s made of boyfriend material.”

“Oh Jesus.” I shake my head.

“Come on! Okay, this will definitely make you laugh. Did you just fart? ’Cause you blow me away.”

I snort.

“See, I fucking knew you’d like that one! Wait, I got more. Do you work at Subway? ’Cause you gave me a footlong. And another: if you were a Transformer, you’d be Optimus *Fine*.”

I'm totally laughing now, but he isn't stopping. The man is on a roll.

"Wait, this is the créme de la créme of lines. I saved the very best 'til last. You ready for this?"

I nod because I can't speak; I'm laughing so hard. My eyes are watering from it.

"Okay, here it is … I hear you're looking for a stud. Well, I've got the S-T-D, and all I need is *you*."

"Fucking hell," I choke out. I'm full-on belly laughing now. Tears rolling down my face. Not practical when I'm driving a car. "Dude, you gotta stop." I hold my stomach. "Or I'm gonna crash!"

Or pee myself. But there are some things I'm not willing to share with a hot guy like Nick.

"Okay. Well, I treasure my life, and I'm out of lines anyway. That was my last one." He sits back, looking mighty pleased with himself.

I'm wiping tears from my eyes. "Where in the hell did you even get those from? They were truly fucking awful."

He laughs. "One of my best friends, Cash. He's notorious for his bad one-liners. Those are some of his finer ones."

One of his best friends. So, he has more than one. And I also know the name of one of them now—Cash. I file that info under One More Thing I Know About Nick Slater.

"Well, I'd say your friend needs new material. But the only question that really matters is, do those chat-up lines actually work for him?"

He looks over at me, that damn brow raised. "All the damn time."

We both burst out laughing again.

Our laughter only dries up when I pull into the department store's parking lot. I slide my car into a space and turn off the engine.

"Well, that was fun. Now, we shop."

We both get out of my car and walk over to the department store. Nick opens the door for me, letting me through first.

Hmm. So, underneath the leather and tattoos lies the heart of a gentleman. And I don't care what anybody says; deep down, every girl wants a man who will hold open a door for her.

And lay his heart on the line for her.

But we don't all get lucky enough to get the latter.

I stop just inside the store. "Okay, men's is up on the second floor. I'll leave you to go get what you need. Women's is down here, so I'll go grab what I need, including Gran's hairspray. And I'll meet you back here in … how long will you need?"

"Twenty minutes?"

"Twenty minutes." I squint up at him. "You sure? That's not very long."

He slides his sunglasses on. "Stevie, I'm a guy. Twenty minutes is longer than we need in any store."

"True." I nod my agreement. "Okay. See you back here in twenty."

I walk away from him, this man that I've known only hours, with this warm, full feeling in my chest that I can't even begin to explain.

I only know it feels good.

So damn good.

Almost twenty minutes later, I'm done shopping, so I walk back to the entrance where I said I'd meet Nick. But he's already standing there, waiting for me. A couple of bags in his hand.

"Damn, you do work fast," I say, approaching him.

He turns and smiles at me.

That smile hits me in all the good places.

"Told you," he says. "You got everything you needed?"

"Uh-huh." I nod up at him. "So, do you want to head back to the B&B? Or we could grab a coffee?"

"Coffee," he says. "Always coffee."

"I hear ya. Coffee is life. There's a Starbucks just around the corner. My best friend, Penny, works there. She'll caffeine us up. Shall we put the bags in my car?"

He agrees with a nod, so we walk back to my car and deposit our purchases in the truck.

After I lock my car back up, we start the short walk to Penny's work.

Aside from getting a caffeine fix, I really want to bring Nick to meet Penny. She will shit a brick when she sees him.

I couldn't have the hottest guy ever to come to our town and not let Penny see him. What sort of friend would I be?

We reach the coffee shop, and Nick steps ahead, opening the door for me again.

A girl could really get used to this.

The place is busy, like usual. I spot Penny behind the counter, serving a customer.

She sees me and waves. I watch her eyes move to Nick standing beside me, and they widen almost comically. I have to stop myself from laughing.

"What's your coffee of choice?" I ask him.

"Americano. And this is my treat."

"No way. I'm getting them."

"Stevie." His hand touches my forearm.

The third time we've touched since we met, and holy hell, haywire electrons are firing under my skin.

Just imagine how it would feel if he put that hand on other parts of your body.

"You just took time out of your day, not only to come rescue my ass from the side of the road"—I open my mouth to argue that it was technically work, but he cuts me off with a look—"but you also just drove me out here, so I could get some stuff—and don't say you were coming here anyway." It's like he's taking the words straight out of my head. "So, paying for your coffee is the least I can do."

I press my lips together and pout. "Well, I was going to have something sweet too, maybe cake …" I let that pout turn into a smile.

His hand reaches out and tucks some stray tendrils of hair behind my ear. "I'm sure I can manage something sweet."

His fingers linger a moment before moving away.

I don't even think he realized that he did it. Did he?

But I'm realizing and … holy shiz!

The way he just touched me. That's intimate, right? Or am I being a total numbnut and reading that wrong?

But the way he's been looking at me …

And I know he was thinking about kissing me earlier, back at the B&B.

Maybe he likes me.

Or maybe he just wants to fuck you.

Probably the latter.

We've known each other for the smallest amount of time. He's only passing through town. Nick is not here to stay.

And you don't do one-nights.

Although I'm starting to revise my thoughts on that.

Shallow as it sounds … he's really hot. But I like him too. He makes me laugh.

And I mean, really, what kind of damage could a one-night stand do to me? Hopefully, the good kind of damage from being thrown around by the big guy.

Seriously though, the worst that could happen is I'd have a couple of orgasms because Nick looks like a-couple-of-orgasms kind of guy, or is that my wishful thinking? Nah, he definitely looks like he wouldn't leave a girl unsatisfied. And after, I'd feel a little sad when he was gone.

But that's it.

My heart wouldn't get hurt.

I'd be fine.

And I'd have one hell of a memory to think about when I was forty and still single.

I lead the way over to the counter, Nick following, and wait behind the person being served.

Pen's green eyes keep flicking to Nick as he peruses the pastries. She looks like she has a nervous tic. I'm dying to laugh. I know this is killing her.

I can practically read her thoughts …

Holy shit, he's hot. Who is he? Has Stevie finally gotten over her dry spell? God, he's hot.

And a little more about him being hot.

I'm grinning to myself.

One of Pen's colleagues, Gary, comes over to serve me. "Hey, Stevie. What can I get you?"

Pen's going to be pissed that Gary beat her to us.

"I'll have a blonde, vanilla-bean, coconut-milk latte and a confetti sugar cookie, please, Gary. Nick?" I say.

When he doesn't respond, I turn my eyes his way.

The way he's looking at me with total amusement curving his lips has me saying, "What?"

"That's quite a drink."

"Well, I'm quite a girl." I imaginary flick my hair off my shoulder.

He's staring at me behind those sunglasses he's still wearing. I wish I could see his eyes. Know what's in them as he looks at me.

Then, he nods. "That you are."

He pulls his eyes from me, and I allow myself to breathe.

Holy shiz!

"I'll take an Americano and a slice of pumpkin loaf, please, man."

"For here or to go?" Gary asks us.

"Stevie's staying," Pen calls out, answering for us. "And I'll bring them over to your table."

Laughing, I say to her, "Do I get a say?"

"Nope." She smirks.

Her eyes go to Nick again before coming back to me, and her eyebrows lift in question.

I just shrug, smiling, giving away nothing.

She's totally going to grill me about him. And she won't be shy about asking questions in front of him either. Diplomatic Penny is not.

"So, I'm taking it, the redhead is your friend Penny," Nick says as we take our seats across from each other at a table close to the back of the shop that he led us to.

I usually like to sit by the window and watch the world go by. But I don't mind sitting where he wants to.

"Yep," I answer.

"How long have you been friends?"

"Since kindergarten. Aside from my family—well, Pen is my family too—she's the best person I know."

She's witty, smart, awesome, and she totally gets me.

We're very similar in traits as well as looks. Same-ish height, except Pen's got an inch on me. Same build, slim with boobs and an ass. The only difference is, I'm blonde, and Pen is a redhead. I tan, whereas she's pale. She has freckles on her face and shoulders that she hates, and I'm totally envious of them.

"So, Nick Slater"—I put my elbow on the table and prop my chin in my hand—"do you always wear sunglasses inside?"

Really, I'm just asking because I don't like not being able to see his eyes. They're so damn pretty.

He shrugs. "Bad habit, I guess." He takes them off, putting them on the table.

I notice the first thing he does after removing them is glance around the room, almost self-consciously. Then, he angles his body, giving most of his back to the rest of the room. He also seems really uncomfortable.

Huh?

Not that I've known him long, but he seems to be a confident guy, and this seems out of place for a confident person. This is more the action of a less than confident person. Maybe a person who doesn't like to be in social situations.

Maybe he's not comfortable in social situations, and he uses the glasses as a crutch.

I feel bad all of a sudden.

"I was just teasing about the sunglasses, you know. You didn't have to take them off."

"No. You're right. Only pricks wear sunglasses indoors." He smiles, but it's not his usual smile. It seems a little forced.

"Pricks. And famous people," I point out.

"Yeah. Those too."

Pen appears at our table a second later, tray in hand.

"That was quick," I say to her.

She shrugs. Puts the tray containing our coffees and food down on the table.

Then, she sits down on the chair next to me.

I'm not surprised at all.

Penny hasn't seen me with a guy … well, since my douche-bag ex.

This is a big deal even if Nick and I are only friends. Not that she currently knows that. Or knows that I would like to climb him like a tree.

"You on your break?" I ask her.

"Nope. But I can spare five minutes to chat. I've missed you."

I'm grinning because I know, even if this place was packed to the rafters and she was rushed off her feet, she'd still be sitting here right now. And miss me, my ass. She saw me yesterday. We had lunch together.

"You saw me yesterday," I reiterate my thoughts out loud just to wind her up.

"Yesterday was yesterday. I need my Stevie fix every day."

Grinning at her, I reach for the sugar to put in my coffee. "Aw, you love me."

"Bitch, please. You know I do. Now, aren't you going to introduce me to your new friend?" She gestures to Nick, whose eyes are on me. Not Penny.

Huh.

I've always thought of Penny as the prettier of the two of us. I think that because it's true. She's like a young Julia Roberts in *Steel Magnolias*.

Gah. I love that movie. Makes me bawl every single time I watch it. When Shelby dies … I choke up, just thinking about it.

"Penny, this is Nick Slater. Nick, this is my bestie, Penny Parrish."

"Nice to meet you," he says.

"Nick you say?" Penny's looking at him with serious curiosity. More than *he's a hottie* curiosity.

Huh.

"Yep. Nick." He picks his coffee up and takes a drink.

"Hmm," she murmurs. "You look really familiar though. Like I've seen you somewhere before."

"I get that a lot. I have one of those faces."

"Nick's from LA," I tell Penny, feeling the need to interject.

Her eyes spark with something. "LA you say?"

"Mmhmm." Nick nods. He's pulling apart his pumpkin slice with his fingers now. Putting a piece in his mouth, he starts to chew.

"What brings you all the way out here?" Penny asks.

I can see that Penny's questioning is making him feel uncomfortable. She can do that sometimes—make people uncomfortable without meaning to. It's just because her intrusive nature doesn't have an off switch. She means absolutely no harm. She's just similar to Gran in that way—nosy.

"Vacation," I answer for him. "His car broke down. I went to tow him. He's staying at the B&B."

Her eyes come to me. There's a definite smile in them. "And now, you're having coffee together." That translates into, *Are you also having sex together?*

Pen is always on me to start dating again. I'm twenty-four years old, and I've dated one man my whole life. I wouldn't even know where to start. And I don't think I want to.

The thought of having a man in my life again, giving someone else the power and opportunity to squeeze my heart to a pulp …

Er … no, thanks.

Pen says, if I don't want to date, then I should at least give my coochie to a man every once in a while. Keep it alive. According to her, if I don't, it's going to shrivel up and die, and when a coochie dies, there's no reviving it.

I used to think no … but meeting Nick has definitely got me thinking other things.

Thinking maybe Pen is right about the sex thing.

Who are you, and what have you done with Stevie Cavalli?

"Pen!" Gary calls. "Need you!"

"Christ almighty." She sighs. "Coming!" She gets up from her seat. "I'll call you later," she says to me. Meaning she'll call me as soon as her shift here is over, so she can grill me about Nick.

I might not answer her call, make her sweat it a bit.

Not knowing the full details will kill her. Not that there's a lot to tell. It's not like anything has happened with Nick.

Except the *I think he was about to kiss me* thing earlier. And the hair-tucking thing a few minutes ago.

"Nice to meet you, *Nick*."

The way she says his name catches my attention. It was definitely pointed.

Wonder what that was all about?

I glance at Nick, but he's watching Pen as she walks away, a furrow in his brow.

Huh.

If I didn't know better, I'd think they'd met before.

But if they had, Pen would have told me.

Although she was questioning if she did know him from somewhere.

Weird. It's not like Pen's ever been to LA. And Nick hasn't been here to Lake Havasu before, so I can't see how they would have met.

Nick's eyes move to mine. He smiles, but it doesn't quite reach his eyes. "You've not eaten your cookie," he says.

"What? Oh, yeah." My eyes go down to it before coming back up to his face. "Make me a promise before I do?"

His eyes twinkle. Like literally fucking twinkle. "Sure."

"Don't tell Gran I ate a cookie before dinner, or she'll kick my ass."

He chuckles. "Your secret is safe with me."

Smiling, I pick my cookie up and take a bite of the sugary goodness, enjoying the feel of the sprinkles dissolving on my tongue.

15
STORM

The friend made me.

I could see it in her eyes. She recognized me, but she couldn't figure out where from. Won't take her long to realize.

For fuck's sake.

I was enjoying my anonymity. Actually enjoying it is putting it mildly. I was fucking loving it.

I like Stevie not knowing who I am. Just having her get to know me. The real me.

Part of me thinks it won't matter to Stevie when she finds out who I really am, but then who really knows for sure?

I didn't think my family would keep something as big as what had really happened the night Jonny died, but they did. So, Stevie could completely change the way she is with me when she finds out I'm Storm Slater.

I probably should just tell her. Get it over and done with. Before her friend tells her. But I'm a selfish bastard, and I want to keep riding this Nick wave and enjoy having her treat me just like I'm any other regular guy.

I'm not ready for the disappointment I'll feel if she turns out not to be the person I think she is.

The kind of person who won't give a shit whose son I am, what I do for my job, or that my life details are a regular in the tabloids.

I've had enough disappointment today to last me for a while. I'm not in the mood for more.

It's crazy to think that, this morning, I was in LA, doing an interview, finding out a long-hidden secret, and feeling like my world was about to fall apart. And, tonight, I'm in a B&B in Arizona, spending time with this crazy, beautiful girl who makes me feel things I've never felt before.

Life is strange at times.

And ain't I glad for it?

And for whoever was looking down on me today when they put Stevie in my path right when I needed her.

Maybe it was Mom's doing.

I've barely thought about what happened while I've been with Stevie. She seems to take the bad shit right out of my head. I can honestly say I haven't laughed as much as I have with her in … well, ever.

She makes me laugh like no one ever has before.

She's fucking awesome.

We got back to the B&B a few minutes ago after leaving the coffee shop. Stevie had us singing Whitesnake songs all the way home. I don't think I'll ever be able to listen to "Here I Go Again" without thinking of her terrible singing.

She totally crucified the song.

And here's me, smiling at the thought.

Who would've ever thought the sound of terrible singing would have me grinning like an idiot?

But everything Stevie does makes me smile.

Dropping my bags on the bed, I kick off my boots and pull my jacket off, tossing it next to my shit on the bed. Taking my new toothbrush, toothpaste, and shower gel, I go into the bathroom and turn on the shower.

I parted ways with Stevie downstairs, so we could both freshen up before dinner. It's the first time I've been away from her since I met her.

And, weirdly, I'm eager to get back to her.

Go figure.

I strip off my clothes and step under the spray, turning my face up to the water.

Finishing in the shower, I turn it off and wrap a towel around my waist. I brush my teeth. When I'm done, I dry off, leaving the towel in the bathroom.

I dress in the pair of jeans I bought and a white T-shirt.

Sitting down on the edge of the bed, I get my cell out of my jacket.

Palming it, I stare down at the black screen.

I've kept it off all day. I only turned it on when I had to call the garage. Turned it straight back off again.

I know there'll be a bunch of messages and voice mails on there.

I'm just not ready to listen to them yet.

My parting words to Jake, Tom, and Denny echo in my ears.

"As far as I'm concerned, the three of you are as dead to me as Jonny is."

It was a shitty thing to say.

I feel like a total prick for saying that. I didn't mean it.

I was just mad as hell.

I'm still mad.

But I can't bring myself to talk to them yet.

I know I will at some point. But not today.

And it's not a conversation to be had over the phone. I'll have to go back and face them at some point.

But that day isn't today.

It's not like I can leave anyway.

My car is here.

I can't go anywhere until she's fixed.

Yeah, you keep telling yourself that, Slater.

It has nothing to do with Stevie or the way she makes you feel when you're around her. Or the fact that you want to nail her.

Okay. I could leave anytime. I could get a rental and drive back and have my car sent to me when she's fixed.

But I like being around Stevie. Like the way she makes me feel when I'm with her.

I'm not ready to leave that feeling quite just yet.

And, honestly, I think the break from LA will do me good.

I do need to let the boys know though.

I'm sure the news of me assaulting that journo has hit the press. The boys are probably wondering what the fuck is going on.

I turn on my phone and wait for it to come to life.

The screen lights up, and it instantly starts buzzing in my hand with incoming messages.

I don't look at them. I swipe the screen up and go to the Call app. I hit Raze's number, put the cell to my ear, and wait for it to connect.

He answers on the second ring. Raze never answers his phone that quick. He must be worried.

"Where the fuck have you been? I've been calling you all day. Cash and Levi too. You hit a journo, man. What the fuck happened?"

I sigh. "I didn't hit him. I just … roughed him up a bit. It was a setup. He told me stuff … about Jonny. Goaded me. He wanted me to hit him."

"Jake called, looking for you. He didn't tell me anything. But it's all over the news. The video of you and the journo. The stuff about Jonny … I'm so sorry, man. I can't believe Jonny knew about you. That's fucked up. You okay?"

"Getting there." I sigh.

"Where are you? Come to mine. We'll sink some beers, talk it through."

"That'll be difficult … I'm in Arizona."

"The fuck!" He chuckles. "What the hell are you doing there?"

"I went to TMS Records, saw Jake, Tom, and Denny … it didn't go well."

"Fuck … I can imagine," he says low.

"After that, I got in my car and just started driving. Somehow ended up in Arizona."

"Well, get your ass back!"

"Can't. My car broke down."

"No fucking way."

"Yeah. It's in the garage as we speak."

"Where are you now then?"

I glance around the room. "I'm at a B&B."

"A B&B?"

"Yep. The owners of the garage, it's their B&B. Their daughter runs it with her gran."

"Daughter, huh? She hot?"

I find myself not wanting to say anything. I don't want to share Stevie with anyone back home for some weird reason. "She's … nice."

"Fuck off!" He laughs. "She's either hot or not. Which is it?"

"Fine. She's hot. The hottest girl I've ever seen."

"Shit. Really?"

"Yeah."

Silence hangs between us for a few seconds.

"So, you gonna tap that then?" Raze asks.

"Hmm. Not sure. She's not like the women we're used to."

"You mean, easy."

"Pretty much." I laugh.

"Gonna make you work for it, this one."

Hopefully. "Yeah." I chuckle.

"So, how long you think you'll be in Arizona for?"

"Not sure yet."

My cell starts to beep in my ear. Call waiting. I pull my cell from my ear and check the screen. It's Belle. Can't say I'm up to talking to any of my family at the moment, but I'll never ignore a call from one of my siblings.

"I've got another call," I tell Raze. "It's Belle. I'd better take it."

"All right, man. Check in soon. And relax, okay? Take a few days, get your head straight, and then come home."

"Will do. Let Cash and Levi know what's up, will ya?" I'm sure they're wondering what the fuck's going on as well.

"Will do."

Hanging up with Raze, I answer Belle's call.

"About damn time!" she huffs in my ear. "I've only been calling you forever!"

"Hi to you too."

"Where are you? You're not home. Mom's already been there to check. We've been worried sick!"

"I'm … somewhere."

"Where?" she pushes.

That's Belle all over. Doesn't take no for an answer. Gets it from Jake.

"I'm out of LA. I just need some space."

Silence.

"But you're okay, yeah?"

"Yeah, I'm okay," I tell her.

"Mom and Dad are worried about you."

"Tell Tru and Jake I'm fine."

"Why do you do that? Say their names like that? It's like you're trying to tell yourself that we're not really your family. We are. So, suck it up."

She's so fucking smart sometimes. She knows when I'm doing shit before I even realize.

"I know you're my family, Belle."

"So, start acting like it then. Family doesn't up and run when shit gets hard."

"Family doesn't lie to each other either," I snap.

I close my eyes and pinch the bridge of my nose with my fingers.

"Dad told us," she says quietly into the phone. "Me, Billy, and JJ. He told us what happened. He feels real bad, Storm."

I drop my hand from my face. "I'm sure he does."

"They all do. Dad, Uncle Tom, and Uncle Denny. They made a mistake, not telling you about your dad. But ignoring them isn't going to help either."

I sigh. "It's not that easy, Belle. When you're older, you'll—"

"Don't give me that crap. I'm not a kid."

"You're fourteen."

"I might be fourteen, but I'm more mature than you are."

Can't argue that. It's true.

"I'm just not ready to talk to them, okay? I just need a bit of time to sort my head out. Tell them not to worry. I'm fine. And I'll be in touch at some point."

There's a pause.

"Okay," she acquiesces. "And don't worry about that journalist. Dad's handling it."

Of course he is. That's Jake. Always fixing things.

I clench my teeth, grinding them.

"Storm?" Belle says when I don't speak.

"What?" I grit out.

"He only does it because he cares."

I relax my jaw a little. "I know."

Another silence and then, "Did you really pick that guy up off the floor by his throat?" Her voice has lowered to a whisper, and I wonder where in the house she is.

I'm not sure how to answer that, but it'll be all over the internet anyway, so it's not like she won't be able to see the video.

"Yeah." I sigh.

"Not that I condone violence in any way … but that's totally badass."

I can't hold in my smile. "I'm hanging up now."

"Call Dad soon," she says quickly.

"Belle …" My voice has a warning tone.

"I know he messed up, but he's hurting. He loves you, you know. We all do."

Another sigh. "I know. I'll speak to you later."

I hang up before she can say any more.

I stare at my phone in my hand for a moment.

Then, I turn it off. Standing up, I leave my cell in the room and head downstairs in search of Stevie.

I'm placing the cutlery on the table when Nick appears in the dining room.

"Hey." I smile at him. My mouth all of a sudden dry.

He looks … amazing. I mean, there's nothing different about him from the first time I saw him—well, except for he's wearing a shirt.

He's all freshly showered, hair still damp from it. Boots on his feet, blue jeans covering his ass, and a white T-shirt that shows off the ink covering both arms.

He has so many tattoos. I've never dated a guy who has tattoos before.

You're not dating this one, doofus.

Only in your head.

"Need a hand?"

He moves closer to me. My heartbeat kicks up a notch.

Just his nearness has my body going into overdrive.

"Nah. I got it. Dinner's nearly ready. Gran's just finishing up. We all usually eat in our kitchen. But we're going to eat in here with you, if that's okay? Gran has this thing about people eating alone."

He smiles. "It's fine with me."

"Cool."

I'm just awkwardly standing here, gazing at him like a teenager standing in front of her first crush.

I am totally crushing on him.

I even made more of an effort tonight in my appearance. Not too much so it's noticeable. If I did, Beck would catch it straightaway, figure out it's because of Nick, and tease me mercilessly.

And I really don't want to go to prison for murdering my brother.

I just put my hair in a sleek ponytail instead of my usual messy bun. A little mascara and lip balm. And I have on pale blue jeans with no rips and my white ruffle-sleeved, baby-doll top.

I realize we actually match. Both wearing blue jeans and white tops.

Except his jeans are a darker blue and his top is a T-shirt and—

Christ, shut up, Stevie.

"You look really nice," he says like, once again, he just read my mind. "Pretty," he adds, and my stomach riots along with my chest.

"Oh, uh"—I touch a hand to my hair—"thanks. You too. Okay, so why don't you take a seat? And I'll go grab some drinks." I gesture to the table.

He's still smiling at me, and it's making me even more flustered and heated.

"Any specific seat?" he asks. "Or …"

"Sit anywhere. We're not precious."

I watch Nick take a seat at the six-seater table, leaving the heads of the table open, probably for Dad and Gran.

I don't know why, but I really like his respectful ways.

I was raised to always treat others with respect.

Gran always said to me, growing up, "Treat people the way you want to be treated, Stevie. You give kindness; you'll get it back."

Although that didn't actually work out that way for me with my ex. I treated him like a king. And he shit all over me.

Still, I won't ever change my ways because of a narcissistic asshole like him.

"Right, well, what can I get you to drink? There's beer, wine … Dad and Beck usually have a beer with dinner."

"What do you usually have?"

"Beer." I smile, and so does he. "Gran's the wine drinker in this house."

"Then, I'll have a beer too."

And why him wanting to have the same drink as me does funny things to my heart, I'll never know.

I turn on my heel, heading back into the kitchen, my heart pounding.

"Nick's here," I tell her.

"Good. It's ready. Can you call your brother and dad for me?"

I slide my cell from my pocket and call Dad. I'm not walking clear across the B&B to get him when I have the power to tell him right there in my back pocket.

"Dinner ready?" Dad says on the answer.

"Yep."

"Coming now."

I slide my phone back in my pocket and open the refrigerator. I get out four beers and the wine. Grab a glass and pour Gran's drink. She only ever has one glass a night. Two if it's a special occasion. I pop the caps on the beer. Tucking two of them under my arm, two in one hand, and the glass of wine in the other, I carry them through to the dining room.

Nick looks up as I walk through the door. Our eyes seem to crash into each other's. It makes me falter a step.

I walk toward the table. Putting down the glass first, I place three bottles on the coasters set around the table, and then I hand Nick's bottle to him.

Our fingers touch, the barest hint. And I feel that touch everywhere. Like he just ran his hands all over my body.

"Thanks," he says. His voice sounding lower, deeper, gruffer.

Does he feel it too? The way I feel when we touch?

I can't be the only one feeling this way.

It's like nothing I've experienced before.

It's confusing and exhilarating. And absolutely fucking terrifying.

"I'm just gonna go help Gran with the food." I thumb over my shoulder, taking a few steps back, unable to break eye contact with him.

In the end, I have to force myself to turn; otherwise, I'd have been walking backward the whole way to the kitchen, and that would have looked weird or obvious that I couldn't take my eyes off the man.

Food is on plates when I go back in the kitchen, so I collect three plates, leaving Gran to carry two—mine and hers.

Gran opens the door with her hip, and I follow her into the dining room.

When we appear, Dad and Beck are seated at the table, chatting with Nick.

I walk over to the table, balancing the plates like a pro. The only problem when you're carrying three plates is that it's not easy to put them down gracefully.

When I'm near the table, Dad reaches out and takes one from my hand, putting it down on the table in front of him.

"Thanks, Daddy."

I put Nick's plate down in front of him, hand Beck's over, and then take the only available seat next to Nick.

"This looks amazing," Nick says to Gran.

She cooked them roast lamb. She'd already checked with Nick earlier to make sure he wasn't vegetarian like me or had any dietary requirements.

"You're not having the same?" Nick asks me, nodding down at my plate.

I've got a cranberry, feta, and quinoa–stuffed butternut squash instead of lamb.

"I'm vegetarian," I tell him.

"Ah. So, the cigarette butt lecture makes more sense to me now."

"Oh Christ. She's lectured you about that as well?" Beck says, laughing. "After she read that damn article, we all got the lecture. She's been tryna get me to go to a beach cleanup with her. But if I'm going to the beach, I'm chilling, not cleaning it up."

"Have fun, lying on a beach surrounded by butts."

I hear the words back right before Beck laughs and says, "Sounds like a perfect vacation to me, being surrounded by butts."

Even Gran and Dad laugh. Nick too.

Ugh.

"You're gross."

"I'm fucking hilarious," Beck says.

"Language at the dinner table," Gran chides. "We have a guest."

"Don't worry about me," Nick says, forking food into his mouth. "I've heard worse. And I'll go to a beach cleanup with you," Nick adds, glancing my way, shocking the hell out of me.

"You will?" I know my eyes are bugging and have just lit up like the Fourth of July.

"Sure. You let me know when the next one is, and I'll be there."

The possibility of spending more time with Nick in the future …

Wow. Just wow.

Though he probably doesn't mean it. He's probably just saying it to be kind.

And if that thought doesn't make me deflate like a balloon.

So, I do what I always do when I feel like this. I throw out a jokey comment.

"And you'll stop smoking as well?"

He huffs out a laugh. "I'll promise to dispose of them responsibly."

I teasingly roll my eyes. "Suppose it'll do."

"So, I had a quick look at your car before I left the garage," Beck says to Nick, changing the subject.

I find my muscles locking up tight, bracing in anticipation of what Beck is going to say.

Because when Nick's car is fixed, he'll be leaving. He has no other reason to stay.

I'm not even going to address why that makes me feel like I've just accidentally squished a ladybug.

Yes, that actually happened. I was seven. I was on the trampoline we used to have in the garden. I was bouncing, having fun. I saw the ladybug but couldn't stop myself from landing on her.

It was death by my butt.

I cried for a whole day. Dad even did a funeral for her for me. The cross Dad made out of Popsicle sticks is still there, next to Gran's rose bushes.

"What's the damage?" Nick takes a swig of beer.

"Still too early to tell. Diesel cars have stronger ancillary equipment because diesel is so much thicker and corrosive than gas. If I'd have been looking at gas in a diesel, piece of cake. Saying that, worse we're looking at is a new fuel pump, possibly a new catalytic convertor. But I'll go in early and flush out the diesel, change the filter, and run her through, see how she holds up."

Is it bad that I'm praying for a new fuel pump and catalytic convertor?

"Just to give you a heads-up," Beck continues, "if you need new parts, I'll have to order them in. None of our local suppliers have Maserati parts. Could take a few days to get, a day to fit."

"That's fine. I'm in no rush."

I glance at Nick, unable not to, and his eyes are on me.

I feel a jolt in my chest and heat between my legs.

Dragging my eyes from his, I grab my beer and take a swig.

Dad launches into a conversation about our local high school baseball team and their upcoming game. Beck used to play for them when he was in high school. Which then moves on to the Diamondbacks and their chances this season and Dad asking Nick which baseball team he supports.

I tune them out and talk to Gran instead about her day, and she fills me in on the gossip she picked up today while at the hairdresser.

Soon enough, dinner is over.

"That was amazing. Thank you, Stella," Nick says, resting back in his chair.

"Awesome as always, Gran." Beck gets up out of his seat.

"Um … where are you disappearing off to?" I frown at him.

Beck pauses, resting his hands on the back of the chair he just vacated. "I've got a hot date."

I snort. "Since when do you date?"

My brother is notorious for his noncommittal ways.

"I don't. But I didn't want to say in front of Gran that I'm going to hook up with this hot college chick I met earlier."

The mention of college girls even now makes me bristle a little.

"Ugh." I pull a disgusted face.

"Well, you asked."

"I didn't," Gran says, a look of mild distaste on her face.

"Sorry, Gran." Beck grins at her.

"Well, before you disappear, you're helping clean up," I tell him.

"Ah, come on!" he complains, glancing at the time on his Apple Watch. "You're gonna make me late."

"Aw, poor Beck. Gonna be late for some random hook-up. My heart bleeds."

"Oh, let him go." Gran waves him off.

"You're the best." Beck slaps a kiss on her cheek. Then, he gives me a winner's smirk.

I stick my tongue out at him.

"Later," he calls, running out of here like his ass is on fire.

Well, as gross as it is, at least one of the Cavallis is getting some.

Nick pushes his chair back, taking his plate with him. "Let me help clean up."

"No way." Gran waves him back down. "You're a paying guest. You'll take that plate into the kitchen over my dead body. Bryan, Stevie, and I have got this. You go relax."

"Uh … well," Dad pipes up, "I did say I'd go meet Pete at the pub for a beer."

Gran shoots Dad an annoyed look. I guess grandkids get off easier than kids do.

Honestly, I don't know why either of us is surprised. This is a regular occurrence around here. Gran and I are usually left to clear up after dinner.

"Go on then. Off with you," Gran chides him.

"Thanks, Mom." Dad kisses her cheek. Then, he comes around and kisses the top of my head. "Later, baby girl."

"Have fun, Daddy."

"You too."

Yep, I'm going to be having all the fun, washing dishes and cleaning the kitchen down.

"Looks like it's just you and me, Stevie," Gran says after Dad's left the room.

"Like always." I give a jokey eye roll.

"Are you sure you don't want me to help?" Nick says again. "It's really no biggie."

"Dead body," Gran reiterates, getting to her feet, and Nick chuckles.

I love the sound of his laughter. It does crazy things to my insides.

"Okay, well, I'm just gonna head outside for some fresh air." Nick pushes his chair back, getting to his feet.

I stand too, taking my plate with me. "That's code for, you're going to have a cigarette?"

He grins. "Am I that obvious?"

"Nah, I'm just that smart." I smirk. "You know … unless you snuck a cigarette in when I wasn't looking, you haven't smoked since I picked you up from the side of the road this afternoon."

"Yeah. And I'm about to die if I don't have one soon."

"Smoking kills," I remind him, grinning.

He shakes his head, laughing. "I won't be long."

I watch him go out through the door, and I help Gran collect up the rest of the plates and take them into the kitchen.

I'm just wiping down the countertops, and Gran is drying off the big pans that won't fit in the dishwasher when Nick appears in the doorway, closest to me.

I get a faint whiff of cigarette smoke and mint from him.

And the smell weirdly doesn't repulse me like it normally does.

It just makes me think of him.

Huh. Interesting.

I wonder if I'll always associate the smell with him now.

He smiles when his eyes meet mine. "I just thought I'd let you know, I'm gonna head to bed." He stifles a yawn with his hand at his mouth. "It's been a hell of a long day."

Nick. Bed.

I wonder if he bought any pajamas from the store today or if he actually does sleep naked like he said earlier.

Sweet Lawd.

"Good night, Nick," Gran calls to him. "See you in the morning. Breakfast is between eight and nine."

"Eight and nine. Got it. Night, Stella." His eyes come to rest on me again. "So, I'll see you at breakfast then?" It's a definite question.

And it makes butterflies storm into my stomach.

I nod, holding his stare. "I'll be here."

His smile reaches all the way up to his eyes. "Great. Okay. So, I'll see you then. Sleep well, Stevie."

"You too."

He gives me one last smile before disappearing back through the door.

I'm still staring at said door when Gran speaks from behind me, "That boy likes you."

"Huh?" I turn to look at her.

"Nick likes you," she reiterates.

"No, he doesn't," is my response with a laugh. It sounds awkward.

And now, my heart is going *ba-boom!* in my chest with excitement at the mere prospect of Nick liking me.

"You mark my words, he does. I saw the way he kept looking at you at dinner. And just then. That boy has the hots for you."

"Gran, please never say 'hots' again."

She laughs. Drying her hands on the tea towel, she walks over to me. "He likes you. And why wouldn't he?" She cups my chin in her hand, staring me in the eyes. "You're as pretty as the sun at rise. You're smart, funny. And you have the kindest heart of anyone I've ever known. I know that little asshole hurt you bad—"

"Gran …" I cut her off.

"Just let me say my piece, and I'm done. I know he hurt you. But don't let his past actions get in the way of your future happiness."

"Gran, I barely know Nick. And he's just passing through town. He's not here to stay."

"He doesn't need to stay, honey. He just has to put a smile back on your face. And from what I've seen, he's done that already. I'm not saying, marry the boy. I'm saying, he's hot as blazes. He thinks you're hot, and you should … make use of that fact. There's a bottle of whipped cream in the refrigerator, its expiration coming up. Make use of it before it goes bad."

"Gran!" I exclaim, nearly choking.

Gran isn't ever shy about saying stuff, but there are some words you never want to hear come out of your gran's mouth, and those are words involving hot boys and whipped cream.

"What? Your grandpa used to love it when—"

"And let's just stop right there," I cut her off with a groan.

She chuckles and gives my chin a gentle squeeze. "Just think about it."

"I'll never think of whipped cream the same ever again. You've ruined it for me."

She laughs again. "I meant, Nick. Enjoy yourself while you're young. You don't want to look back when you're old and have any regrets about missed opportunities." She kisses my cheek. "I'll go lock up. You get yourself to bed … or Nick's." She winks before breezing out of the kitchen.

And I'm left standing here, my heart beating quickly, wondering if she could actually be right—that Nick does like me. And whether I should actually be brave and go up to his room.

Sans whipped cream, of course, because … *gross.*

I didn't go to Nick's room last night.

Because I'm not that brave.

I mean, what if I had gone up there, knocked on his door, and I had read things totally wrong and he didn't like me in that way?

I'd have looked like a total idiot.

Looking like an idiot and being rejected are two of my least favorite things in life.

So, I went to my own bed and stared at the ceiling for most of the night.

Fun times.

"Stevie?" I hear Nick's voice calling from the dining room. "You around?"

Christ, just the sound of his voice gives me goose bumps. I'm so screwed.

"Coming," I call back.

If only.

"He probably wants breakfast," I say to Gran, who's just washing up the dishes from our breakfast.

We ate early with Dad and Beck, who were up and out so they could get a start on Nick's car.

I walk through to the dining room, and he's standing there in the middle of the room, looking like a dream.

I'm pretty sure he's gotten even better-looking since I saw him last night.

"Hey." He smiles, and it reaches all the way to his eyes.

"Hi." I tuck a stray hair behind my ear, giving him what I'm pretty sure is the goofiest smile known to man. "Did you sleep okay?" I ask through my cotton mouth.

"Better than okay. That bed is seriously comfy."

Nick. Bed.

Dirty thoughts incoming.

"Good. Great," I croak. I clear my throat. "Glad to hear it."

He's staring at me, and I'm staring at him, right into those blue eyes of his. And I'm starting to feel all hot and giddy and turned on.

Sweet Jesus. Pull yourself together, Stevie.

"Breakfast," I blurt.

"What?" is his response.

"Breakfast," I repeat. "What can I get you?"

"Oh. Right. Sure. Well, what's on the menu?"

Me.

"Waffles, pancakes, bacon, eggs any way you want them, fruit, toast, cereal ..." I reel off.

He thinks for a moment. "Can I get waffles topped with fruit?"

"Sure. Any particular fruit?"

"Strawberries."

"Whipped cream?" The words are out before I even register them.

Then, I do.

Gran's suggestion ...

I can feel my chest and face going red.

"No. No whipped cream."

Thank God.

"So, just waffles topped with strawberries. You want coffee too?"

"Absolutely." He nods.

"Black?" I say, remembering his order at Starbucks yesterday.

He smiles at me again. "Yep."

"Cool." I take a step back toward the kitchen door. "Well, sit yourself down, and I'll bring it through—when it's ready, of course. Which will be in about five minutes. Ten at the most."

Christ, Stevie, stop jabbering on.

I turn on my heel and hightail it out of there, my heart beating out of my chest.

God, the effect he has on me is nuts.

No man has ever affected me in this way before.

I'm practically panting by the time I reach the kitchen.

"What does Nick want for breakfast?" Gran asks me.

"Waffles with strawberries. And coffee."

"You make the coffee. I'll do the waffles."

I walk over to the cupboard and get a fresh filter. Take the old one out of the machine, throw it in the trash. Put the new one in and fill it with coffee. I've just filled the machine with water when Pen comes walking in through the back door.

"Hey," I say to her.

"Don't you *hey* me. I've been calling you since last night." She points an accusing finger at me.

"I know." I smile.

"Morning, Penny," Gran says.

"Sorry. Morning, Gran." Her eyes briefly go to Gran before coming back to me. Her gaze narrows. Her hands go to her hips. "What do you mean, you know? Why didn't you answer?"

I stick a cup under the coffee machine and get it going. "Because I knew how much it would annoy you."

Her mouth pops into an O.

I laugh. "You were just calling to grill me about Nick, but honestly, there's nothing to tell." *Except I want to kiss his face off of him. And do other things. To his hot body. Possibly lick his abs.*

"Well, see, if you'd bothered to answer your phone, you'd know that I wasn't going to grill you about him. Actually, I have oodles to tell you about *Nick*." There she goes, saying his name in that way again.

Although I am distracted by her word choice. I cock my head to the side, grinning. "Oodles?"

"Yes, oodles," she says primly, flipping me the bird, making me laugh.

"Oh, I'm here for the gossip," Gran says, leaving the waffle mixing in the KitchenAid and coming over to us.

Pen takes a deep breath, like she's about to deliver a speech in front of the entire nation. The hairs on the back of my neck start to prickle. I don't have a good feeling about this.

"Nick-is-Storm-Slater," she blurts out.

I glance at Gran, who shrugs.

"Pen, I got none of that. Nick is what?"

"*Nick*, the Hottie McTottie you brought into Starbucks yesterday, is *the* one and only Storm Slater. Lead guitarist in Slater Raze. Only child of Jonny Creed. I friggin' knew I recognized him yesterday, but I just couldn't put my finger on where from. Then, it came to me when I was making Mrs. MacIntosh's hot chocolate. Bam! Hit me like lightning. I was like, *That dude is Storm Slater*!" She slams her hand on the kitchen counter.

I glance at Gran again, but she's looking at Pen with interest. At least one of us knows what she's going on about.

"Pen, all I got from that was Nick. Guitarist. Something about a storm and lightning and Mrs. Mackintosh's hot chocolate." And now, I want a hot chocolate.

Pen lets out a sound of exasperation. She looks at Gran helplessly. "You're her DNA. Maybe she'll get it, coming from you."

Gran turns to me. "Honey, what Penny's trying to tell us is that Nick isn't Nick. He's actually Storm Slater."

My brow furrows. "Who's Storm Slater?"

"Storm Slater," Pen says, "is the lead guitarist in Slater Raze, one of the hottest bands around. Total celeb! He's Jonny Creed's son. He was raised by Jake Wethers. He comes from music royalty."

"Dude, you're throwing all these names at me, but I still don't have a friggin' clue what you're talking about."

"I'm literally going to cry right now," Pen says to Gran, who consolingly pats her on the arm. "I'm seriously questioning our whole friendship."

Pen reaches in her bag and pulls out her cell. She taps the screen and then hands it to me. "Read that. If you don't get it after this, then I give up."

I take her phone from her. It's a Wikipedia page. The name at the top says *Storm Slater.*

> *Storm Slater (born September 30, 1994) is an American musician, singer, and songwriter. He is the lead guitarist of the American hard rock band Slater Raze, with whom he has achieved worldwide success. He is the only son of the late Jonny Creed.*

I scroll to the picture beneath, studying it.

It's Nick.

So, Nick's real name is Storm Slater. He's a guitarist in a rock band.

Huh. Go figure.

I hand the phone to Gran, so she can read it.

"Well?" Pen says to me.

"Well … I don't know." I shrug.

I go and turn off the KitchenAid because the sound is driving me nuts.

"Dude, you have a bona fide rock star in the house, and you don't know!"

"Will you keep it down?" I whisper-hiss. "He's right in there." I point in the direction of the door leading to the dining room.

Pen's eyes go to the door. "He's in there? Right now?"

I move in front of her path to the door. "Yes. And no, you are not going in there."

"Ugh. You're a total buzzkill, you know. We have a celebrity in our midst. And not even a B-lister. We are talking A-lister here!"

"We're talking about a person, Pen. A person who lied about his real name. He did that for a reason." *No reason I can think of right now.*

"Oh, I maybe know why." Gran raises her hand likes she's in class.

"Me too!" Pen bounces on her toes. "That was my next bit of gossip!"

Gran hands the phone back over to me. I take it. The screen is now showing a news website.

BREAKING NEWS!

THERE'S ONE HELL OF A
STORM HAPPENING!

Storm Slater was captured on film in an apparent physical altercation with journalist Jasper Marsh. Marsh had allegedly revealed to Storm during an interview that Storm's father, the late Jonny Creed, was heading to the airport the night he died to meet the son he hadn't known he had.

Now, as we all knew, before his death, Creed was supposedly unaware that he had a son.

But it's been exclusively revealed that Creed had received a call from an anonymous source hours before his death, revealing Storm's paternity. It is said that Creed was in his car on his way to the airport to go meet his son.

A meeting he tragically never made.

As you all remember, Jonny Creed died when his car crashed into a ravine late at night. His blood toxicology was later revealed to have been through the roof, leading many to believe that Creed might have actually committed suicide. Something the TMS clan vehemently denied. We now know it's because they knew the real reason that Creed was in his car that night.

And it wasn't just us they kept the truth from.

Storm too.

Shame on them!

Storm was last seen fleeing TMS Records in downtown LA after a confrontation over the death

> *of his father with Jake Wethers, Tom Carter, and Denny Daley.*

> *We've contacted all representatives. But no word back at the time of publication.*

I stare down at the screen, my heart hurting for him.

Jesus. Poor Nick—I mean, Storm. His dad died before he ever met him. And he thought his father never knew of his existence for all those years.

And then hearing it from a journalist and having the intimate details of his life splashed all over the news like this? I can't even imagine how that feels.

Christ, no wonder he didn't tell me his real name. Probably wanted to hide for a bit. Pretend to be someone else. Can't say I blame him.

"Crazy, huh?" Pen says to me.

I hand the phone back to Pen. "No. It's sad," I say, my chest tight with emotion for him.

"I remember that young man dying," Gran tells us. "It was all over the news. You were around four or five at the time, Stevie. And that boy in there is his son." Her eyes go to the dining room door. "So sad."

"But exciting!" Pen says way too loudly.

I hush her again, my eyes darting to the door.

"Come on, you have Storm Slater sitting in your dining room," Pen says, exasperated.

"Waiting for his breakfast." My eyes flash to Gran, who leaps into action.

"On it!" She grabs the batter and pours it into the heated waffle maker.

"Are you not even a little bit excited?" Pen asks me as I take the coffee-filled cup from the machine.

Well, I was excited because Nick was sitting in there. And I like him. More than anyone should after a day of knowing a guy.

But now, I don't know. I guess … I still am excited.

I mean, he's still him. Even if his name isn't what I thought it was.

Storm Slater.

Which is a really cool name.

"Am I excited about Nick—I mean, Storm being a rock star? Nope." I shake my head. "But you clearly are."

Pen's hands go to her hips. "So, you mean to tell me that if Jim Kerr from Simple Minds was sitting in your dining room right now, you wouldn't freak out? Or the one from A-ha who's still hot."

"Morten Harket."

"That's the one." She clicks her fingers. "Total DILF."

"True dat. And yeah, I might freak a little. But that's different."

"How?"

"I don't know." I shrug. "It just is."

Her gaze narrows. "It isn't, and you know it."

She's totally right. It isn't different at all. And now, I feel like a total douchecanoe and a massive hypocrite because I would freak if it were Jim Kerr or Morten Harket sitting in there.

And that makes me no different to Penny and how she's reacting now.

But he's just … Nick. I mean, Storm. Damn it!

"Fine, you're right. It isn't any different. But at the end of the day, he's just a guy, Pen. A really nice guy from what I know of him." *Really fucking nice and hot and gorgeous and everything in between.* "Who's had a shitty time of it. And yeah, he's famous, but knowing that doesn't mean I'm going to treat him any differently. And neither are you." I point at her. "Or you." My finger travels to Gran, who laughs.

"Stevie, I have far better things to do with my time than go giddy over a rock star. Penny's the one you need to worry about."

"Hey!" she says indignantly. "I have some self-control. Well, okay, I don't," she says at my and Gran's expressions.

"But I can be cool. And anyway, I think Raze Rawlins is hotter," she adds with a toss of hair.

"Who's Raze Rawlins?" I ask.

"Christ almighty, Stevie," Pen sighs.

"Raze is the singer in Storm's band," Gran tells me while getting the now-freshly-made waffles out of the maker.

How does Gran even know all of this stuff?

"See, even Gran knows!" Pen exclaims. "Babe, I love ya. But you really need to spend more time out of the eighties."

I lean my hip against the counter. "And why would I do that when all the best music came from that decade?"

"I wouldn't say that to your boyfriend in there."

"Shut up! He's not my boyfriend." *And I'm five years old and back in the school playground.*

Pen laughs. "You're totally crushing on him. I could tell yesterday."

"Whatever. He's good-looking. And since I last checked, it's not a crime to crush on a good-looking guy."

"No, it's not. And it's definitely about time."

I give Pen a look. "I said I was crushing. Not that I was going to do anything about it."

"I told her she should," Gran imparts while getting the strawberries from the refrigerator to top Nick's—*Storm's, damn it!*—waffle.

I roll my eyes. "Thanks for both of your input, but I can handle my love life"—*or lack of it*—"myself. And as for Nick—Storm, or whatever the hell he's called, we keep silent. We do not let on that we know his real name. He wants us to call him Nick, so that's the name we'll call him."

"What if he wants you to call him Daddy?" Pen says, and I nearly choke.

"Jesus, Pen!" I splutter.

"Just saying, I'd call him Daddy if he asked me to." She shrugs, grinning.

"Me too," Grans says.

And I actually die on the spot.

Fucking. Die.

Pen bursts out laughing. Same goes for me.

Screw keeping our voices down. I can't hold anything in after hearing that.

"Christ almighty, Gran!" I gasp, holding my stomach with my hand.

"Just saying." Gran grins before chopping the strawberries, setting me and Pen off again.

When my laughter calms, I try again. "Okay, so we agree to say nothing. We do not call him Storm—or *Daddy*." I snort. "We call him Nick. The guy has had a rough time. His private business is all over the news. He clearly wants privacy. So, privacy is what we'll give him."

"So, basically, what you're saying is that I can't tell one single person that Storm Slater is here in town and staying at the B&B?" Pen looks less than impressed.

"In a nutshell." I nod.

"You're killin' me, Smalls. This is the news of the century."

"I know. But think about it. If people find out that he's here, journalists will turn up, he'll get harassed, and he'll have to leave. He leaves, and you won't be able to fangirl over him."

"Well, it's not like I can fangirl over him because I'm not allowed to let on that I know who he really is." She folds her arms over her chest, lips pouting.

And that's when I know I have her. She'll keep quiet.

And me asking this of her has absolutely nothing to do with me not wanting him to leave.

Nope.

Okay, maybe a little.

But, mostly, it's for his benefit.

"Thanks, Pen. I appreciate it."

She shoots me an unhappy look. "Fine. But I'm only keeping quiet 'cause I love you."

"I know. Love you too." I turn to Gran, who's just finished placing the strawberries on the waffles. "Gran, I can count on you not to say anything, right?"

"Of course." She smiles, picking up Storm's plate.

For a woman who loves her gossip, she's a damn good secret-keeper when necessary.

"You want to take this through?" she asks me.

"Sure." I take the plate from her and pick up his coffee.

Moving through the kitchen, I fix Pen with a stare. "Stay," I tell her.

I push the door open with my hip, and there he is, still sitting at the table, reading the Sports section Dad left there earlier.

Nick. But not Nick.

"Hey. Sorry it took a while."

He glances up at me and smiles.

That smile hits me square in the chest.

Honestly, he could be called Lucifer, and I wouldn't care.

I like him.

Just him.

"No problem," he says, folding the paper up and moving it aside.

I've just put the plate down when the door opens, and I know just who's walking in through it.

Fucking hell, Pen!

"Hey, Nick!" She comes striding over. "Thought I'd come and say hello."

I'm glaring at her. She is, of course, blatantly ignoring me.

I'm going to kill her.

"Sure. Hey. Penny, right?" he says to her.

She giggles.

Actually giggles.

I've never heard that girl giggle in her life.

"Yep. That's me. Penny. Stevie's best friend. And you're Nick."

He nods slowly, staring at her. "Didn't we already cover that yesterday?"

"Duh. Of course we did. Silly me." She flicks her hair and giggles again.

Christ almighty.

He's still staring at her. His brows pinched together.

Then, his eyes dart to me.

I freeze in his gaze.

He holds it there. Then, I watch as his eyes dim before moving down to his plate.

My heart sinks. He knows we know.

He picks his coffee up and takes a large drink.

"Thanks for breakfast," he says quietly, dismissing me.

Fucking hell, Penny! I'm literally going to murder her.

"No worries," I say, forcing brightness into my voice. Then, I flash Pen a look that means retribution.

She just shrugs and mouths, *What?*

"Enjoy your breakfast," I tell him. "Say bye, Penny."

"Bye, Penny," she says, her voice way too high to be normal.

I grab her arm and pull her back into the kitchen.

"Fucking hell, Pen," I hiss. "I told you to stay put."

"I'm sorry." She pouts. "I just wanted to see the rock star."

"You saw him yesterday!"

"But I didn't know who he was then," she whines.

I let out a hint of frustration. My eyes swing Gran's way. "You couldn't have stopped her?"

Gran's hands go up in surrender. "She snuck past me when I was in the pantry."

I pin Pen with a stare. "You're officially banned from the B&B."

"What?" Pen yelps. "No fair!"

"Until *Nick*," I emphasize the name, "has left or you can learn to behave yourself, you're not allowed to come here."

She pouts again, arms folding. "You're being mean."

"I'm being a good B&B manager and protecting my guest from a crazy fangirl."

"Hey!" she exclaims. "I'm not a fangirl."

"No?" I do a girlie giggle, imitating her a moment ago, and flick my ponytail. "*Hi, Nick. I'm Penny. Total fangirl*," I say in a high-pitched voice. I add another hair flick for good measure.

She's glaring at me, less than impressed. But I'm not feeling so impressed with her myself right now.

He's probably sitting in there, feeling shitty because he knows we know who he really is.

I just need to tell him it doesn't matter to me who he is, and I'll keep his identity a secret for however long he wants me to. And so will Penny, if I have to gag and bind her and lock her in the garage.

We're in a staredown at the moment. I know I'll win because Pen is shit at the staring game. She always cracks first. Me, I could go on until the end of time.

"Fine!" She blinks. "I was totally obvious. I didn't mean to be. But he's so famous, Stevie. And you know I've never met anyone famous before. He's this famous rock star with abs that go on for days! And you know abs make me stupid. I mean, come on, have you seen his abs?"

"Actually, yes." I fold my arms over my chest, eyes narrowing. "When did you see them?"

"Calm down, tiger." She rolls her eyes. "I saw a pic of him shirtless online. He was photographed on the beach last year." She mimics me, crossing her arms over her chest, and fixes me with a look. "But more importantly, when did you see them?" I open my mouth to speak, and she cuts me off, "And do not say online 'cause I'll know you're lying."

"Fine," I huff, dropping my arms. "I saw them yesterday. When I went to tow him. He didn't have a shirt on because he'd spilled coffee on it. He was just wearing his leather jacket."

"I saw them too." Gran waves her hand again from her spot by the coffee machine that she's now cleaning down. "He took his shirt off in the gas station when I was there. That's where he spilled the coffee on himself."

"Sweet Jesus." Pen fans herself. "You're telling me that he had on just a leather jacket? And those abs?"

"Yep," I answer.

"How did you not maul him on sight?"

"Because I'm not an animal."

"Dude, we're all animals. If those abs were put in front of me, I would have climbed that eight-step ladder all the way to sex god heaven."

I laugh despite myself. "You're a perv."

She grins and shrugs. "I just really like abs."

"Don't we all?" Gran says on a sigh, making Pen and me chuckle.

"You should totally go for it with him," Pen says to me. "He likes you. I could see from the way he was looking at you when you brought him to my work yesterday. Jeez, an A-list rock star wants to bone my bestie." She fans herself again.

"He does not want to bone me." I roll my eyes.

Totally not feeling giddy at that thought.

But also, I'm crushing on a man who doesn't want me to know who he really is.

That's not messed up at all.

"Pen's right," Gran says. "He does. I told you this last night."

My eyes flick to Gran. "You did not say he wants to bone me. You said I should go up to his room and take the whipped cream with me. Although I don't know which is worse to hear."

"Whipped cream? Go, Gran!" Pen claps her hands together.

"Don't you need to get to work?" I say to her.

Her eyes go to the clock on the wall, and she sighs. "Ugh. Suppose I'd better go. Don't want Gary getting his panties in a twist if I'm late."

I follow her to the back door. Pen collecting her bag and cell on the way.

"Later, Gran," she calls, opening the back door and stepping outside onto the driveway.

"Bye, Penny," Gran calls to her.

I hold the door open, leaning against it.

"Seriously though, babe, you should go for it with him," Pen says to me. "Opportunities like this don't come along … ever for girls like us. The chance to bang a rock star. Dude, do it, or you'll regret it."

"I don't care that he's a rock star."

"I do."

"No shit, Sherlock," I deadpan, and she chuckles.

"Okay, rock star aside, you like the guy. He likes you. He's hot as hell. And you deserve hot after prick-face Josh."

I bristle at hearing my ex's name.

Fucking Josh.

I'm over him. But that doesn't mean I like hearing his name—ever.

"If I were you," Pen continues, "I'd ride that rock star for days. Or let him ride you. Either way, you deserve a good riding."

That makes me laugh. "Go to work," I tell her.

"Promise me you'll ride the rock star," she whisper-shouts, walking to her car. "Do it for the both of us! It's the only chance we'll ever get!"

I shake my head, laughing.

"Say you'll do it!"

"Bye, Pen." I wave, giving her nothing.

She slaps a hand to her chest before getting in her car. "You're killin' me, Smalls!"

I roll my eyes, holding back a smile.

"Love you!" she calls before shutting her car door. "And bang the rock star!"

I close the back door to the sound of her engine starting and car reversing off the drive, still chuckling to myself.

"So, you think Pen gave the game away?" Gran asks as I walk back into the kitchen.

I glance at the door to the dining room and sigh. "Yeah, I think she did."

"That girl." Gran shakes her head, smiling. "She always was overexcitable. Means no harm though."

"No, she doesn't," I agree.

I wouldn't be friends with her if she did.

"What do I do now?" I ask Gran. "Do I go in there and play it cool, wait and see if he says anything to me? Or do I just tell him I know who he is and get it over and done with?"

Gran shrugs, wiping her hands on a towel. "I'd just go in there and play it by ear."

"Play it by ear. Right. Got it."

I walk over to the door and pause.

I wipe my hands on my thighs, smooth my ponytail back, take a deep breath, push open the door, and walk into the dining room.

The now-empty dining room.

18

STORM

"Hey." Stevie's sweet, soft voice comes from my left.

I turn my head to look at her. "Hey." I smile, but it's weak as fuck.

A mix of feelings hits me in this moment. Disappointment because she knows who I am even though I knew this was coming. I guess I just didn't want it to come so soon. I wanted a little more time. Happiness at seeing her because I'm always happy when I see Stevie. And anxiety at what's to come.

I don't think things will change. I don't think she will change or treat me any differently.

But then what the fuck do I know?

I didn't know everyone had been lying to me for years.

So, how would I know how this girl, who I've known for a day, is going to react toward me now? Now that she knows who I am.

And there's no doubt in my mind she knows.

It was written as clear as day all over her friend's face back in the dining room.

And the discomfort I saw in Stevie's eyes as she stood beside her just confirmed it for me.

I move my eyes from her and stare across the street. I take a drag of my cigarette and let the smoke out through my nose.

Stevie comes and sits next to me on the wall outside the B&B where I parked my ass ten minutes ago. I'm also on cigarette number two. But let's not share that with her.

She's so damn short.

Whereas I've got my ass resting on the wall, legs stretched out, feet resting on the pavement, Stevie had to hop up on it, leaving her legs dangling, not touching the floor.

God, she's so fucking cute.

Please don't let this go to shit.

Please don't change.

Treat me the same as before.

She's silent next to me. Which isn't like her at all.

I mean, it's a good thing she's not freaking out on me, going all fangirl. But her silence is equally unnerving.

I take another drag of my cigarette. I let my words out with the smoke, "Must be bad. You're not giving me shit about smoking."

She laughs softly. "Oh, I'm totally gonna give you shit. I just wanted to make sure you were okay first."

"And why wouldn't I be okay?" I turn my eyes to her, waiting to see what she says next. A lot depends on this.

"Well, you make shit music, so …" She grins, and my fucking heart soars.

Laughter bursts from me.

Relief. Elation. What-the-fuck-ever it is, it's because of her.

This fucking girl.

She's amazing.

She's everything.

I tap the ash from my cig to the pavement. "So … you've heard my music?"

"Christ, no. I'm guessing no tambourines, triangles, or electric synthesizers were harmed in the making?"

I chuckle. "Fuck no. Just plain old guitar, bass, and drums."

"Ah, well, bummer for you." She grins and bumps her shoulder against mine.

I feel that quick touch of her body against mine, like she just put her hand on my dick. Heat suffuses in my groin.

I tilt my head her way, looking at her. "So, you're not mad that I lied … about my name?"

Her brows draw together, confusion lying between them. "Why would I be mad?"

I shrug. Another drag of my cigarette.

"If it makes you feel any better," she says, "I had no clue who you were when Pen told me. Still kinda don't. My sixty-six-year-old grandmother knows who you are. Me, not so much. Not sure what that says about me though."

"It means, you're fucking awesome."

"Ah, well, tell me something I don't already know."

She grins at me, and all of my remaining tension melts away.

How does she do that? Make me feel so at ease in my own skin.

Untangle the complicated and make it seem not so messy anymore.

"I've gotta say though, Storm is a pretty fucking cool name. I mean, it's no Stevie, but no one can achieve that level of awesome."

"Thanks. I think." I'm smiling an honest-to-God smile. And I'm pretty sure I've only ever smiled this way with her. Because of her.

There's a beat of silence between us. I feel a shift in the air around us. It makes me tense because I don't know what's brought it on.

"Storm?"

"Yep?" It feels weird, hearing her say my name. But I also like it a fuck of a lot.

Another pull on my smoke, and I brace myself for what she's about to say.

"I need to be honest with you about something."

And here we fucking go. "Hit me with it."

"I feel like a total dick for this, but … I read about you online. I know it's tacky as fuck. I feel bad for it."

I let out a laugh of relief. *That's what's bothering her.*

Christ. And there was me, thinking it was gonna be something bad.

She just keeps on surprising me.

"Stevie, it's fine. I'm used to it."

"You shouldn't be." She frowns. "And I shouldn't have read it. I should've just spoken to you as soon as Pen told me about you. Well, to be fair, Pen had to give me your Wiki page to read because I just wasn't getting it at first."

That makes me laugh again. Only Stevie.

"But, by choice, I did read the news article Gran had shown me."

"Okay …" I say slowly, bringing my eyes to her. "And what did it say?"

"That you assaulted a journalist."

"That's true." I nod.

"Did he deserve it?"

I sigh. "Yeah. But I still shouldn't have done it."

She shrugs. "We do what we have to when necessary."

I'm still staring at her when I ask, "What else did it say?"

She exhales a soft breath that I want to inhale for myself. I just want her goodness inside of me. And I want to be inside of her so fucking badly.

I just want her, full stop.

"It said things about your dad. Jonny, right?" She glances at me for confirmation, but all I can manage is a nod. "It mentioned how he died. How you never knew him and you thought he didn't know you. But he did and that you just recently found that out, that he had been coming to see you the night he died."

"That's pretty much it in a nutshell."

"I'm sorry he died. Sorry that you never knew him."

I sigh again. "Yeah. Me too."

I might resent Jonny in many ways, resent his ghost, the memory of him. But would I have wanted to know him, given the chance?

Of course I would have.

"It also said you had a disagreement with your family …" She leaves the words hanging, giving me the option of whether I want to say more or not.

"Yeah." I sigh again. "Jonny—my dad—and his best friends, they were in a band together. I'd tell you who they are, but chances are, you wouldn't know."

"Probably." She grins, making me smile.

"To cut a long story short, when Jonny died, for a long time, no one knew why he had been out in his car that night. He was high—Jonny had a serious drug problem. A lot of people thought he'd committed suicide, driving his car into that ravine. Turns out, he was driving to the airport to come see me. He'd found out that night that I existed. Jake, Tom, and Denny—my dad's best friends—they never knew about me or what happened that night. They found out about me eleven years ago. Found out the truth about Jonny's last moments the day of my mom's funeral."

"You lost your mom?" she whispers. "I'm so sorry."

I shrug. Because it's all I can ever do when my mom comes up. "It's okay. It was a long time ago." Another pull on my cigarette. I blow out the smoke. "They never told me the truth. I found out yesterday morning. That journalist I assaulted, he told me. I went and confronted them. Said … some shit." *Some awful shit.* "Walked out, got in my car, and started driving."

"Pulled up at a gas station, put the wrong fuel in your car, and here we are."

I rest my chin against my shoulder, staring at her. "Yep. Here we are."

I hold her eyes. I feel the exact moment the air changes. Everything seems heightened. The scent of her perfume. The way her hair blows gently in the breeze. The flush in her cheeks, spreading down her neck, across her beautiful chest. The heat that suffuses her eyes.

Fuck, I want her. More than I've ever wanted anything.

A car horn beeps down the street, killing the moment.

She looks away.

And I want to go punch whoever hit their car horn.

I take a final pull on my cigarette and put it out against the wall. I stuff the butt back in the packet, next to the other butt I just had before she came out here.

"Um … that's you disposing of your cigarette butt responsibly?"

I grin, unable not to. I get off on her giving me shit. Sick fucker that I am. "Yeah …" I say slowly.

"Dude." She frowns, her brows puckering. "That's not even close to disposing of it responsibly."

"Is this the point where I'm supposed to say sorry?"

I'm still grinning because this is what she does to me. She makes me happy as fuck.

She huffs, a little puff of air escaping between her lips. "No. It's fine. The marine life will forgive you this one time." I don't tell her it's not just this one time. "And I owe you a free pass anyway because you didn't give me shit for reading the news story about you when you should've."

I give her a look. "Stevie, I told you, it's not an issue."

"It is an issue. I shouldn't have done it. Also … I have another confession while we're at it." She bites the corner of her lip. "I was gonna go along with the lie. About your name. I wasn't going to tell you that I knew who you were. I figured you hadn't told me for a reason, and that was because you wanted your privacy. So, I was going to give that to you. I'm sorry Pen messed it up. Next time, I'll gag her."

I'm just staring at her, wondering where the hell she came from and how I had the damn good fucking luck to meet her.

She thinks that's bad. That's about one of the nicest things anyone could have done for me.

"Where have you been all my life?" The words are out before I can stop them.

She looks surprised. Her eyes drop down to her feet.

I've embarrassed her. Probably scared the shit out of her.

Fuck.

I've known this girl a day, and I go and say something stupidly fucking forward like that.

But in truth, it feels like I've known her forever.

And what I just said feels an awful lot like the truth.

I'm stumbling over words in my brain, figuring out how to take it back, knowing that I don't want to. "Stevie, I—"

"Right here," she says softly, her eyes lifting back to mine. "I've been right here." She smiles.

And my heart fucking jets. It skyrockets out of my chest. And I'm pretty damn sure it lands back down, right in the palm of her hand.

"Spend the day with me," I blurt.

"Spend the day with you?"

"Yeah," I'm quick to say. "Can you do that … or are you busy?" I tip my head back in the direction of the B&B.

"Yes. I mean, no." She shakes her head. "I'm not busy." A smile lifts her lips, lighting her eyes. "What do you have in mind?"

"Anything," I tell her honestly. "As long as I'm with you, I don't care."

19

Stevie

"*Where have you been all my life?*"

"As long as I'm with you, I don't care."

Yep, those sentences have been on repeat in my head ever since he said them.

It's not often a girl hears those words.

Especially not this girl.

And I'm still trying to figure out in what capacity he meant them.

Where have I been all his life—as a friend?

As long as he's with me, he doesn't care—as a friend?

You can't throw these kinds of bombshell statements on a girl and then leave her hanging. I need answers.

Not that I'm going to ask him for answers.

I'm brave. But not that fucking brave.

Storm left it up to me to choose what we'd be doing today, and as I didn't think he'd want to spend the day around people in case he was recognized, I figured we'd do the one thing we could where he'd be ensured privacy.

Take my dad's boat out.

So, I told Gran I was going to take Storm out on the boat. And I ignored the excited gleam in her eyes.

She'll be at the B&B today because she doesn't have any plans, so it's worked out well. And considering Storm is our only guest until tomorrow when more guests arrive, there's not a lot to be done, except ready their rooms, which I can do later.

I didn't tell Storm where we were going. I thought I'd let it be a surprise.

So, I packed up a picnic. The water isn't usually warm this time of year, but it is an unseasonably warm day today at eighty degrees, so the water should be okay to swim.

I borrowed a pair of Beck's swimming trunks for Storm to wear. And I'm not considering going swimming, so I can see Storm's bare chest again.

No siree.

Although swimming does mean wearing a bathing suit in front of him.

Not nervous about that at all.

I've let Storm have control of the stereo. I was feeling generous. Not my usual MO to give up music control in my car. But when a guy asks where you've been his whole life, then he can pretty much have whatever he wants. Coochie included.

So, we're currently listening to one of his favorite bands, Avenged Sevenfold. "Afterlife" is what I think he said the song's called.

It's not my thing, just a lot of noise if you ask me, but he seems happy, and that's what matters.

He's singing along to the song, which means I get to hear him sing, which of course is a bonus.

He has such an amazing singing voice. It surprises me that he doesn't sing in his band.

"How come you don't sing in your band?" I echo my thoughts, turning onto the street that will lead us to London

Bridge, taking us over the water to the island where the marina is and where Dad keeps his boat.

"I do. Well, I sing backup."

"Why don't you sing lead?" I briefly glance at him.

He's watching me with those intense eyes of his. I catch a shrug before I look back to the road ahead.

"I guess it's just always been that way. Raze sings. I play guitar."

Raze. That's the one Pen thinks is hot.

"So, Raze is the singer. You play guitar. Who else is in your band?" I ask.

He chuckles, making me ask, "What?"

"I'm just not used to someone asking me these kinds of questions. Especially not a girl."

Another glance at him. "Because they always already know?"

"Pretty much," he says. "But I like that you don't know, if that makes sense."

I smile, feeling happy at that. "It makes perfect sense."

"Thank you," he says in a quiet voice.

"For?" I pull up to a set of lights, allowing me to look at him properly.

His eyes meet mine.

He shrugs again. He seems shy, which is at total odds with the confident man I've come to know.

"For not … caring. About who I am out there." He tips his head to the window, indicating the world outside.

I swallow. Then, of course, I make a joke. "I've never been thanked for not caring before."

He chuckles, smiling at me. "Well then, I'm officially the first person to ever thank you for not caring."

"I feel like I need a badge to commemorate it. Or maybe a certificate. Framed, of course."

"Of course."

"Certificate of Achievement awarded to Stevie Cavalli for being the first girl to not care that Storm Slater is a rock star."

"Has quite the ring to it."

"I think so." I grin at him, earning me one of his gorgeous smiles that I feel all the way down to my toes.

The car beeps its horn behind me, making me realize the light has changed.

I put my car in drive and set off moving.

We drive over London Bridge, and I tell Storm about how it was the original bridge that spanned the River Thames in London. Built in the 1800s, it was bought by a founder of Lake Havasu in the 1960s when they built the bridge they have in London now. It was dismantled and shipped here and reconstructed over the water to link the island to the main shore in the early '70s. He seems interested in the brief history lesson, and I'm relieved that I didn't bore him to death.

We reach the marina, and I park the car.

"A marina?" Storm asks as we get out of the car.

"Ever been on a boat before?" I ask him, heading to the trunk of my car.

Then, I hear my words back.

Of course he's been on a boat before, dummy.

God, I ask the stupidest questions at times.

"Yeah … I've been on a yacht." He seems to wince. Like he's embarrassed by this. He shouldn't be. Having money is nothing to be ashamed of. "Not mine," he adds quickly. "It was this guy's yacht. He's a big deal in the music industry."

"Please tell me it had a helipad. Because I'm not calling it a yacht if it didn't." I pop the trunk and get out the picnic basket and bag with our swimming gear.

He chuckles. "Actually, it didn't." He takes the picnic basket and bag from my hands.

"Pfft. Doesn't count then. Not that Dad's boat has a helipad." I start walking toward where the boats are moored on the jetty. Storm follows. "Or its own bathroom," I add. "It doesn't even have a downstairs, and it has a permanent fishy smell to it 'cause Dad mostly uses it to go fishing. So, actually, your music man's yacht sounds a lot better, even without the helipad."

He's laughing the whole time I'm talking. "Have I ever told you that you, Stevie Cavalli, are the best kind of nuts?"

I grin up at him, feeling this warm glow in my chest. "Eh, once or twice. But feel free to keep saying it."

We walk down the jetty to Dad's boat. I climb onboard first. Then, Storm hands me the picnic basket and bag before getting onboard.

"You ever driven a boat?" I ask Storm, moving toward the front of the boat.

Dad's boat is an open bow, meaning it has a seating area at the front of the boat, which I mostly use to sunbathe when I do come out on the boat with Dad. I set the stuff down on one of the two padded bench seats.

"Nope. Never."

"Well, I'd offer to let you have a go today. But I don't feel like dying."

"Hey." His eyes spark with mischief. "I'll have you know, I'm a fast learner. And I'm good at most things."

Hands to my hips, I cock my head to the side. "Only most things?" I tease.

Something hot and dark flashes in his eyes. "Things that matter. I'm really *fucking* good at the things that matter."

Oh. Wow.

Shit. Wow.

What do I say now?

Breathe. Swallow. I'm totally flustered. "Well, if you're really good at the things that matter, maybe I'll trust you to have a try then."

"You should."

And there's that dark, heated stare again.

And I'm also sure that we're not talking about boats anymore.

I'm pretty sure he's hinting at me letting him drive *me* instead. Or drive into me. Or I need to stop with the shitty analogies and say that he's basically hinting at fucking me.

Sweet Lawd.

"Okay then. Cool." I'm walking toward him, but I can't look at him. If I look at him, I might die. Or jump him right here on the boat, on the jetty. "You can have a go. I mean, drive the boat. Later. On the open water."

Jesus. Shut the fuck up, Stevie.

He's standing at the entry to the walkway. I have to sidle past him to get through because he doesn't move to make space for me to pass. And he could. There's plenty of space.

I decide to go past with my back to his front. Chest-to-chest seems like a bad idea for some reason I can't quite fathom in my head.

I just didn't think of the fact that my back to his front means my ass brushing over his groin.

I feel him stiffen behind me. Literally.

I swear to God, he groans.

Or was that me?

I'm hot and turned on and wondering if bringing him on the boat was the worst idea in the history of ideas.

I'm confining myself to a small space with him for a good few hours. And I'm also planning on getting us both into bathing suits and in the water.

Okay, so I never said I was the smartest person in the world.

But I'm not an animal. I can control myself.

I'm not going to have sex with him on my dad's fishy-smelling boat.

There's always the water.

Sweet Jesus.

I can survive a bit of sexual tension.

Okay, not a bit. A nuclear power plant's worth of sexual tension.

And yeah, I'm pretty sure at this point that he wants to have sex with me. But I'm still not sure if I'm the kind of girl who can have a one-time thing.

Especially with how much I like him as a person.

Hotness aside, he's funny, smart, sweet, and kind.

Pretty much all a girl wants in a guy.

I don't know if my heart would be able to separate the sex from my feelings for him.

I go to the back of the boat, and reaching over, I unmoor it from the jetty.

When I turn around, I see Storm quickly look away.

Yep, he was totally looking at my butt.

I hold back a smile. It was clearly the right choice, putting on my denim shorts this morning.

I take my seat at the helm. He sits in the chair next to me.

I take my cell out of my pocket. Select my music app. Scroll my playlist and press play on the only song a girl needs to listen to when she's out on her daddy's boat—"Summer of '69" by Bryan Adams.

Storm smiles at me. "Good song choice," he says.

"I know." I grin at him.

Then, I start the boat up. Maneuver it out of its spot on the jetty and drive it out of the marina and into the open water.

20

Stevie

I take the boat up to Copper Canyon. It's great for swimming, and it's pretty as hell. It's a popular spot around here, but at this time of year, it should be fairly quiet.

And I'm right. As I turn the boat into the canyon, I only see a couple of other boats here.

"I thought we could stop here for a bit," I say to Storm. "Have something to eat. Swim if you want. I brought some of Beck's swimming trunks for you to wear."

"You'll be swimming too?"

I give him a funny look. "Well, I didn't plan on sending you in on your own."

"Then, I'm definitely up for swimming."

Huh. Weird.

Why will he only swim if I'm going in? Does he have a fear of the water or something?

"Are you afraid of the water?" I ask him.

It's his turn to give me a funny look. "No. Why?"

"Just … you don't seem to want to go in the water without me."

He laughs a low sound. "No. I just wanted to make sure I'd get to see you in a bathing suit."

Oh. "Oh."

Christ. I'm going red. I can feel it.

Fucking hell.

I keep my focus ahead and steer the boat into the canyon.

Look at me, I can't even cope with him flirting with me.

He was flirting with me, right? I'm pretty sure he was flirting with me.

Jesus. This is how bad I've gotten—that I don't even know when a guy is flirting with me.

And there's me early-on, thinking about having sex with the guy, and I can't even handle it when he makes a flirty comment, if that's what it even was.

Welp.

I drive the boat to a secluded part, away from the other boats, to give Storm privacy.

Not that I want to get him alone or anything. I mean, why would I want to do that? It's not like I'd even know what to do with the guy.

Turning off the engine, I anchor the boat.

I turn to Storm. He's standing in the walkway of the seating area, looking out at the water.

"Swim first or eat?" I ask him.

He turns to face me. Eyes meet mine. There's something almost playful in them. So, I'm not wholly surprised when he says, "Swim."

Okay.

Bathing-suit time.

At least I put my bathing suit on beneath my clothes. So, it's just a case of me removing them, and I'm good to go.

But still, I'm going to be wearing a bathing suit in front of him.

And for some reason in my wisdom, I decided to put on a two-piece.

It's black. Nothing fancy. But still, it only covers the girls, my coochie, and my butt.

The rest of my skin is going to be on show.

And I am not a girl who feels the need to cover up at the beach. I'm fairly confident about my body. Are there things I'd change? Of course. But I'm sure that's the same for everyone.

I'm just not confident in front of him.

Because I like him.

And given the way I reacted just a few minutes ago when he said he wanted to see me in a bathing suit … I'm almost certain my whole body will be tomato-colored the moment I strip off down to it.

"I'll grab those swimming trunks for you."

It's when I've gotten them out of the bag that I realize he's going to have to put them on.

Meaning he's going to have to strip naked to put them on.

Didn't think that one through, did I?

And it's not like I can leave the room. I'm literally just going to have to turn around while he changes behind me.

Like when we were in his room back at the B&B and he changed into Beck's shirt.

Why is it always my brother's clothes he's changing into when he's stripping off?

But this is good. Just focus on the fact that he's going to be wearing Beck's trunks. Which is gross because Beck.

"Here you go." I hand the trunks to him. "Obviously, there's not a lot of privacy on here, but it's just us here, and I'll just face this way"—I thumb over my shoulder—"while you get changed."

He's staring at me. His eyes move down my body to my bare legs. Then, back up to my face. A small smile curls his lips.

And my mouth goes dry.

"Okay." He nods.

"Right. Okay. Cool. Sure. I'll turn this way then."

I turn away from him and have to stop my hand from smacking my face.

What the fuck was that?

"Right. Okay. Cool. Sure."

Jesus Christ.

I unfasten the button on my shorts and lower the zipper, completely aware of the fact that Storm is getting naked behind me.

Naked as the day he was born.

All those rock-hard muscles, tattoos, and golden skin on show behind me.

Not to mention, his cock will be also out, on show.

Beck's trunks. Beck's trunks.

I'm chanting the words in my head, but it's not working.

He's stripping off his jeans and T-shirt and boxer shorts—does he even wear boxer shorts? God, I hope so. I don't think my heart will take it if he's a commando kind of guy.

Focus, Stevie.

I take a deep breath, clear my mind, and set to the task of undressing myself. I kick off my shoes, push my shorts down over my hips, and shimmy them down my legs. I step out of them, kicking them aside. Then, I grab the hem of my T-shirt and pull it over my head. My hair's still in its ponytail, but I decide to take it out for swimming. More so that I can cover my bare shoulders with my hair, use it as a bit of a shield. I pull the tie from my hair and let it fall down my shoulder. Putting the tie on my wrist, I run my fingers through my hair, tidying it up a bit.

"Turn around." Storm's gruff voice comes from behind me.

"What?" I say.

"I mean, you can turn around. I'm decent."

I know you're decent. That's the fucking problem.

Swallowing down my nerves, I bend down and pick my clothes up from the floor, and then I turn around.

Sweet fucking Jesus.

Just abs. So many abs. And muscles. And tattoos. And smooth golden skin where there're no tattoos. And just fucking hotness.

So much hotness.

If I died right now, I'd go happy as a pig in dirt.

"You look …" He blinks. Then, shakes his head. And blinks again.

I look, what?

Nice? Okay? Bad? Terrible?

WHAT?

"Pretty," he says, voice still rough.

His eyes lift to mine. Heat unfurls low in my belly.

"So fucking pretty."

He thinks I look pretty.

Of course, I go red. I can feel the heat spreading over my chest.

"You too. I mean, nice. Good. Not pretty. What's the dude word for pretty? Handsome? Yeah, you look handsome."

For. Fuck's. Sake.

I'm just going to hurl myself in the water now and get it over with.

Dying of mortification, I busy myself with putting my clothes on the chair.

When I straighten up, Storm is watching me. And he doesn't bother to hide the fact.

I swallow down. "Shall we go in the water?" *Could I be any more awkward right now?*

"Sure."

"Jump in?" I suggest.

"Together?" He holds his hand out to me.

I glance at his hand and then back into those blue eyes of his. "Okay." I smile.

I put my hand in his and let him lead me up and onto the front of the boat.

We're side by side, my hand in his. And it's the best feeling ever.

"On the count of three," I say, and he grins down at me.

"One ..." I start.

"Two ..." he says.

"Three."

And we jump together.

I hit the water and—

Fuck, it's cold!

I lose my hold on Storm's hand as we go under.

Kicking my feet, I swim back up to the surface. When I'm clear of the water, I push my wet hair back off my face.

Storm's already surfaced. He's right here in front of me. Not even a foot away. All wet and beautiful and watching me.

My heart starts to thrum in my chest. Heat between my legs.

I lick the water droplets from my lips.

His stare drops to my mouth.

Something dark and wickedly hot flickers through his eyes.

My stomach clenches tight.

He looks back into my eyes.

I'm not sure who moves first.

Maybe him.

Maybe me.

All I do know is, the distance between us is gone. I'm in his arms, and he's kissing me.

21

STORM

I can't stop kissing her. Touching her.

My hands are in her hair. Then, down to her back. Going lower, grasping her thighs as I urge her to wrap her legs around me so I can have her even closer. Even though I don't think I'll ever get close enough to Stevie.

I want to be inside of her in every way that matters.

Inside of her the way she's inside me. She's under my skin.

It's crazy. I've never felt the way I do with her or about her ever before.

Maybe it's lust. But … no. I've felt lust before. And it's never felt this way.

She willingly comes to me. Legs wrapping around my waist, pressing up against me. Her pussy pressed to my stomach. Her tits crushed against my chest. Arms around my shoulders, her hands clutching the nape of my neck.

We're in the water and I'm kissing her and I never want to fucking stop.

Never.

I could stay like this with her forever.

Just me and Stevie, here.

Nothing and no one else.

Sounds like fucking heaven to me.

The kiss slows. She's breathing heavily. So am I.

But we're reluctant to part. I can tell she is with the way her fingers slide up into my hair, clutching the strands.

"I've wanted to do that since the moment I met you," I say against her mouth.

Her gray eyes open, staring straight into mine. I can see the flecks of gold around the irises. So fucking pretty.

"I've wanted you to do that since the moment I met you." She breathes the words inside of me, and I inhale them.

"All this time wasted," I murmur, brushing my lips over hers, kissing her again. "If only I'd known."

She giggles, and it's the best fucking sound in the world.

My hands slide to her ass. She seems to like that because she starts nibbling and sucking on my lower lip. And I definitely like that. Jolts of heat keep shooting to my cock.

"You want to stay in the water and swim or get back on the boat?" she murmurs, pressing kisses to the side of my mouth, moving lower to my jawline and then up to my ear.

Fuck, that feels good. My hands tighten on her ass. And what an ass it is.

"Is that a trick question?" I reply, and she laughs softly. "Stay in the water and swim with you or get on the boat and get to look at your sweet body? Hmm, let me think."

"Boat then?"

"Definitely."

She goes to move, but I stop her, my hands on her waist.

"Stevie, before, on the boat, when I said that you looked pretty, I tamed my words. I didn't want to scare you with what I really thought."

"Okay …"

"I thought—I think that you're fucking beautiful. The most beautiful woman I've ever seen. And seriously sexy. God, so sexy. And I know this probably sounds cheesy as fuck, and you'll totally give me shit for it, but I wanted you to know."

She's staring at me, saying nothing.

Then, without warning, she crushes her mouth to mine.

I don't hesitate to kiss her back. My hand cupping the back of her head as I match her eagerness and desperation, stroke for stroke.

Breaking off, panting, she leans her forehead against mine, eyes closed. "If I said even half the things I'd been thinking about you, I would definitely scare the shit out of you."

She laughs softly, and I chuckle.

"I don't scare easily, babe."

Her eyes flash open at the term of endearment. There's a warm look in them that I feel deep inside my chest. She cups my jaw with her palm and runs her thumb over my lower lip.

She pecks me once more and then says, "Let's get on the boat."

We swim around to the back of the boat where the ladder is.

Stevie goes up first, of course. I'd like to say it's because I'm a gentleman, but I totally want a view of that sweet ass in my face. I follow up after her.

Stevie pulls two large towels from the bag, handing one to me. She wraps the other around herself, covering her body.

Yeah, not so keen on that.

I dry myself off with the towel and then toss it aside.

I reach out and give her towel a little tug at the point where she tucked it in. It drops to the floor at her feet.

"Much better," I say. Then, I pull her to me and crash my lips back down to hers.

Without breaking the kiss, I back up, taking her with me, until I'm sitting down. I bring her down onto my lap, so she's straddling me.

Legs on either side of mine. Her pussy pressed against my hard cock. Only two thin pieces of material separating us. I can feel the heat of her through the fabric.

I have one hand in her hair, keeping her mouth to mine. Not that she's going anywhere. Stevie is as into this as I am. Thank fuck.

I let my other hand trail up her side, loving the way she shivers. I wrap my hand around her rib cage, just beneath her tit. My thumb lightly strokes the underside of it.

She moans into my mouth.

I didn't think my dick could get any harder.

I was wrong.

I cover her tit with my hand, taking it slow. I don't want to rush her into anything. She rushes it for me. Pressing herself harder into my hand.

Fuck yeah.

I brush my thumb over the peak of her hard nipple through the fabric of her swimsuit.

She shudders under my hands. Pressing herself harder against my aching cock.

She's turned on. I'm turned on.

I really want my mouth on her. I want to pull that string on her bikini top and take her nipple into my mouth.

And I know we're secluded, and no one is around. But Stevie is shy.

I don't want to freak her out by pushing things too quickly.

I'm not in this to just fuck Stevie and be done. This wouldn't be a one-time thing for me.

I don't know when this happened or how it happened. All I do know is that I want more from her. I want all of her.

I don't want just one night with Stevie.

I want all her nights.

And, honestly, I'm just happy, being here with her, kissing her.

I move my hand up from her tit, sliding it up her chest.

She makes a sound of protest, and I chuckle darkly. I love that she wants my hands on her 'cause I sure as hell want to be touching her all the damn time.

My hand circles around to cup the nape of her neck, my thumb pressing gently against her throat.

Her hands come to rest against my chest. One of her palms moving to brush over my nipple, making me shiver.

She smiles against my mouth. "You like that?"

"I like you. And everything you do. Period." And I mean it.

I don't say this shit lightly. And there is definitely nothing light about the way I feel for her, especially in such a short space of time.

It's crazy.

I know it's crazy.

But I also don't fucking care.

Because this is *everything*.

She is everything.

Stevie is the end game as far as I'm concerned.

I just hope she feels the same way about me and that I'm not in this on my own.

22

Stevie

It's mid-morning and a beautiful day. My hand is in Storm's as we walk back from the grocery store. In his other hand is the bag of groceries. We went to pick a few ingredients up for Gran that she needs to make dinner tonight. He's also wearing his sunglasses and a baseball cap. The last thing he wants is to be recognized at the grocery store.

I love the feel of his callous palm against my skin. Crazy how such a small act as hand-holding can feel so important.

Storm seems to like to hold my hand. He reaches for it all the time.

I would never have had him down as the touchy-feel kind of guy. But he seems to like touching me. He hasn't had his hands or mouth off me pretty much since that day on the boat when things shifted from friends to … well …

We haven't discussed what this is that's happening between us. But to me, it does feel an awful lot like dating.

I mean, we've spent almost all our time together since we met.

But Storm hasn't said anything, and I definitely will not be bringing the subject up.

And I'm not complaining because I'm liking this … whatever it is that's between us. It feels natural and right.

It makes me feel happy.

He makes me feel happy.

Am I crazy? For the way I'm feeling about him.

I barely know him but feel like I've known him my whole life.

And the chemistry between us is off the charts.

It never felt this way with Josh. We were kids when we got together. But even still, it never felt so right, as I feel the way I do with Storm.

We just click. Like two parts fitting together.

I never believed in soul mates.

But I'm starting to wonder …

And there I am, getting way ahead of myself.

I don't even know if what we're doing is dating. We haven't even slept together, for Christ's sake, and here's me, saying the guy could be my soul mate.

Yep. There's been no sexy time.

We've hit second base, and that's it. And even that is PG-rated. I'm talking hand-on-boob-over-clothing action and nothing more.

We kiss tons, but he hasn't even once attempted to de-clothe me.

I think he's trying to be respectful.

I'm ready to rip his clothes off.

Storm's phone starts ringing. He lets go of my hand and pulls his cell from his pocket. He glances at the screen before looking at me. "It's Beck," he tells me before answering. "Hey, Beck. Yeah. Cool. Okay. That's great."

My stomach starts to sink.

There is only one reason Beck would call. Because the part they need to fix his car has arrived. Beck had to order it in. It's arrived earlier than expected.

Just my frigging luck. When you want something, it takes forever and a day to arrive. When you don't want something to come, it shows up early.

"Thanks, man. I'll see you later." Storm ends the call and pockets his cell.

Our walk has slowed to a stop.

He turns to face me. "The part for my car is in."

And there it is.

I swallow down my feelings. Because I knew this was coming. Even if a little sooner than I hoped.

"That's great news." *It's awful news.*

I smile up at him. It's a weak-as-crap smile, and he knows it. I can tell in the way his brow furrows ever so slightly.

Pull it together, Stevie. Don't get upset. This was always going to happen.

He was never here forever.

He has a life in LA. His band is there.

"Yeah … Beck said he'll fix it today. My car will be ready … tonight."

I love my brother, but I could kick him for being so damn efficient at his job.

I can't speak because the words won't come without the waterworks, so I force my smile bigger and brighter.

Storm pulls off his sunglasses and pockets them. His eyes look bluer than ever. They look conflicted. "Stevie—"

"This is good news, right?" I take a step back, putting some distance between us.

He frowns.

But distance is what I need to get through this.

"Your car being fixed means you can get back to LA. Which is good. It's great. I'm happy for you." I'm officially smiling the widest smile I've ever smiled. I must look deranged. But I'm desperately trying not to burst into tears.

Which is stupid.

I'm stupid.

I've known this guy for a short period of time.

I knew this was temporary.

He was never mine to keep.

Storm lowers the grocery bag to the floor. Steps closer, reclaiming the space I put between us, and takes my face in his hands. I close my eyes.

I can't have him this close, touching me like this, and not cry.

Funny because, only moments ago, I was feeling happy.

Shows you just how quickly things can change.

"Stevie … look at me." His voice is low and commanding.

I blink my eyes open. His stare is focused and intense.

"I don't care that my car is ready. Because *I'm* not ready to go yet. I want more time with you."

Yet.

That one words says everything.

He's not ready to go *yet*. But he will be at some point.

My mouth is dry. My chest aches.

I do want more time with him. But won't it just hurt more when it does come time for him to leave?

Because, inevitably, it will happen.

He said it himself. *Yet.*

He will eventually leave.

He presses his forehead to mine. "Tell me you want me to stay."

Conflicting feelings have my mind and heart at war.

He stays, and it only prolongs the inevitable. The longer I'm with him, the more I'll feel. The more it will hurt when he goes.

But sense has never been my strong point. And knowing he wants to stay, even if just a bit longer, makes me find it harder to care about my own feelings.

I'll deal with the pain when it's time.

I wet my lips, exhaling a breath. "I want you to stay."

He groans, and it sounds an awful lot like relief. Then, his lips find mine, and he kisses me right here in the street.

It's deep and wet and intoxicating. And it feels like a claiming.

I'm clutching on to him for dear life, kissing him back equally as desperately.

He breaks off, breathing heavy. He tilts his head back, staring into my eyes, his own bright with some unnamed emotion. His hands still cradling my face. "You want me to stay?" he checks.

"Yes."

"Then, I'm staying." His words sound final, but we both know they're not. Because left unsaid was for how long he's staying … another day or a week or a month.

He kisses me again. Softly this time. Light, feathery kisses over my mouth, along my jaw. Then, he pulls me tight into his arms, holding me.

And I grip on to him, praying that my heart can take it when he does finally decide that it's time for him to go.

23

STORM

It's early evening, and Beck has brought my car from the garage to the B&B for me. She's all shiny and beautiful and working.

I used to think she was the most beautiful thing in the world.

I was wrong.

Stevie is.

"Thanks, man," I say as Beck gets out of my car, handing me my keys.

"No problem. She was a dream to drive. Back to new, like nothing ever happened."

But it did happen, and I'm so fucking glad it did because it brought me here to Stevie.

"How much do I owe you?"

Beck pulls the bill from his pocket and hands it to me. "Just settle it up later with me."

I open up the bill. Not bad. Could've been worse. But, honestly, I'd have paid anything to meet Stevie.

"It's fine. I've got the money on me. Let me pay now." I grab my wallet from my pocket and pull the hundred-dollar bills, adding extra to it.

Beck takes the money from me, briefly counting it. "There's too much here," he tells me, trying to hand back the extra bills I put in there.

"The extra is a thanks for fixing her."

"That's my job. And it's not like I didn't charge for labor." He laughs. "Because I did."

"Beck, it's fine. Take it."

He eyes me for a moment. "This isn't because you're …" He trails off. "*With* Stevie, is it? Because I ain't buyable, man. I don't give a shit who you are. You hurt my sister, and I'll kick your ass, just like I did the last one who screwed her over." He holds the extra money out for me to take.

He kicked her ex's ass. I'm glad someone did.

Since Beck and Bryan, Stevie's dad, found out who I really am, neither of them have treated me any differently. But then, they're Stevie's people, so I didn't expect any less.

"No, man, it's not because I'm with Stevie. It's a thanks for fixing my car. And I'm glad you kicked her ex's ass. And if I do anything to hurt her, I'll fucking stand there and let you beat the shit out of me."

He's still watching me carefully.

"I think Stevie is fucking amazing. I don't know where this thing between us is going." *Somewhere, I hope.* "But I do know I would never do anything to purposefully hurt her."

And I do know that. Because I think the world of her.

The man who came here isn't the same man that I am now.

In the past, I wouldn't have given a shit how a woman I was with was feeling. Only how she was going to make me feel when I got to fucking her.

God, I was a total prick.

In some ways, I'm just as bad as that shithead ex of hers. Except I'm no cheater.

No, because you've never committed to anyone to be able to cheat on them.

True. But even still, I know me … and I would never cheat. Especially not on a girl like Stevie.

I might not know where this thing between us is going.

Her life is here. Mine is in LA.

But I do know how I feel about her. And she feels an awful lot like she's mine.

Beck sighs and pockets the money. "Fine. I'm taking you on your word. Stevie is sweet and trusting. She comes off as tough, but she's not. Not really. She hurts. And if she hurts, I hurt whoever made her cry. So, you ever do anything, on purpose or not, and I will beat the crap out of you. And I'll also stuff this money where the sun don't fucking shine."

Nodding, I say, "I accept that."

Because if someone ever hurt Belle, purposefully or not, I'd do the exact same.

The back door bangs open. I turn to see Stevie. My face breaks out into a big smile at the sight of her, and I was just with her literally minutes ago.

I'm so screwed.

"You got your car back then." She's smiling back at me, but it's missing that Stevie spark. It has been since the conversation of my car being fixed came up.

We were living in a bubble until that point.

Now, my car being back and working has put an end date on this thing between us. But I really don't want there to be an end date. I just can't figure out how to keep Stevie and go back to LA. And I have to go back for the guys. We made a pact in the beginning. If one of us goes, we all go.

There's no Slater Raze without the four of us.

And I've been writing songs since I got here, and I haven't written anything decent in a long time.

It's because of Stevie. She fucking inspires me.

And this is different material. Really good music.

The boys will love it.

But for them to hear it, I have to go home, and right now, that feels hard to do.

But I know I have to leave here at some point.

I love the guys, the music. So do Levi and Cash.

But we could go on without it.

Raze couldn't. The band is his life.

And he's my best friend.

So, I have to return there.

I just don't know how to do it. Go back to LA and keep Stevie. I don't know how to get everything I want.

But right now, I have her, and I'm going to make the most of it.

I grab hold of her around the waist. Swinging her around, I plant a kiss on her lips.

Beck mutters something about, "Don't need to see this shit," and disappears inside the house.

"Come for a drive with me?" I say, pressing individual kisses to her mouth.

"You're offering to drive me?" She blinks dramatically, and I chuckle.

Stevie has been driving me everywhere since my car has been out of service.

"Yep. I want to introduce you to the other woman in my life. Show you your competition."

She laughs, pressing her hands against my chest, leaning back to stare into my eyes. "Dude, there is no competition. I'm awesome." She shrugs, smiling.

"Yeah, you are." I pull her back in and plant one more kiss on her lips.

Then, taking her hand, I lead her around to the passenger seat. I open the door, and she gets inside. Once she's in, I close the door behind her and round the car to the driver's side and climb in.

Stevie's already got her seat belt on, ready to go.

I pull mine on and start my baby up.

She purrs to life.

It's like fingers sliding over my skin. Feels almost as good as when Stevie touches me.

"Where are we going?" she asks as I reverse off the driveway.

"Where do you want to go?"

She shrugs. "Don't care. As long as I'm with you."

I smile at her. Pick her hand up and kiss it. I don't let go. I keep her hand in mine, resting it on my thigh.

I head toward the 95, so I can take her out on the highway and open her up.

The sun is setting, giving the sky a reddish glow. My window is down. The radio is playing. The girl I'm crazy about is sitting beside me.

Life doesn't get any better than this.

"Who sings this song?" Stevie asks about what's currently playing on the radio.

It's the acoustic version of "I Don't Care."

"Ed Sheeran."

"Who's he?"

I chuckle. "Singer from England. Good guy."

"You know him?"

"Met him a couple of times."

"And what's this song called?"

" 'I Don't Care.' " I glance across at her, momentarily taking my eyes off the road. Her brow has furrowed. I laugh. "That's the name of the song, not that I don't care." *Because I care about you. A fuck of a lot.* "Why?"

"No reason."

"Stevie …"

"Yep?"

"You like it, don't you?"

Her lips purse, her eyes narrowing. "I never said that."

I laugh again. "You didn't say you didn't either. Holy shit, Stevie … you like it. You like a song that's not from the eighties. I don't know whether to high-five Ed Sheeran or be offended that you like his music and not mine."

Her nose wrinkles. "I haven't heard your music."

"Again. Offended or not …" I chuckle.

"I'll listen to it if you want?"

"Let me think on that for a little while."

"Why?"

"I don't know if my fragile ego could take the criticism."

"Hey! I'm not critical."

"Nope. Just honest. And so far, you like cheesy eighties pop and Ed Sheeran. I don't think I stand a good chance."

"One song, dude!" She sticks her index finger up. "One! It's just a catchy tune, is all." She pouts, and it's fucking adorable.

"So, you admit you like the song?" I deadpan.

She scowls at me. "You ass … you tricked me into that."

I shrug. "I'm smart. Can't help it."

"You're a butthead, and you can help that," she mutters, making me grin. "I just like the words. That's all. Doesn't mean anything."

I'm laughing now. "Course not, babe." Then, I give her a sobering look. "But you know, on the original chart release of this song, he sings it with Justin Bieber."

Her hand covers her mouth, her eyes going wide. "You're shitting me?" The words come out between her fingers.

"Nope." I grin.

"Oh God, I'm a Bieber fan. Pen will be so proud."

"You wanna hear the Bieber version?"

She pauses. Then, she glances around like there're people around us who might hear. "Yeah, I kinda do." She sighs.

And I'm laughing again. Like I always do when I'm with her.

"You can't tell anyone. If you do, I'll put your nuts in a shredder."

I shudder. "That sounds fucking awful."

She gives me an evil grin. "Exactly."

Smiling, I lift her hand to my mouth and kiss it again. "Your secret's safe with me." I release her hand and search through my music until I find the Sheeran and Bieber collab version. I hit play, and the music fills the car.

"I'm such a dirty cheater." She sighs. "But, damn, this is a good song. I don't know if I prefer this version or the first version … probably the first version," she adds a moment later.

"You'll probably like more of Ed's songs. I'll introduce you to them."

"Hey, calm down there." She lifts a hand in a stopping gesture. "Don't be getting all crazy. I like this song. But I'm not sure if I'm ready to go all full-blown affair and cheat on the eighties with this Ed guy."

This Ed guy.

God, she cracks me up.

"Stevie Cavalli, you are the best kind of nuts," I tell her, and she smiles, seeming to like that.

I'm staring at her, grinning, my eyes flickering between the road and her because I can't *not* look at her. Because she's beautiful and sexy and fucking awesome.

And I'm hard. Yep, that's right; my dick is hard. Because this is what she does to me. I've never known anyone like her before.

I get hard from hearing her laugh. From laughing with her. I'm either losing my fucking mind or this is how it is for everyone when they meet *the* girl.

And she is *the* girl.

She's my girl.

I come off the 95, taking the turn heading for the bridge, to drive us onto the island where the marina is and where her dad's boat is kept. There are some nice beaches on here. Not that we'll be able to see them. The sun has set now, and night has come in. But then I'm not coming here to look at the beaches.

I want to make out with my girl in my car.

I follow the road round the island and park the car up in a space facing out over the water. There are no other cars around.

It's just me and her.

I turn off the engine, plunging us into darkness, leaving the music playing.

I shove my seat back as far as it will go. "Come here," I say to her, holding out a hand.

She takes my hand and climbs over into my lap, tucking her legs between mine.

I cup her chin in my hand and kiss her. Softly at first. But it quickly turns into more. Deeper. Wanting.

Because I want her all the damn time.

I've been holding back with her even though I've felt her pushing for more.

I haven't wanted to rush things with her.

But now, I'm feeling the time that I have left here with her. Like it's slipping through my fingers.

Her hand slides into my hair, gripping. She moans into my mouth. It's like a lightning rod to my dick.

Def Leppard's "Hysteria" is now playing on the radio, and I'm feeling every single one of those fucking lyrics.

Because that's how I feel about her. Hysteria when she's near. Like I'm coming out of my skin with wanting her.

It's amazing and scary and fucking intense.

But I want all of these feelings.

I want all of her.

My hand slides up her bare leg to her thigh, fingers inching under the hem of her denim skirt.

She shifts restlessly in my lap. Her ass pressing against my hard, aching dick.

I suck on her tongue, at the same time grazing the underside of her tit with my thumb, knowing it drives her crazy.

She squirms against me.

Then, she grabs ahold of my hand and guides it down, putting it between her legs. "Touch me," she whispers. "*Please.*"

I almost come out of my seat. And my dick.

I haven't suffered premature ejaculation since I figured out what my cock was for. But I have a feeling I'll be coming in my pants like a preteen the second I put my hand on her.

Leaving my hand where she put it, I rub my thumb up and down against her skin. I bring my other hand around the back of her neck, cupping it. My thumb presses against her pulse.

It's beating wildly.

I stare into her eyes.

I need to know she really wants this.

I'm so nervous with her. All my confidence is gone. I've got nothing.

I'm never nervous with a woman.

But with her, I am. Because she means so much to me.

I don't want to fuck this up. And I am absolutely stellar at fucking things up.

But I can't mess this up with her. She's too important to me.

I could sit here and say it's not a big deal, that it's just fooling around in my car with a girl.

But it is a big deal. It's Stevie.

I could say I'm not falling for her. But it'd be a lie.

Because I am.

It's fast. Fucking lightning fast.

I also don't care.

Her fingertips touch my lips. She replaces them with her mouth.

"Don't … you want me?"

My head jerks back. I stare into her eyes. "You are all I want. I just want to do this right. I don't want you to regret anything."

She sucks her lower lip into her mouth, biting on it. "I could never regret anything with you."

I also don't need to be asked twice.

I turn Stevie, putting her back to my chest. I pull her skirt up and part her legs with my hands on her thighs, spreading her open for me.

Starting at her chest, I run my hand down between her tits, down over her stomach, until I reach her pussy.

I let my fingers brush over the cotton fabric of her panties.

She shudders against me.

She's soaked.

"This for me?" I ask.

She nods.

"Do you like these panties?" I say against her ear.

"I can live without them." Her words are breathy. She's panting.

I can smell her lust from here. It's fucking intoxicating.

I lick the shell of her ear, making her groan. "Good." I grip the elastic with my hands at one side and snap it. I do the same with the other side, and the fabric is gone. Tossed aside and forgotten.

I cover her pussy with my hand.

Her head falls back against my shoulder, her pussy bearing down on my hand, needing the contact.

"Storm …" she moans.

"I've got you, babe. I'll take care of you."

She's hot and wet and everything I've ever wanted.

I slide a finger inside her.

She's so fucking tight.

I pull my finger out and put it in my mouth, sucking her off my skin, needing to taste her.

Her head is turned to mine, eyes wide and on my mouth.

I grin.

My hand goes back to her pussy, and I slide my finger between her soaked folds.

I bring it back to her mouth.

"Taste yourself." I run my finger over her lips, coating her mouth.

Her tongue darts out and licks her juice from her lips.

"You taste so fucking good," I tell her right before I cover her mouth with mine and plunge my finger back inside her pussy, fucking her with it.

God. The feel of her body pressed up against mine. The sweet scent of her perfume. The hint of crisp apple that I can smell in her hair.

The way she tastes … like pure sex.

Her skin.

Her mouth.

Her.

She's everything.

I feel drunk off her. And it's not just her body. It's her mind. Her smart mouth. Her zero tolerance for my bullshit.

She's a fucking queen.

And I adore her.

Pushing up her shirt, I pull down the cup of her bra and roll her nipple between my finger.

She's panting and groaning, her hips moving restlessly against my hand.

I add another finger, sliding it inside her, widening her up.

"God, Storm," she groans. Her head turning into my neck, she starts kissing me there.

"That's it, baby." I tug on her nipple, increasing the pace of my hand, speeding up, letting the heel of my palm press against her clit with each return back into her pussy I make.

She moves, hitching her hips forward, and her hand snakes between us. She cups my cock through my jeans, squeezing it.

"Fuck, baby," I moan.

Stevie tugs down the zipper and gets my dick out.

Her hand is on me for the first time.

And I've died and gone to fucking heaven. I feel like I'm being touched for the very first time.

I grab her chin and turn her face back to mine, and I kiss her. Hard and heavy. Thrusting my tongue in her mouth the way I'm thrusting my fingers in her.

I drag my thumb over her clit. She cries out into my mouth.

I start circling her clit with my thumb, teasing her.

Her hand squeezes my dick and starts pumping it up and down in the limited space we've got, urging me on, wordlessly telling me to give her more.

So, I do. I stop teasing and stroke her clit, giving her what she needs.

The only sounds are of our hot, wet kisses and out-of-control breaths. My hand slapping against her pussy with each drive in my fingers make. My low groans with each squeeze and stroke of my dick.

What I wouldn't give to be able to spread her out right now and eat her pussy. Make her come with my mouth.

But nothing will get me out of my car with her. I'm going nowhere, and neither is she until she's screaming my name and I've got her cum all over my hand.

And also, my cum all over her hand and back. Because I am so fucking close to coming, it's not even funny.

I sink my teeth into her lower lip. "You keep doing that, and I'm gonna come, babe."

She squeezes my dick. "I want you to come."

"You come first. That's just the way it is."

I drag the tip of my callous thumb over her clit. She shudders.

"You like that?" I ask.

"Yes," is her breathy response, and she gets even wetter against my hand.

My fingers are soaked. And it's so fucking hot.

"Faster," she tells me.

I give her what she wants. I move my thumb faster, gliding it over her clit.

I can tell she's close. So, I pinch her nipple with my fingers, gently tugging on it, giving her more, taking her there.

I kiss her neck, licking and sucking on her skin.

"Storm … please … I'm close … so close …" Her incoherent words ramble off into nothing.

I feel the instant her orgasm hits. Her hand stops moving on my cock. She squeezes it hard, and it's pleasure-pain.

Her pussy tightens around my fingers. Her body stiffening against mine. She cries out my name, and it's the hottest fucking sound in the world.

I pump my dick in her tight fist and spill a few seconds later, coming all over her hand and back so fucking hard that I'm pretty sure I black out for a few seconds.

"Fuck," I breathe against her neck, pressing kisses against her skin, unable to stop touching her.

"Yeah," she agrees.

"You okay?" I ask, reluctantly sliding my finger out of her. I cup my hand over her pussy, still needing that contact.

Her eyes turn to mine. "I'm more than okay." She gives my cock, which is now flying at half-mast, a gentle squeeze.

Jesus, I've just come, and I'm still semi-hard. That never happens. It's her. Because of her.

"Are you?"

I smile and brush my lips over hers. "The best I've ever been. Although we are kind of messed up." I indicate to the stickiness between us.

She laughs. "I don't care. It was hot. It is hot."

And I don't disagree with that. Because it was hot.

It was the single hottest sexual experience I've ever had. And I've had a lot of experiences in my time.

Who knew fingering Stevie to orgasm while she jacked me off in the front seat of my car would be it for me?

But it is.

She's it for me.

If this is all I ever have with her, I will die a happy man.

But also, now that I've had a taste, I definitely want more.

Just imagine what it'll be like when we do finally have sex.

It'll be fucking explosive.

One thing I do need to know now though …

I reach over and turn on the overhead light.

She squeals in protest at the blinding light, covering her eyes with her hands. "What are you doing?" she complains.

"Just checking something."

"What are you checking?" She drags her hands from her face.

I peer down at her chest. *Yep, it's red.* And I don't know why, but that makes my dick rock hard all over again.

I drag my finger over the red skin on her chest. "From the moment I met you and saw how you blush on your chest, I wondered if it also went red when you orgasmed. It does."

She blinks back at me.

"It's really fucking hot," I tell her. I drag the palm of my hand over her tit, cupping it, and press my hand up hard against her pussy.

I watch her pupils dilate. Her fingers flexing against my hard cock.

"You in a rush to get home?" I ask her.

She shakes her head. "No."

"Good, 'cause I'm nowhere near done with you." I slide a finger back inside her, loving the sound of the surprised gasp she makes, catching it with my lips and swallowing it down.

"Turn the light off," I tell her. "So, I can make you come again."

24

STORM

Stevie and I are out in town, getting ice cream together. We just went to the cinema, and when we got out, she had a craving for peanut butter cup, so here we are.

We've been going out more together over this last week on dates, for dinner, picnic in the park. We've even been out on her dad's boat again.

It's crazy to think I've been here almost two weeks. It feels like longer, but it's still not enough time either.

But then all the time in the world still wouldn't be enough with Stevie.

I have been getting more relaxed around here, not worrying so much about getting recognized. And if anyone has figured out who I am, no one seems to care.

I like this town. I'd like it even if Stevie wasn't here.

But I like it even more because she is.

Ariana Grande is playing in the background—"God Is a Woman." And I'm thinking she might be right because Stevie is pretty fucking heavenly.

And … the cheese just keeps coming.

I swear, if Stevie heard half the shit I thought about her, she would piss herself, laughing.

I'm smiling at the thought while watching her lick the ice cream off her spoon, wondering how soon I can get her home and get my tongue on her, when my cells starts to ring.

Getting it from my jacket pocket, I see that it's Zane calling.

Something heavier than rocks drop into my stomach.

There's only one reason he'd be calling, and it's not for a chat.

"I gotta take this," I tell her, standing from my seat. I press a kiss to the top of her head. Walking out of the ice cream parlor, I answer the phone as I go, "Zane."

"So, you do know how to use your fucking phone."

I let out a breath, readying myself for this conversation. "Sorry I haven't been in touch. I've been taking some time off."

"Yeah, I know. You done?"

"I don't know …"

He laughs without a shred of humor. "That was me giving you the chance to say the right thing. You didn't. So, now, I'm fucking telling you that you're done. You're gonna get your ass back here and get this album written, or I'm bringing in songwriters, and you'll be playing someone else's music for the foreseeable future."

"But—"

"Shut the fuck up, Storm. There're no buts. You come back to LA and get in the studio, or you can kiss good-bye to any artistic control over the songs that go on the album."

"Jesus, Zane. Come on. The date we're supposed to start recording isn't until—"

"A month's time."

Shit, is it?

Pulling the phone from my ear, I glance at the date on my phone.

Fuck, he's right.

I put my cell back to my ear. "Look … you don't need to bring anyone else in. I've been writing while I've been here. It's good stuff. Really good. You'll like it."

"You'd better fucking hope I do. Bring the songs into the studio with you tomorrow."

"Tomorrow?" I almost fall over in shock. "Zane, I can't—"

"Do I sound like I'm asking? Your boys have been covering for you for the last few weeks. But, ultimately, you're the songwriter. Get your ass back here and do your fucking job."

Pausing, I sigh. "Have you spoke to Jake?"

"I speak to Jake more than I speak to my wife. Your fucking point is?"

"Well … is this him telling me to come home?"

Zane laughs. "I'm not Jake's fucking errand boy. Whatever the hell family shit you have going on, *I don't care*." He enunciates each word clearly. "This is me, the VP of the label your replaceable band is signed to, telling you to get your ass back to LA and start working on this fucking album ASAP. We invested money in you. I expect to see a return on it."

Jesus. I have to go home.

Swallowing down, I say in a quiet voice, "There's no movement on tomorrow at all?"

"No. I'm running a business here, Storm, not a fucking preschool." Then, he hangs up on me. Which is usual protocol for Zane.

Fuck. I have to go back tomorrow.

Fucking fuck!

I'm not ready to leave Stevie.

But if I don't go … the album will be screwed. I can't have other people writing the songs. We write our own music. We always have.

Fucking Zane.

Though I can stand here and blame him, he's only doing his job. Doing what I've seen Jake do to other bands over the years. The world doesn't stop turning just because I decide I need to step off for a while.

And I do need to go back and face Jake, Tom, and Denny. I have to sort things out with them.

I might still be angry with them over what they did. But they're my family.

The only family I have.

Palming my cell, I open up the Messenger app.

I open the group text with the boys, firing off a message, letting them know that I'll be back tomorrow afternoon and to meet me at the studio.

I'm not leaving tonight. I want one more night with Stevie.

I'll drive back early tomorrow morning.

An ache pierces into my chest at the thought of driving away from her tomorrow.

Don't think about it.

Just focus on what needs to be done.

I open up another message to send to Jake, Tom, and Denny, asking if I can see them tomorrow night to talk.

I don't bother to wait for the replies to come back in.

I've got this one night left with Stevie. I'm not wasting a second of my time with her.

I've also got to figure out a way to tell her that I'm leaving.

Even though I know she knows it's coming at some point, the coward in me—the one who doesn't want to say the words out loud because when I do, it makes them real—doesn't want to tell her.

But I know I have to.

I take a deep breath. Pull the door open and walk back inside.

Stevie's still sitting right where I left her.

Pain lances across my chest, almost taking my breath away.

I knew leaving her would be hard. I just didn't realize how fucking hard.

"Hey." I sit back down across from her.

She puts her spoon down in her bowl.

"Hey." She smiles, but it doesn't quite reach her gorgeous eyes. "Everything okay?" she asks, referring to the phone call.

No, babe. It's really not.

I should tell her right now.

But I don't want to do it here. I'll wait until we get back to the B&B.

So, I force a smile, reach over, take hold of her hand, and say, "Yeah, babe. Everything's fine."

"*Everything's fine.*"

That's what he's said twice now when I've asked if he's okay.

But it's clearly not fine. He's been off since he took that call half an hour ago at the ice cream parlor.

He was quiet the whole car ride back. He smoked two cigarettes on the way back with his window rolled down.

He didn't even ask me if I minded.

That's not like Storm.

And I said nothing. Which is unlike me. I didn't even give him shit when he flicked both the cigarette butts out of the window.

I did make a mental note whereabouts he ditched them, so I can go back and pick them up.

Just because we're having problems doesn't mean the marine life should suffer for it.

And now, we're walking up the stairs to his room at the B&B, and the tension is palpable.

I feel like I'm walking the green mile, heading for my execution.

Honestly, I would rather be picking up his cigarette butts from the roadside right now than walking up these stairs with him.

My legs feel like lead. Hands clammy. Heart heavy in my chest. Rocks in my stomach.

Because I know what's coming.

This last week, I've felt it coming like the sands of time. The grains have been slowly slipping away into the bottom of the hourglass.

And whatever the phone call was … it was the last grain to fall.

Time has run out.

He's leaving.

He's going back to LA.

Storm hasn't been able to look me in the eye since he came back in the parlor. And that's not like him. Usually, he can't keep his eyes or hands off me. It's one of the things I like about him. How tactile he is.

But there's been nothing.

And it's fine. I was expecting this.

Okay, it's not fine.

But it will be.

I think.

Maybe.

Probably not.

Fuck.

We reach his room, and he unlocks the door and lets us inside.

I step aside, and he shuts the door behind me.

Usually, I'd kick my shoes off and climb onto the bed. Storm would jump on me, and we'd make out for hours. That, or I wouldn't even make it to the bed before he was tackling me onto it.

Guess those days are over with now.

Because right now, I'm hanging by the door he just closed.

He's crossed to the other side of the room without even looking at me.

The silence is evident. It's painful. I could carve my name into the air; it's that thick.

I silently watch him as he takes off his jacket. Hangs it on the back of the chair. Kicks off his shoes. Empties his pocket of his cell and wallet and the ticket stub from the cinema. He puts them on the table. Then, he takes off his ball cap and places it on the chair. Runs his fingers through his hair.

Basically, he's doing everything but looking at me.

It's painfully obvious what's happening.

I just wish he'd get it over and done with.

I bind my hands together in front of me.

Finally, he turns to look at me, and part of me wishes he hadn't because it hurts to look at him.

All the unsaid words are in his clear blue eyes.

My heart starts to ache.

Unlinking my fingers, I wrap my arms around my stomach. I wet my dry lips with my tongue and knowingly nod my head. "You're leaving."

He's staring at me. Time seems to stretch out, dragging on, before he finally confirms what I already know. "Yes."

That one simple word.

Yes.

I've never been hit before. But I'm pretty sure this is how it would feel if someone punched me in the stomach.

I actually wince at the ache I feel in my abdomen.

And it's stupid. I'm stupid. This isn't a surprise. It was always coming. He was always going back to LA.

Why the hell are my eyes watering?

I blink back the tears, ignoring the burn in my throat.

"Stevie—" He steps toward me, but I lift a hand, stopping him.

"It's fine. I mean, we both knew this wasn't forever, right?" I grab hold of my ponytail. Wrapping it around my hand, I tug on it to direct the pain away from my heart to my head. "So, when do you leave?"

"Tomorrow morning."

That I'm not prepared for. I thought I'd have a couple of days to come to terms with it.

But … tomorrow.

God … it hurts.

No. It's fine.

This is good. Rip the Band-Aid off.

I'm fine.

"Stevie—fuck. This isn't—"

"It's fine! Tomorrow is good." My voice sounds abnormally bright and high-pitched. It must be clear as day to him that I'm close to the breaking point.

I mean, there's no point in prolonging the inevitable. And we had a good run, right? It's been … fun.

Fun? What the fuck is wrong with me? It's been the best time of my life, being with him. And I currently feel like someone just uppercut me in the heart. And that's all I've got.

He's staring at me. I can see the indecision in his eyes. In a way, it's good to know I'm not completely alone in this. That it is hard for him too.

But he's the one leaving you.

My sneaky subconscious rears her ugly head.

I hate that my mind does that.

Puts doubt into what I know.

Because he does have a life in LA. Just like I have a life here.

I can't expect him to give that up for me. Just like he couldn't expect me to give my life up here for him.

"That's what the phone call was about?"

His eyes sweep the floor before coming back to meet mine. They are the brightest I've ever seen them. They remind me of the blue fire you see on a Bunsen burner.

"Zane … the VP at the label. That's who called. I'm expected back. The album … we've a month before recording. The songs aren't written. The boys write some … but predominantly, I write them. I have to …" He sighs, a sad sound. "I have to go home."

"I know." I nod, still fighting back those fucking tears.

God, I need to get the hell out of here. I can't cope with the way I'm feeling right now. It hurts too much to be around him. I need some space to clear my head, and then I'll be fine.

"Okay … so …" I'm blindly reaching back, trying to find the door handle. "I … have … some stuff to do." *Got it. Thank you, Jesus. I need to get out of here before I break down and do something stupid, like beg him to stay.* "I guess … I'll catch up with you later. Before you leave."

I'm out of that door and closing it behind me and running back down the stairs. I'm out of the house and in my car. I back out of the driveway and hit Call on my phone.

Pen's voice fills my car, "What's up, chica?"

At the sound of her voice, I burst out crying.

"Stevie?" She sounds worried.

"God. Sorry, Pen. I'm just …" I sniffle, wiping my face with my sleeve. "Storm's leaving. He's going home. I'm being stupid. I know I am. I knew this was coming. I just … it hurts, Pen. More than I expected."

"Where are you?"

"In my car."

"I'm at home. I'll be waiting with alcohol. What level of alcohol are we talking here—beer, wine, or vodka?"

"Tequila."

"Tequila." Pause. "Okay. But I'm out of lemons. I'll go to the store. It'll take me two minutes."

"Don't worry. I'll go. I've got a couple of stops to make first before I come over."

There are some cigarette butts that need picking up from the roadside. Tossed there by a rock star in a Maserati.

Sounds like there's a joke in there somewhere. Something about my heart getting tossed out of his car too.

Or maybe that isn't a joke.

Maybe it's just the truth.

26

STORM

It's close to two hours ago since Stevie practically ran out of here. I've been kicking around the room, unsure of what to do.

I wanted to go after her, but what would I have said? *Don't leave. I know I'm leaving soon. But don't leave.*

Basically, there was fuck all I could say, so I had to let her go.

So, I'm here, sitting, listening to music, like I always do when I feel like this …

Sad. Upset. Hurt. Confused.

All of the above and more.

I'm trying to figure out what to do.

But there aren't many options …

I stay here. But that means, I leave the band, leave the guys. And I just can't do that.

I leave and ask Stevie to do long-distance. Which is shit and I'd hate it.

I ask her to come to LA with me … which doesn't feel fair. She has a life and family here, and I'd be asking her to leave that for me.

Basically, whichever way I go, I'm screwed.

Guns N' Roses have just started singing "Don't Cry" when a knock comes on the door. It's not a quiet knock. It's determined.

Stevie.

I'm off that bed and pulling open the door a second later.

"Stevie, I—"

My words are cut off when her body and mouth collide with mine.

She literally jumps me.

And it takes me zero seconds to respond back.

My arms go around her. Grabbing her thighs, I pick her up. Kick the door shut and press her back against it.

And I kiss her. I kiss her desperately. I kiss her with every-fucking-thing I feel for her. Which is a lot.

But an alarm is also going off in the back of my head.

Then, I register the taste of alcohol on her tongue.

I pull back, looking into her gorgeous eyes. They're dilated but from lust, not liquor.

I don't think she's drunk, but still, I ask, "Have you been drinking?"

She gives me a look. "A shot of tequila and a beer over an hour ago."

"Please tell me you're not drunk."

"I'm not drunk."

"Thank fuck." I slam my mouth back down on hers. I really didn't feel like being the good guy right now.

My hand drags up her body, taking her shirt with it.

She lifts her arms, and I pull it off, tossing it aside.

Reaching back, I grab hold of my own shirt and pull it off over my head.

Stevie's already removed her bra.

We're naked from the waist up, and I'm as hard as stone.

Kissing her again, I carry her over to the bed and gently lay her down on the mattress, supporting my weight with my hand.

I lick a path around her nipple before taking it into my mouth, knowing how sensitive she is there.

Her hips lift, pressing against me, seeking contact.

I kiss my way down her stomach, stopping when I reach her jean shorts.

I pop the button on them, drag down the zipper, and remove them along with her panties in one go.

And then she's here, naked, on my bed, and I have no fucking clue how I'm going to walk away from her tomorrow.

Wasting no time, I drop to my knees and bury my head between her legs.

I run my nose up the small landing strip of hair on her pussy, and I inhale deeply.

I fucking love the way she smells, the way she tastes.

Like she's mine.

Parting her lips with my fingers, opening her up to me, I run my tongue up her center.

She cries out, hips jerking, but I hold her still with a hand on her hip and suck her clit into my mouth.

She grabs hold of my hair, tugging on it, and I fucking love it.

I push a finger into her and then another. I slowly fuck her with them, paying special attention to her clit.

She's panting and writhing and so fucking tight around my fingers.

She's always responsive to me, but her orgasm comes even quicker this time, surprising both of us. Her muscles clamping down on my fingers, I feel her orgasm against my tongue. She cries out my name, and I promise myself that it won't be the only time I hear it tonight.

I might have to leave in the morning.

But tonight, she's mine.

I rock back on my heels, wiping my mouth on my hand, as she sits up, resting on her elbows.

Her hair is tousled, mouth swollen from my kisses.

She looks beautiful. And it fucking hurts.

Sitting up further, she comes to me.

There are no words spoken.

It's not like us.

Usually, we have a lot to say to each other.

Reaching for me, she slips her hand around the back of my neck and kisses me, and I'm all about that.

I suck on her tongue, and she moans. The sound vibrates through me.

My hands go to her tits, but she stops me.

"Stand up," is all she says.

My legs are fucking shaking as I stand.

Stevie unfastens my jeans and pulls them down, taking my boxers with them. I kick them aside.

And we're both naked.

We've been naked together before, but something about this time just feels different. Knowing this is the last time I'll be with her makes everything seem...*more.*

More important. More pronounced.

She takes my cock in her hand. She's looking up at me when she leans forward and slides my dick between her lips.

I almost come out of my skin.

I've watched her suck me before. Of course I have. I'm a guy.

But she's never looked up at me in this way before.

Stevie's shy. And it's like, in this moment, all her shyness has gone away.

Her hand is wrapped around the base of my dick, her mouth covering the rest, eyes on mine, as she jacks me and sucks me. And I feel like I'm going to fucking die.

I can feel my orgasm building already. My balls tightening up, the tingle at the base of my spine.

I grip her head with my hand.

And she pulls away.

Her hand and mouth gone.

I watch as she climbs back onto the bed, sitting on her knees, her hair down and loose around her shoulders.

She's like every single wet dream I've ever had.

"Do you have a condom?" she says the words so softly that I wouldn't have heard if I hadn't been paying close attention to her, like I always do.

Honestly, I almost come right then on the spot.

I knew this time was different. I just didn't know it was going in this direction.

We haven't had sex yet. We've done everything but. And I just figured, with me leaving tomorrow, that it wouldn't happen.

But it seems Stevie has other plans.

"You want to have sex?"

She looks me in the eye. "No. I want you to fuck me."

My heart sinks. I know what she's doing, and I'm not down for it.

She's trying to detach herself from the situation, so she won't feel. I've done it a hundred times before.

"No. I won't fuck you." I step up to the bed and take her face in my hands. I stare down at her. "I'll have sex with you. Make fucking love to you. But I won't fuck you, babe."

Her eyes close. She's hiding her feelings from me, and I hate it.

I hate this whole fucking situation, but I don't know how to make it better.

"Look at me."

Her eyes open. I can see the glisten of pain in them.

It makes my chest feel like it's cracking wide open.

I lean down and press my lips to hers. "I'm sorry," I say against them.

"Don't, Storm … *please.*"

I hear the tremble in her voice, so I do as she asked, and I don't say the words I want to say—*I'm sorry I have to leave. I don't know how I'm going to when the time comes. I wish things were different.*

"Just be with me tonight," she whispers. "I want to feel you inside me."

God, I want that too.

But, honestly, I don't know if I'll survive it.

It feels hard now, knowing I'm leaving her.

What the hell will it feel like once I know what it's like to be inside her?

But I also know I'll regret it forever if I don't.

I press my forehead to hers, and looking into her eyes, I say, "Okay."

I get a condom from my wallet, and when I turn back, Stevie is still waiting on her knees on the bed, where I left her.

Her eyes on mine.

I climb onto the bed on my knees, facing her. I put the condom on the mattress beside us. Then, I cup her head in my hands. And I kiss her. Deep and wet and wanting.

There's no finesse or thought here. I've handed myself over to my feelings.

Our bodies are molded together. My dick pressed up against her stomach. Her tits crushed against my chest. My hands holding her head, angling it, so I kiss her deeper. But still, it doesn't feel like enough.

I release a hand from her head and run it down her back, over her ass. I slip two fingers inside her pussy from behind.

She's soaking wet for me. My dick pulses between us.

I fuck her with my fingers the way I'm going to with my cock.

She's moaning and bearing down on my hand. She's ready for me.

I guide her down to her back.

Grabbing the condom, I rip it open and make quick work of putting it on.

I don't take my eyes off her the whole time, and she doesn't take her eyes off what I'm doing.

When the condom is on, her eyes finally lift to mine.

She doesn't say anything. She doesn't need to.

This is it.

I'm going to make love to her.

I've never made love to anyone in my life before.

I've fucked plenty of women.

But no feelings have ever come into sex for me.

All I have for Stevie is feelings.

Too many to handle.

I move over her as she parts her legs. I fit myself between them.

Then, I take her face in my hands, and I kiss her. Because I can. Because I won't be able to soon.

I swallow back the ache that thought brings, and I focus on the now.

The feel of her beneath me. The apple scent in her hair. The way she tastes. The little moans she makes when we kiss.

I move my hand to her tit, cupping it. I drag my thumb over her nipple.

Her hips lift. Her pussy pressing against my cock, seeking it.

"Please, Storm. I need you," she whispers.

I run my hand down her side. Taking hold of her thigh, I lift her leg, opening her up for me.

Her eyes are closed. I want them on mine when I slide inside her. I want to remember the way she looks in this moment. "Look at me," I say, my voice commanding.

She blinks open her eyes, staring into mine.

I pull my hips back. Then, I plunge my dick partway inside of her.

She cries out at the feel of me.

She's small, and I'm big. If I went all the way in one thrust, I'd hurt her. I might not be able to stop this situation from hurting either one of us. But I will never hurt her intentionally.

God, I'm not even all the way in, and she feels so fucking good.

With each retreat I make, I inch more of my cock inside her. Until I'm fully in. And it's everything. She's everything.

We're both gasping and panting.

And she's so fucking tight. Squeezing me like a fist.

"Fuck, Stevie. You're so tight."

Closing my eyes, I press my forehead to hers, trying not to come. But she's not making it easy for me. She hooks her legs around my back, increasing the pressure on my dick.

I groan.

It's pleasure-pain.

"Just give me a minute, babe. You feel so fucking good. I don't want to come like a preteen."

She laughs, and it's the best fucking sound I've heard all night.

My eyes flash open to hers. And finally. Fucking finally, I see her in there.

My Stevie.

Not the Stevie who's hurting because I have to leave.

But my Stevie. The happy, beautiful, laughing Stevie.

And fuck it if I come in three seconds. I don't care. I'm going to do this to her all over again tonight. Multiple times if possible.

My control snaps, and I start moving, pumping into her.

"Yes! God, Storm!" she cries out.

I lower my head, capturing a nipple between my teeth and give it a gentle tug.

She cries out again, "Harder! More!"

So, I give her more. I rear back onto my heels. Grab her hips and start pumping my dick in and out of her.

And the view from up here is like nothing I've seen before.

Her blonde hair fanned out on the pillow. Her face and body flushed.

My dick sliding in and out of her.

I press my thumb to her clit, circling it.

Her eyes are on mine, glazed with lust. She's never looked more beautiful than she does right now.

"Storm … please … yes … I'm going to … come!" The last word screams out of her.

Her muscles clamp down on my cock, triggering my own orgasm.

I'm pretty sure I lose consciousness for a moment; it's that powerful. I fall forward onto her, unable to keep myself upright, catching my weight with my arm, pumping my dick in and out of her, riding out my orgasm.

My mouth seeks her, and I kiss her. Our bodies shuddering, still moving together, slowing.

We're sweaty, our skin sliding against each other, like our tongues are doing.

And I can't get enough of her.

I've just come harder than I ever have before in my life, and I don't feel done. And neither does she by the way her hands are still moving all over my body.

I'm inside her, and I still want her so fucking badly.

I've wanted her since the moment I met her.

I can't imagine not ever wanting her.

And I can't see how I'm going to be able to drive away from her tomorrow.

I don't want to.

I really don't fucking want to.

I pull back and stare into her eyes. "Come with me," I blurt out. "Come to LA with me. Move there with me. Live with me."

27

Stevie

I stare back at him, shocked.

Of all the things I expected him to say, it wasn't that.

Move to LA with him? God, I want to.

My heart really wants to. She's over the fucking moon, elated and beating wildly.

But my head … my stupid, practical head says no.

The B&B. Gran. Dad. Beck. Penny.

I can't leave them.

Especially not Gran. She needs me here to help run the B&B. And I owe her everything. She paused her life to help Dad raise me and Beck, and not once has she ever asked for anything in return.

I know she would encourage me to go.

But I can't. I can't leave her.

He must see it in my eyes because his expression dims.

I place my hands on his cheeks, loving the feel of the bristles of his stubble against my palm. "I … can't. I'm sorry."

"I shouldn't have asked. It was too much." He moves his eyes from mine.

I can feel him pulling away from me. I'm not ready for him to leave me yet. He's still inside of me, for God's sake, and I'm not ready for it to end yet.

I just need a little more time.

"No," I tell him, pulling him back to me. "It was everything."

His eyes move back to mine. I press my thumb to his lips, tracing the contour of them.

"I just … I can't leave Dad, Beck, and Gran … the B&B. I would come with you to LA in a heartbeat if I could."

An absolute heartbeat. Christ, I'd be packed in under ten minutes and waiting at the door for him.

His fingers move over my face, the gentlest of touches, his eyes following his movements, like he's memorizing it.

Maybe he is.

I know I've memorized every inch of him. Every moment we've spent together. And this moment … the sex we just had … the feel of him still inside me … the way I can feel his heart beating against mine … even the music playing in the background, which couldn't be more fitting if I'd picked the song myself—Whitesnake's "Is This Love."

All of it is forever etched into my brain.

His fingers drift down my neck to the hollow of my throat. His hand slides behind my nape, fingers pushing into my hair. "Would you consider"—he pauses and swallows—"long-distance?" His eyes meet mine. "I'm just not ready … for this to be over yet."

It's my turn to swallow. My eyes start to burn.

Because I know my answer. Long-distance never works.

"I …"

"Don't say long-distance doesn't work," he cuts me off, reading my damn mind, like he always does. "Because we'd make it work."

"For how long? And then what? We'd both still live in different states."

"You don't know the future, Stevie. Things could change."

"Are you planning on leaving your band at any point?"

His eyes hold mine. He shakes his head.

"And I'll never leave here. It won't be long before Gran is too old to do anything around here, and then I'll take over the B&B fully. My life is here, Storm. God, do I want to say yes to long-distance and be with you for however long we can. Of course I do. But I also know we'd be delaying the inevitable. I know me, and I know I'd be unhappy because I wouldn't be with you. I'd have half of you and even less of your time. And I don't want to be unhappy. I want to be happy. Do I want a relationship with you? Yes. But I want a proper relationship. Not half of one. I'm sorry …"

"Don't," he stops me. "You have nothing to be sorry for."

"Neither do you," I tell him, knowing what he's thinking. He blames himself because he's the one leaving when the truth is, it's neither of our faults.

It just fucking sucks. And I hate that it does.

I want him so badly, and I can't have him.

Life is cruel sometimes.

He presses his forehead to mine, staring into my eyes. "I don't want us to be over."

Tears fill my eyes again. "I don't either. But—"

"Don't," he stops me, closing his eyes. "Just … don't say it. Please."

I press my lips together, keeping in the truth we both know. A tear runs from the corner of my eye. Another quickly following, soaking into the pillow.

"Stay with me tonight," he whispers.

His mouth moves down to mine, lips brushing lightly against mine.

"Okay," I whisper.

Our hips are moving against each other. His cock, hard again, is slowly sliding in and out of me.

"I need to take this condom off. Get another," he says, still kissing me. "But …"

"I'm on the pill," I whisper.

His eyes open on mine, bright with lust. "Are you sure?" He's still slowly fucking me.

"Yes."

He reaches down between us, briefly pulling out of me. I hate the loss of him, even for just these few seconds. He removes the condom and rids himself of it.

Then, eyes on mine, he slowly slides back inside me.

He's hot and hard and perfect.

"I … I've never done this before. I've never gone without a condom before."

My chest squeezes, as I know that he's doing this with me. That I'm his first.

He closes his eyes. "Jesus … you feel … I just … fuck, Stevie." He captures my lips with his and kisses me deeply. As deeply as he's fucking me.

He grabs my hands and pins them to the bed above my head, and then he starts fucking me with reckless abandon. Almost frantically. And I meet each frenzied thrust. Because I feel the exact same.

This sex is different from the last time.

It's wilder. Hotter. Inflamed.

It's like we're on fire.

My nails rake down his back.

He bites and licks and sucks my skin.

He makes me scream.

And I drive him crazy.

And this is how we spend the rest of our last night together. With Storm bare and deep inside me, fucking me and making love to me, until dawn shows up. And she comes way too quickly.

He pulls me to him, my back to his front. He wraps his strong arms around me. His chin on my shoulder, his mouth against my ear. "When I started driving that day, I thought I was running away from all the stuff I couldn't deal with," he says quietly to me. "Turns out, I knew jack shit. I was driving straight toward you, Stevie. And even if I never see you again after today, I'll never regret it. Never. You're the best fucking thing that's ever happened to me."

My eyes fill with tears again. I feel like I'm going to be doing a lot of crying for the foreseeable future. I swallow down, getting control of my emotions.

"I'll never regret it either," I tell him on a whisper. "Even if you do have the shittiest taste in music." Of course, I had to go with humor. It's either that or burst into gut-wrenching tears.

He laughs deep. I feel it vibrate against my back, hum in my ear, and wrap around my heart.

He pulls me tighter up against him. I slide my fingers between his, holding his hand.

I close my eyes at the feel of him around me.

When I open my eyes a few hours later, he's gone.

The closet empty of his clothes.

His car gone from the driveway.

Gone like he was never here.

And, finally, I break down and cry.

28

STORM

Welcome to Los Angeles, the sign says.

Fuck LA. And fuck my life.

I have never wanted to be here less than I do right now.

The drive back from Arizona has been fucking horrendous.

I almost turned around a hundred times and drove back to Lake Havasu. Back to Stevie. The only thing stopping me was the thought of Raze, Cash, and Levi. Letting them down.

I can't let them down. They're my best friends.

And I need to see Jake, Tom, and Denny too. Speak to them. Apologize for what I said and hash this shit out. Get back to where we were before it all happened.

But if it had never happened, I'd have never met Stevie.

And if there's one thing in my life I'll never regret, it's her.

I'll just always regret leaving her.

Getting out of that bed and walking out that door and climbing in my car was the hardest thing I've ever done.

And I've done some hard things in my time. Watching my mother being buried is one of them.

I've been listening to an eighties station the whole drive. I'm *that* hooked on her. I'm listening to shitty music, so I can be close to her in some way.

Hooked. And pathetic.

Clearly, because I'm currently singing along to "Glory of Love" and agreeing with every damn word Peter Cetera sings.

God, if the guys could see me right now, they would give me shit for the rest of my life.

So would Stevie.

Jesus. How am I going to get over her when she's in every other thought I have?

Although I bet Peter Cetera would never leave the girl he's singing about. I bet he wouldn't slip out of bed and leave like a coward while she was sleeping because he didn't know how to say good-bye to her.

Just like I left Stevie.

And then it hits me.

I snuck out on Stevie just like I used to with all those girls I'd screwed and not wanted to have the morning-after conversation with.

I treated her exactly like I had those girls.

And she deserved so much better.

Fuck.

Fuck my shitty fucking life.

I drive to TMS Records and park my car in the building's parking lot.

I don't get nervous often, but I'm nervous now, walking up to the building.

I'm seeing Jake, Tom, and Denny first before I go to the studio to meet with Zane and the guys.

I'm definitely in a different place than I was the last time I was here. Funny how much can change in a few weeks.

In a few hours.

A handful of hours ago, I was in bed with Stevie. She was in my arms.

And now, I'm here. In LA. Alone. Without her.

I pull open the door to the building and walk inside. I wave to Patty as I walk through reception, heading for the elevator.

I take the elevator up to the top floor where Jake's office is.

The door pings my arrival, and I step out into the foyer.

There's only Jake's and Zane's offices up here.

There's an empty office up here too. It was Jonny's office.

They've never reused it.

It's been sitting there empty for nineteen fucking years.

I glance down the hall in the direction of it.

My feet are moving toward Jonny's office before I even realize I'm moving. But when I do realize, I don't stop walking. I keep going.

I push the door open and walk inside.

It doesn't smell stale in here, like some offices do when left for a while. Jake probably has it cleaned regularly.

It still looks the same as I remember. Just less stuff.

I came in here once years ago when I first moved to LA. Jake brought me in to show me where Jonny had spent his days when he wasn't in the studio or on the road, touring.

There's nothing particularly special about it. It's just an office.

All that's in here now is an empty desk and a chair. Some discs hanging on the wall and pictures of Jonny, Jake, Tom, and Denny. And a couple of other pictures of him with famous people.

The only other thing still in here is his guitar, sitting on its stand.

That guitar would be worth a lot of money to people.

But not to me. To me, it's just another thing that Jonny left behind when he died.

I remember running my fingers over the strings that day when I was a kid and wishing I could have met him. Wishing I could be a great guitarist like him.

How fucking laughable.

Because I am a great guitarist.

I know I am. It's just a shame no one else fucking sees it.

Well, except Raze, Cash, and Levi, that is.

And probably Stevie if she ever heard me play. Although she'd probably give me shit about it first.

I wonder if Jonny would have thought I was good.

He was coming for me that night. He wanted me. He wanted to know me.

That's the first time I've let that actually sink in.

All this anger I've felt toward him over the years for dying, for getting in his car when he was high. And he did that because he wanted to meet me.

I don't feel responsible for his death. Rationally, I knew I never was.

I just feel … sad.

Movement behind me has me turning around.

It's Jake, Tom, and Denny.

"Hey," I say to them, moving to rest my ass against the desk. "I was just coming to see you. I got … sidetracked. How'd you know I was in here?"

Jake smiles. "The room's alarmed, and there's a camera." He tips his head up to the far corner, where I notice the security camera for the first time. "I get a notification when anyone comes in here. And the only people who come in here are the cleaners, every second

Monday, and us sad fuckers when we're drunk." He refers to himself, Tom, and Denny.

"It's true," Tom says, grinning. "I haven't been in this room sober since Jon died. Actually, I probably wasn't even sober when I came in here when he was still alive."

I laugh at that.

Then, my laughter dies, and we're all just kind of standing here, saying nothing.

And since I texted them, asking to talk, I should probably be the first to speak.

"So …" I say. "I just wanted to apologize for what I said the other week—about you being as dead to me as Jonny is …" I feel weird, saying it in here, in Jonny's office. "I didn't mean it. I should never have said it. It was shitty and wrong of me. And I'm sorry for that. But I'm not sorry for the other stuff. You all lied to me, and you were wrong."

"You're right. We were." Tom steps forward, coming a little closer to me.

"In our defense, we thought we were doing the right thing at the time," Den says. "In the space of a few short months, you'd just found out that Jonny was your father, and your mother passed away. We didn't want to give you more to deal with."

"But," Jake interjects, "we should have told you after things settled. We messed up. Really fucking messed up, and we're sorry as all hell."

"We are," Tom adds. "And it's no excuse, but as time went on, it just got harder and harder to tell you. We knew you'd be pissed that we'd kept the truth from you. And … I guess … we didn't want to lose you."

Fuck. I didn't expect that.

My throat is burning.

And I know this isn't anything they didn't say to me two weeks ago, without the addition of them not wanting to lose me. But the difference now to then is, I'm not mad anymore.

"Okay." I nod.

"So … we're good?" Tom checks.

"We're good." I smile because, sometimes, it's just that easy.

"Thank fuck for that." Tom bounds over and bear-hugs me. "Missed you, kid." He thumps me on the back with his fist.

"Missed you too," I tell him, and I have. I just didn't realize how much until now.

Den comes over and ruffles my hair. "Hasn't been the same around here without you," he tells me. "It's good to have you back."

"It's good to be back," I say, only half-meaning it. Because there's a Stevie-shaped hole in my chest.

Tom finally releases me. I turn to Jake.

"You're okay?" Jake asks.

"Yeah." I smile. "I'm okay."

He puts his arm around my neck and pulls me in for a hug. "We fucking love you, son. No matter what happens, don't ever forget that, okay?"

"Okay," I choke out.

I'm nearly in fucking tears.

Jesus. Christ.

I pull out of Jake's hold and turn away, walking over to the window, giving myself a moment to sort my shit out and stop acting like a pussy.

When I hear the strumming of strings, I turn to see Tom standing in front of Jonny's guitar, his fingers running over the strings.

"Why is this still in here?" Tom turns to Jake and Den. "Actually, why the fuck is any of this stuff still in here? I thought we had it cleaned out years ago?"

"We did," Jake answers him. "I just left a few things in here. I guess I didn't want it gone of Jon completely. But you're right; we should get rid of the rest of it. Donate it to charity or something." Jake glances at me. "Unless you want anything out of here?"

In the past, I always refused anything of Jonny's that Jake offered to me. I didn't want anything of Jonny's back then. I guess I was an angry kid, who turned into an angry adult.

I don't feel so angry anymore.

And that's because of Stevie.

She made everything so much simpler.

She made me happy.

And I walked away from that happiness.

I walk over to the guitar and pick it up. "I'll take this, if that's okay," I say to Jake.

"It's more than okay," he says, smiling.

"So, are we getting the fuck out of here and going for a drink?" Tom slings his arm around my shoulders, leading me toward the door.

"Can't. I've gotta be in the studio in ten minutes, or Zane will kick my ass from here to kingdom come."

"Jake, call Zane and tell him that Storm won't be going in the studio today."

"I'm not fucking ringing him." Jake laughs from behind us.

"Come on!" Tom turns to face Jake, taking me with him. "It's your fucking label. Call him, say, *Storm's not coming to make music today because there's drinking and strip bars to go to.*"

Laughter bursts from Jake and Denny.

"Oh, yeah, sure, you're going to a strip bar." Jake nods, smirking. "Let me just call Lyla and check on that with her."

"Fuck off!" Tom flips him off.

"Strip bars?" Den chuckles. "Really, Tom? Christ. It's like I've flashed back twenty-five years."

I don't bristle when Den says that. I don't feel like he's comparing me being here to Jonny being with them all those years ago.

And even if he were, maybe it wouldn't be such a bad thing, being compared to Jonny.

God, I never thought I'd think that.

I guess things have changed.

And two weeks was all it took.

Two weeks with Stevie.

And now, I've left her behind, and I'll never again get to feel the way I did when I was with her.

I just … I wish I knew a way where I could have Stevie … and have my music.

But I don't.

So, this is the way it has to be.

And I fucking hate it.

29

STORM

It's been four days since I got back to LA.

Four days without Stevie.

And I'm climbing out of my fucking skin.

So many times, I've picked my cell up to call her, just needing to hear her voice.

My fingers fucking itch to text her.

But I can't.

What the fuck would I say?

I miss you. I need you.

I know you can't come to LA, and you won't do long-distance. I understand all of this. But … I just fucking miss you. I'm desperate for you, and I need a fix.

Four days, and I still feel as empty as the day I left her there in bed and got in my car and drove home.

Only … LA doesn't feel like home anymore.

It just feels lonely and empty.

I'm surrounded by people.

And all I want is her.

I just wonder if she's missing me like I am her.

I'm driving home after another day in the studio. Me and the guys have been working on what I already wrote because I've got nothing else.

The words have dried up. I can't find a goddamn thing to write about.

When I was with Stevie, the words flowed easily.

Without her, I've got nothing.

Usually, after a day in the studio, me and the boys would go grab a drink after to wind down and relax.

They've been going without me. I keep making up bullshit excuses as to why I can't go.

But the truth is, I don't feel up to socializing. I'm too stuck in my own head. I'm not really feeling very fucking rock 'n' roll these days.

I pull my car into my space in the building's lot and turn off the engine. I open the door, and I'm just getting out when something down the side of the seat catches my eye.

Something white.

I reach my hand down, and my fingers grab hold of what feels like fabric. I pull it out and stare at it.

Stevie's panties.

The ones I ripped off her.

How have I not noticed them there until now?

They've been there since the night I tore them off her body.

The day I got my car back, and I took her for a drive and parked.

The first time I made her come. The first time I felt her. Tasted her.

God, I miss her.

I lift the torn panties to my nose and inhale. Her scent is all over them. Memories flash through my mind.

Sliding into her for the first time. How she felt around my bare cock. Feeling her come around my dick. Squeezing me so tight.

Her soft skin.

Kissing her.

Laughing with her.

My chest aches with missing her.

Fucking hell.

I've officially hit my lowest. I'm in my car, sniffing her panties.

Even still, I'm not parting with them. I stuff them in my pocket. Leave my car and head to the elevator.

I let myself in my apartment, kick off my boots, and slump down on my sofa.

Getting my cell out of my pocket, I unlock the screen, open Photos, and stare at the one picture I have of Stevie.

I took it one day when she was lying on my bed. Hair fanned out on the pillow. That gorgeous smile on her face. She was wearing one of my T-shirts. She was also giving me shit about something—I forget what now. But I know I was laughing, like I always did when I was with her.

I thought she looked so fucking beautiful in that moment, so I grabbed my cell and snapped a picture of her.

I'm still staring at the photo thirty minutes later when there's a knock on my door.

There are only a handful of people it could be, who are on my authorized list. Everyone else has to be announced.

I click off the picture, pocket my cell, get up from the sofa, drag my ass across the room, and open the door.

Raze, Cash, and Levi are standing here, holding a couple of six-packs and some pizza boxes.

"Didn't I just get rid of you fuckers an hour ago?"

Not that I'm unhappy to see them. But I was looking forward to lying around on my sofa all night, torturing myself with that picture of Stevie, while listening to eighties music.

And, apparently, I've turned into a teenage girl.

"Yeah, and we fucking love you too." Grinning, Cash blows me a kiss as he walks past me into my apartment.

Raze and Levi follow him. I shut the door behind them and follow them into the living room.

Pizzas and beer are dumped on my coffee table. Raze grabs the remote and turns the TV on. I sit down on the sofa, and Levi tosses me a bottle of beer.

"Cheers, man." I pop the cap and take a drink.

"So, what the fuck is going on with you?" Cash asks me, getting straight to the point, like always.

"Nothing."

Cash frowns. "You're walking around like someone killed your dog."

"I don't have a dog."

"Shut the fuck up. You're as moody as a preteen who hasn't discovered what his dick is for. Does it have to do with this girl? The one you met in Arizona."

My eyes go immediately to Raze, who shrugs. He's the only one I've talked to about Stevie. And I haven't told him a lot.

"They asked what I thought was up with you. I figured it has to be the girl. Not that you've told me much about her."

Because talking about her makes it real … reminds me that I no longer have her. And it hurts like a motherfucker.

"So, you met this chick and what?" Levi asks.

I fell in love.

Holy. Fucking. Shit.

I fell in love with her.

How am I only just realizing this now?

I love Stevie.

I'm in love with her.

"Well, it was … awesome. Stevie's fucking amazing. She's different to the kinds of girls we know. She's just *real.* Smart as fuck and so beautiful—but like a natural beauty, you know? She doesn't take my shit. If anything, she gives it to me. And she doesn't care about the stuff other girls do. She had no fucking clue who I was when I met her."

"What?" Cash looks confused. "She didn't know who you were?"

"Nope." I shake my head, smiling at the memory. "Stevie's not into … recent music. She likes the old stuff."

"Huh," is Cash's response.

"Yeah," I say. "And when she did find out who I was, she still didn't give a shit. I guess"—I sigh—"I was myself around her, and I really fucking liked who I was when I was with her."

They're all staring at me like I've lost it.

Maybe I have.

"So … basically, you love this Stevie chick, and you're walking around like you lost your dick because you miss her." That's Cash.

And he's just hit the nail on the head.

"Basically, yeah." I take another swig of my beer.

"Well, go back there and get her. Bring her back to LA." That's Raze.

"I can't …" I swallow down my embarrassment at admitting this. "I already asked her. She said no."

"She knocked you back?" Levi looks like I just told him Santa wasn't real.

"She runs a B&B with her grandmother," I'm quick to explain. "Stevie pretty much runs it now. But she'll take over full-time when her gran is ready to retire."

"Okay … but she knows you're loaded, right?" Cash asks.

I shrug. "I guess so." I mean, I figure she knows I have money from the car I drive and then when she found out what I did for a living. "We just never really talked about it. Stevie's not really into money."

"Everyone's into money. Even the people who say they aren't," Levi adds.

I shrug. "I don't know what to tell you. Stevie's just not a materialistic person."

Levi and Cash look at each other. Then, they look at Raze like he has the answers, but he just shrugs, looking equally perplexed.

"So, when you said she's different," Cash says slowly, "you meant, she's actually different."

"Yeah, man. She's actually different."

There's silence in the room.

"And she doesn't want your money?" That's Levi.

"No." I laugh, exasperated.

"Or your fame? Or to spend your money? Or live in your big apartment? Or drive your nice car?" Cash asks.

"Fuck's sake, man! No! She's not interested in any of those things."

"Well, what does she want then?" Cash asks.

"Nothing." I shake my head. "She didn't want anything." *Except for me.*

She wanted me.

And I left her.

I take another pull on my beer. Holding the bottle between my palms, I stare down into it.

"Those songs you brought to the studio," Raze says, bringing my eyes to him, "you wrote them while you were there? While you were with her?"

It's not a question because he knows. But I still answer, "Yeah."

"They're fucking good, man. *Really* fucking good."

I stare back down to my bottle, hoping the answers I seek are in there somewhere.

"So, we've established that you're miserable as fuck without her. And that you write really good fucking songs when you are with her," Cash says.

I laugh without humor. "Pretty much."

"So, what the fuck are you doing here?" That's Raze, and it brings my gaze back up.

"If you're miserable without her, go back to Arizona. Be with her."

"I can't. I need to be here."

"Says who?" Raze challenges.

"Zane. I came back because he said if I didn't get my ass back here and we didn't get in the studio and start putting this album together, he'd bring in songwriters to do it, and we'd lose all creative control."

"Fuck what Zane said!" Cash says. "Well, actually, don't fuck what he said because he's our paycheck at the end of the day. But why do you have to be here to do the album?"

I give Cash a stupid look. "Because you guys are here. The studio is here."

"And Arizona is what, four hours away in a car? An hour on a plane? Commute. Or what-the-fuck-ever. You're rich; buy a fucking plane. Write the songs there in Arizona. Because, honestly, the shit you brought to the studio is the best you've ever written, and if that's because of this Stevie chick, then I'll marry you guys myself. You move there, be with your girl, and then fly back here to record the album when needed. And when it's time to tour, just figure that shit out as it comes. That's the beauty of music, man. You can make it anywhere. Even in Arizona."

Huh.

Okay.

Write the songs in Lake Havasu. Commute to LA. Why the fuck didn't I think of that before?

I feel this excitement start to bubble in my gut.

But …

"What if Zane won't go for it?"

"Why the fuck wouldn't he?" Raze says. "He doesn't give a shit where you live just as long as the album is done and you don't waste the label's money. Don't ask him, man. Tell him how it's gonna be."

"And what about you guys?"

"What about us?" Raze says.

I shrug. "We've just … we've always been together."

"Hate to break it to you, but I've been trying to cut the apron strings for years. You've just never fucking gotten it," Cash says.

"Fuck off." I laugh.

"We've got your back," Levi tells me. "We're friends first. Band members second. We've always said that. We want you happy, man. And you ain't happy. You haven't been for a while."

Levi's more perceptive than I gave him credit for. They all are.

"The only time I've heard you happy in a long time was when you were there in Arizona with your girl," Raze tells me.

I look at the three of them. "So … I'm really doing this? I'm really moving to Arizona?"

Shit.

I am.

I'm really doing this. I'm going back to her.

I'm going back to Arizona.

To Stevie.

But …

"What if she's already moved on? Met someone else?" I blurt.

I can't see it, but you never know. Stevie's beautiful and cool and hot as fuck. Some little prick could have come to stay at the B&B and swooped in and stolen her from me.

Well, whatever. I'll kick his ass and take her back.

Cash grins wide. "Then, you're gonna look like a massive dick when you turn up there and get blown out."

"Fuck off." I flip him off, and he just laughs.

"Look, man, if Stevie is half the person you've told us she is, then she hasn't moved on," Raze tells me. "I reckon she's probably as miserable as you are without her."

God, I hope he's right.

Not that I want her miserable.

But I don't want her to have moved on either.

The guy I was before Stevie … with the one-night stands. The empty, hollow feeling inside of me. The anger I carried.

I don't want to be him anymore.

I want to be the man I am when I'm with her.

I want to be happy. But most of all, I want to make her happy.

I'm going back there to Lake Havasu, to Stevie, and I'm just praying to God that Raze is right and Stevie's not over me and that she still wants me like I want her.

Otherwise, I don't know what the hell I'm going to do.

30 STORM

It's early morning when I pull my car up on the driveway to Jake and Tru's house.

Home.

Even though being with Stevie feels like home to me now, this place will always be home too. It just means something different than what it used to.

I remember the first time I came here. Coming in the car up the driveway, I remember thinking it was the biggest house I had ever seen.

Life was a hell of a lot different back then.

I just hope my mom would have been proud of the choices I've made. Well, maybe not *all* of my choices. But most of them at least.

I know she would have loved Stevie though. She's impossible not to love.

Putting out my cigarette, I put the butt back in the pack.

If I'm going to be with Stevie—and I'm hoping to be with her permanently—then I'm either going to have to find out how the hell to dispose of these things in the right way. Or stop smoking.

I shudder.

Okay, the cigarettes stay for now.

I'll look into the responsibly-disposing-of-them shit.

Getting out my car, I head into the house.

I hear the voices as soon as I enter.

They're all in the kitchen.

I came early, so I'd catch them all at home. I want to tell them I'm leaving.

God, I make it sound so final.

I'm moving four hours away, and I'll be back all the damn time.

I spoke to Zane last night. He was surprisingly okay about it. Well, as okay as Zane could be.

He basically said, "I don't need to hear about your girlfriend problems. I'm not your fucking therapist. I don't give a fuck where you live. Live in a fucking cave in the Antarctic for all I care. Just make sure the fucking songs are written, and your ass is back in the studio every fucking second I tell you to be there."

Then, he hung up on me.

So, yeah, he's okay with it.

And I'm packed and ready to go. My bag's in the trunk, and Jonny's guitar is on the passenger seat. Everything I need is with me.

No, that's a lie. Because the only thing I need is in Lake Havasu, Arizona.

I wander into the kitchen. Jake, JJ, Billy, and Belle are all seated around the breakfast bar. Tru's at the counter, making coffee. She's the first to spot me.

"Hey." She smiles. "What are you doing here so early? Thought you rock stars slept late. You want some breakfast?"

"Hey, don't be rock-star-ist," Jake says. Picking up his cell phone from the counter, he starts tapping on it.

"What the heck is rock-star-ist?" Belle's face screws up.

Jake finishes tapping on his phone and puts it back down on the counter. "*Ist*," he highlights the word, if it even is one. "Like racist, ageist. Your mom was characterizing a person on the grounds of being a rock star. Like all rock stars sleep late. And drink. And smoke."

JJ's brow goes up. "You do all of those things."

"I don't smoke." Jake's voice goes higher at the end.

"Uh-huh, sure you don't, Dad." That's Billy in that awesome sardonic voice of his.

"I don't," Jake exclaims. "Tru, tell our kids that I don't smoke. I used to, but I stopped when your mom was pregnant with you, JJ."

Tru laughs. Coming over with a cup of coffee, she puts it down in front of Jake and kisses him on his cheek. "No, babe, course you don't smoke."

Jake turns to Tru, captures her chin in his hand, and briefly kisses her on the lips.

"Ugh, gross," Belle complains. "Can we stop the PDA? *Please*. And, Dad, we know you hide your cigarette butts in the planter. FYI, you're a terrible hider. But it's okay. We know you only smoke when you're stressed with work. So, we let it go."

God, Stevie would have a hernia if she knew where Jake was disposing of his cigarette butts.

Not that I didn't already know where he hid them. He's been doing it since I came to live here. It's a running joke among all of us. Jake thinks that no one knows that he still smokes occasionally.

Jake glances around all our faces, brows drawn together. "You all know?"

Tru slides her arm over his shoulders and laughs. "Course we know."

"Huh," he says. "So, that means I can smoke freely then?"

"No!" is the resounding answer, and I start to laugh.

I fucking love these people.

It's going to be weird, not seeing them nearly every day.

"So, was it a yes to that breakfast?" Tru asks me, still standing next to Jake.

I shake my head. "No. I'm good." I swallow down.

I feel so goddamn nervous, telling them that I'm leaving. I'm not sure why because they've always been nothing but supportive to me.

"Everything okay?" Tru asks, still smiling at me.

I nod and swallow. "Yeah … I just … I came to tell you that I'm leaving," I blurt out.

No one says anything. And they don't seem surprised either. Which is surprising.

"Well, I met this girl when I was away in Arizona. She's called Stevie. And … well, she's awesome and I'm crazy about her and I want to be with her … so I'm moving to Arizona to be with her. I'm going today. Well, now in fact."

My eyes go to Jake's, who's just looking at me steadily. "I'm not quitting the band," I tell him. "I spoke to the boys and Zane last night. I'm going to keep writing the songs from there and then fly back to record them. It's literally an hour's flight from there to LA, so I can be here at the drop of a hat. I'll be back as often as I'm needed. I won't slack. But I want to be with her. And she's there. She can't move here. So … I'm going there to be with her."

There's absolute quiet in the kitchen, and then JJ says, "So, you met a girl, and now, you're moving to Arizona?"

I look at him. "In a nutshell, yeah," I tell him.

"Weird. But okay. Whatever makes you happy, man."

"It's not weird," Belle says to JJ. She hops down off her stool and comes over to me. She wraps her arm around my waist, hugging me. I look down at her, and she smiles up at me. "I think it's really romantic."

"Well, just so everyone knows, I won't be leaving home for any chick anytime—ever," Billy announces, and I chuckle.

Leaving Jake, Tru walks over to me and takes hold of my hand, giving it a squeeze. "I agree with Belle. I think it's really romantic. You know, I moved halfway around the world to be with Jake, and it was the best thing I ever did."

"Course it was. I'm fucking amazing," Jake says.

"Dollar in the swear jar, Dad," Belle tells him, going back to sit down.

"Jesus, why do we even still have that thing?" Jake complains. "You're all practically grown adults, for fu—God's sake."

"We have it to annoy you." JJ smirks at him.

"And if we're grown adults, that means we don't have to have curfew anymore," Belle adds.

"I said, *practically* grown adults. Not actual grown-ups."

"Semantics, Dad. You can't have it both ways," Billy tells him. "It's one or the other."

"For fuck's sake," Jake growls, rising from his stool.

"Two dollars," Belle singsongs.

Jake shoots Belle a look before walking over to me. "You're leaving me to deal with them on my own?" He's smiling when he says it.

"Sorry." I grin.

God, I fucking love these people. This house.

It'll always be home.

But I need to go be with Stevie.

If she'll still have me, that is.

"So …" Jake says. "You're moving to Arizona."

It's just me and him now. Tru has moved to sit with the kids at the counter.

"Yeah. But like I said, I'll be back in the studio as often as needed. I won't slack off."

Jake puts his hands on my shoulders. "Storm, don't sweat it. It'll be fine. And I get it. I do. I would have given up the whole world for Tru."

"Gross, Dad!" Billy calls, and I chuckle.

"Your mom loves it. Right, babe?"

"Sure do," Tru says back.

Jake focuses back on me. "Do what you need to do, and we'll be right here, whenever you need us."

"Thank you," I tell him. "For *everything*."

"You don't have anything to thank me for." One of his hands goes to the back of my neck, and he looks me in the eyes. "We love you, kid. As long as you're happy, that's all that matters. And I know I'm not your dad, but—"

"You are," I cut him off. "You, Tom, and Den. You're all my dads. But you win Tom and Den out for the top spot, just don't tell them," I mock-whisper.

Jake chuckles. But his eyes fill with some unnamed emotion. "Don't worry about the album," he tells me, his voice sounding rougher than it did a moment ago. "Or your boys or anything. It'll all be okay. Just go to Arizona, to your girl, and be happy. Okay?"

"Okay."

And then I do something I've never done before. I hug Jake.

I was never what you'd call an affectionate teenager. I'd take a hug but never give one.

It was always Jake showing me affection and me taking but never giving. God, I was an asshole.

Jake stiffens in surprise at first but immediately hugs me back. And he hugs me tight.

My eyes start to sting.

"Hey! No hugging without me." Tru jumps up from her seat and comes over, fitting herself into the hug.

And before I know it, they're all here—JJ, Billy, and Belle—hugging me.

And I'm about to start fucking crying. *For fuck's sake.*

"Okay, let's break this up before I start crying and ruin my makeup," Tru says. She cups my cheek and kisses it. "We'll come to Arizona to see you real soon. I want to meet Stevie."

They all walk me to the door. JJ giving me shit for moving to be with a girl I've known for a few weeks.

He doesn't get it now. But he will when he meets *his* girl.

They walk out with me to my car. I hug them all again.

"Drive safely," Tru tells me.

"I will."

I turn to Jake. "Will you tell Tom and Den for me … that I'm moving?" It was hard enough, telling them. I don't want to have to do it another two times.

Jake nods in understanding. "I'll tell them. Just expect a call from Tom, either yelling because you left without saying good-bye or blubbering. Probably the latter. He's a needy bastard like that."

He chuckles, and so do I.

Then, I hug Jake one last time. I hug him tight.

"Love you," I tell them all.

Then, I climb into my car to the resounding sound of, "Love you," from them all.

Seat belt on, I start my car. I give them all one last look. Then, I put my car into drive.

Destination: Cavallis' B&B, Lake Havasu, Arizona.

Well, not quite yet. First, I have a couple of other stops to make. I need to go and see the guys before I go.

31

STORM

I've literally just pulled out of the gates to Jake and Tru's house when I see Raze, Cash, and Levi waiting up front. They're all leaning up against the hood of Cash's car. Raze's motorbike is parked up beside it.

Bringing my car to a stop, I put her in park and get out.

"What're you fuckers doing here?" I ask, walking over to them. "I was just coming to see you before I left for Arizona."

"I bet he was going to your place first," Cash says to Raze. "He's always liked you best."

"That's 'cause I'm prettier than you two ugly fuckers." Raze grins at Cash.

"As nice as this mothers' meeting is, you still haven't told me what the fuck you're doing here," I say.

"You told your girl that you're going back to Arizona to stay?" Levi asks me.

"No." I shake my head.

"He's scared she'll tell him not to come," Cash says, smirking.

Asshole.

"Fuck off. I want to surprise her."

"Well, she'll definitely be surprised when we all rock up there," Raze says.

What?

What does he mean … we?

"It's a long fucking drive for nothing though," Levi adds.

"Nah, it'll totally be worth it to see Storm get knocked back. Never seen it happen before. I'd legit pay good money to watch it," Cash says.

"Hang on." I lift my hand, stopping them. "What the fuck are you dipshits talking about? You're not coming with me to Arizona."

Levi comes over and claps me on the back. " 'Fraid we are. We're all kind of a package deal. Where you go, we go. And considering we've got an album to record, we're gonna be stuck to your ass like glue until it's done."

"But I sorted it with Zane last night. I'm gonna fly back here as often as I'm needed. You don't need to be with me to record the album."

Raze pushes up off the car. "We spoke to Zane and Jake last night."

"Jake already knew I was leaving?" My eyes grow wide.

"Yeah, sorry 'bout that, man," Raze says, holding my stare. "But we all talked after we left your place last night and decided to come with you. So, we spoke to Zane and Jake. Had to tell him, so we could get it all in place. Told them that we're gonna write and record the album down in Arizona. Jake was the one who texted us to let us know you were here this morning. I asked him to."

"And just so you know, you're paying for the studio time," Cash adds with a grin.

They're coming with me?

"You're actually coming with me to Arizona?" My words echo my thoughts.

"Well, yeah. You don't get to ditch us that fucking easy," Cash says. "And it's not like we've got anything else to do right now. And, honestly, man, I really wanna meet this chick who's got you all tied up in knots."

My eyes go to Raze, and he shrugs. "Like Cash said, we've got fuck all else going on in LA at the moment. And we thought getting out of here for a bit might do us all some good."

I look at Raze. Really look at him.

He looks tired. They all do.

Maybe this lifestyle has been wearing them all out more than I realized.

Guess I've been too wrapped up in my own shit to see it. Some fucking friend I am.

And I know things with Raze's dad have never been easy for him, but I'm wondering if they've gotten harder, and he hasn't told me.

I step closer to Raze, my voice lowering. "You okay?" I ask him.

"Of course he's fucking okay." Cash wraps his arm around Raze's neck, pulling him to himself. "He has us. Just like you do, you pussy. We're family. Now, are we standing around here all day, having a heart-to-heart, or are we getting this show on the road?"

I can't believe they're coming to Arizona with me.

It's a lot.

A fuck of a lot.

I'm not a man to cry. Although I've been on the verge a few times this last week. But fuck if this doesn't punch me right in the feels.

My throat starts to burn. And I swear, if I speak right now, I'll cry like a fucking baby, and these bastards will never let me live it down.

"You think he's gonna cry?" Levi says, pretending to whisper to Raze and Cash. "He's got that weepy look in his eye."

"Fuck off," I say, and they all laugh. *Assholes.*

"See you in Arizona." Levi pats me on the shoulder, heading for Cash's car, who follows behind him.

Raze climbs on his motorbike, straddling it, and pulls on his helmet.

"Hey, any of you dickheads actually know where in Arizona you're going?" I ask them, knowing full well they don't.

Cash stops with his hand on his car door and stares over at me. "No."

I laugh. "So, how the hell were you planning on getting there?"

He gives me a stupid look. "Figured we'd just follow your whiny ass there."

"And if you lost me?"

"Then, we'd call you, dipshit," Levi says, holding up his cell phone. "Power of technology." He yanks open the passenger door of Cash's car and climbs in.

Shaking my head, I rattle off the address and zip code for the B&B to them. "Stick that in your GPS, and I'll see you cunts there."

I walk over to Raze, who's just stuck his key in the engine of his bike and kicked off the stand. "Look …" I say to him in a lowered voice. "You don't have to do this, you know. Come with me to Arizona. I fucking appreciate it, man. I do. But I know you have shit going on here." And by shit going on, I mean his dad. He's a fucking useless excuse for a father.

He stares at me. "Remember when we first met?" he says.

"Yeah, course I do," I answer, wondering where he's going with this.

I was in one of the music rooms, messing around on a guitar. Raze came in, asked if he could hang. That was the day we started playing music together.

"My dad was trashed that day. Like usual. But that day, he was being even more of an unbearable cunt. I honestly don't know how he kept his job at TMS Records for as long as he did. But that day, when I was walking around, staying out of his way, I heard someone playing, so I followed the sound, and there you were. I stood outside that room, thinking, *Fuck, this kid can play*, and when I found the courage, I came inside and asked if I could hang. We started playing together, and I felt … happy, man. Like I finally fucking belonged, you know." He shrugs. "This band is my family. *You're* my family. Where you dickheads go, I go."

I stare at him, understanding everything he's saying.

Raze has never had a family. Not a real family. Until me, Cash, and Levi.

And he's not ready to walk away from that yet. If ever.

Cash's car horn beeps, making me jump. "Are we going? Or you two gonna stand there all day, making fucking eyes at each other?" he yells.

"Fuck off." I give him the middle finger. "See you in Arizona." I pat Raze on the back and head for my car.

I hear Raze's bike roar to life just as I start my car up.

And to the sound of Mötley Crüe's "Home Sweet Home," I put my car in drive, pull out onto the street, and head for the highway to take me back to my girl with my boys following behind me.

My cell starts to ring next to me on the bed.

My heart jumps. Like it does every time my phone has rung over the last five days, as I hope it's him.

Storm.

I pick my phone up lightning quick.

I look at the screen.

Beck.

I deflate like a balloon.

Of course it's not Storm.

Why would he be calling me? I haven't heard from him since he left. And it's not like anything has changed.

I slide my thumb across the screen, answering it. "What?"

"You really need to work on your phone etiquette."

"Bite me," I say.

Beck laughs. I swear, my brother lives to annoy me.

"What do you want, Beck? I'm busy here."

"Yeah, busy moping around, feeling sorry for yourself, like you have for the last five days."

"Fuck off. I'm not moping. I'm …" *Lying around, feeling sorry for myself.*

"You want me to kick his ass?" he says, suddenly sounding serious.

I sigh. "No. He didn't do anything wrong, Beck. It was just … our lives are in two different places. But it's nice to know you care."

"I never said I cared. I said I'd kick his ass."

That makes me laugh. "What is it you wanted? Apart from annoying me."

"I need a favor."

"No," is my immediate answer.

"Aw, come on, Stevie. It's just a tow."

"Then, definitely no." The last tow I did for him is the reason I'm lying on my bed, feeling like my heart is slowly dying.

"Please. Dad isn't here, and I'm busy."

I sigh, dragging a hand through my hair. "For God's sake, Beck."

"So, you'll do it?"

"Fine," I huff. "Where am I going?"

"Main Street."

Pause.

"Are you fucking kidding me?"

"Sorry, Stevie." He actually sounds apologetic. At least my thickheaded brother realizes this isn't going to be easy for me. Doing a tow on the very street where I met Storm.

Jesus. Here's some salt. Rub it in my open, bleeding wound.

"Why does everyone break down there?"

"Maybe because it's the main road in town," Beck says, back to his sarcastic ways, and I flip him the bird even though he can't see.

"I don't want to do it." I'm practically whining.

"Come on. I wouldn't ask if I didn't need your help."

That's true. Beck only asks for a favor when he's in a bind.

But still …

"You really need to hire someone to help you. I can't just be dropping stuff here to come help you out." Not that I'm super busy at the moment. Currently just lying on my bed, feeling sorry for myself.

"Last time I'll ask, Stevie. Promise."

"Yeah. Sure it will be. What's the car?"

"White BMW."

"Name?"

Silence.

"Beck … you did get a name, right?"

"I forgot …"

"Christ's sake." I sigh.

"I was busy when I took the call!"

"You always are."

"I do know that it's a guy who has broken down. Actually, there're two of them. I heard the other guy in the background."

"Oh, well, that's great. Two dudes to murder me instead of one."

"Drama queen."

"Buttmunch."

"Whiny ass."

"How about you shut the hell up? If you want me to do this favor for you, then you'll stop flapping your lips right about now."

He chuckles. "Thanks, Stevie. I owe you."

"Whatever." I roll my eyes. "Be there in five to collect the truck."

I hang up on him and sigh the loudest sigh I can.

Someone upstairs hates me. Like really hates me.

I sit up and swing my legs over the side of the bed. I roll my shoulders.

I can do this. It's no biggie.

Main Street is fairly long. I'll just avoid looking at the place where I picked up Storm. Like I'm avoiding looking at anything in this town that reminds me of him.

Ice cream parlor—ruined forever.

Dad's boat—hell might have to freeze over before I go on there again.

The room where Storm stayed—I've sealed it off.

Well, I haven't actually because we can't afford to lose the income on it, but Gran's been cleaning it for me.

But I feel bad. She doesn't need to be cleaning rooms at her age.

I just need to pull up my big-girl panties and get on with it.

Get on with my life.

Like Storm's getting on with his.

Not that I know what he's actually doing.

I'll admit, I Googled his name to see if there was any recent news, but nothing new came up.

I know he doesn't use social media much, but I checked Instagram too.

I know. I've turned into a total stalker.

But … I miss him.

I checked Slater Raze's band page, but there were no new updates. Then, I checked his own personal page. Also nothing.

I don't know whether to be relieved there are no updates or hate that there's nothing to tell me what he's doing in LA.

Without me.

But then, is this going to be my life now, stalking his Instagram for pictures of him?

And what about when he meets someone and moves on? Because, of course, he will. He's gorgeous and funny and smart.

Honestly, I'm just trying not to think about that day.

After Josh cheated on me and I was heartbroken—which coincidentally feels minor in comparison to the way I feel over losing Storm, and that says a lot about Josh and my relationship—Gran said to me, "Stupid men lose smart women."

And I let Storm go. I didn't go with him. I said no to long-distance. I lost him. So, does that make me stupid? Quite likely. Men like him ... what we had between us, come along once in a lifetime, and I didn't even try to keep him.

I should have said yes to long-distance. I would have hated it. But at least I'd still have him. I'd be miserable, missing him. But I'm miserable, missing him now, without the option of being able to call or FaceTime him or know that I would be able to see him again at some point.

God, I'm a fucking idiot sometimes.

My fingers itch to call him. Tell him I was wrong. That I made a mistake. That we should do the long-distance thing.

But I'm scared. What if I call him up and he says he's changed his mind? That the feelings he thought he had for me weren't real? That, with this distance and time, he's realized that?

I'd be crushed.

And I'd really rather not be crushed. So, here I am, stuck in a perpetual limbo of missing him and crying into my pillow every night.

I stand up and grab some shoes, slipping them on. I call to Gran, who's in the kitchen, letting her know where I'm going, and I leave the B&B and walk in the direction of the garage.

It's quiet when I get there, but I know Beck is inside, working.

I pop my head through the door. "Me," I shout. "Just getting the keys." I grab them off the hook just as Beck appears out of the office.

"Hey," he says.

"Hey. Got the keys." I hold them up in my hand. "I'll be back soon."

"Okay." He pushes his hands in the pockets of his coverall and rocks back on his heels.

He's looking at me oddly. He's got this shifty smile on his face. I recognize it well. It always came out when we were kids and he'd broken something of mine.

"What's going on with you?" I cock my head to the side, watching him.

"Nothing."

I glance around the garage, looking for anything out of the ordinary. "Dad's still at the suppliers?" I check.

"Yep."

"Why are you smiling at me like that?"

His brow goes up. "Smiling at you like what?"

"Like you've done something wrong."

"Nope. I haven't done anything."

I narrow my eyes on him.

He smiles wider, showing actual teeth.

"You've totally done something, and I will find out what."

He laughs. "Maybe I'm just happy to see my kid sister."

See, that's weird. Beck would never say something like that. He's not what you'd call an affectionate brother. And I did only see him this morning.

It's my turn to laugh. "Now, I know you're lying."

He just shrugs, still wearing that damn smile.

"Are you dying?"

Laughter bursts from him this time. "No, I'm not fucking dying."

"Are you high then? Drunk?"

"Nope, and nope."

I eyeball him. He gives me an even wider smile.

He's totally done something. Or is up to something. And I'll figure it out when I get back from this tow.

I point a finger at him. "I'm going to do this tow. I'll see you when I get back."

I back out of the garage, swivel on my heel, and walk over to the tow truck.

What the hell was that all about? If he's broken something of mine, I will kill him.

I climb in the cab. Start the truck up. Hook up my Bluetooth and put "Love Is A Battlefield" on. Pat is the only one who understands me at the moment.

I shift the truck into drive and set off to go get this tow over and done with, so I can get back to lying on my bed and feeling sorry for myself. Desperately trying not to think about the last time I was in this truck and who I was with.

Because if I do, I'll probably cry.

And I really don't want to cry anymore.

I reach Main Street and drive down, keeping my eyes peeled for a white BMW.

I locate it not far from the small stretch of industrial space, where I first picked up Storm.

Don't cry. Don't cry.

I can see two guys leaning up against the hood of the car. There's a guy on a motorbike parked up in front, talking to them.

Probably a passing motorist offering assistance.

I pull the truck up in front of the BMW, turn off the engine, and hop out.

I know I look a mess. Jean shorts. T-shirt that I'm pretty sure has bleach stains on it. Sneakers. My hair tied up in a messy bun. But I'm not here to impress anyone.

I walk toward the car. The guys leaning against the hood straighten up. Both are really good-looking. One has dark brown hair. The other light-brown hair. Both have tattoos showing on their arms.

The guy straddling the bike turns his head to look at me.

Wow.

If I wasn't currently a mess and heartbroken over Storm, I'd be in a puddle on the floor.

He's seriously hot. Storm level of hot. But in a different way.

Long dark brown hair, which is tied back off his face. He's wearing leathers, so I can't see if he has any tattoos like the other two guys here.

And since when did I become obsessed with tattoos?

Oh, yeah. Since Storm.

"Hey." I smile. Pushing my hands into the back pockets of my shorts, I rock back on my heels. "I hear you need a tow."

"Actually, they don't."

The voice I hear behind me makes my heart pause. My breath still. My body tremble with nerves.

Storm.

My hands slip from my pockets.

I turn on the spot.

And everything stops. Ceases to exist in this moment.

Because it's him.

He's actually here.

And he looks so fucking beautiful that it physically hurts me.

"You're here …" I breathe, and even I hear the tremor in my voice.

He takes a step closer. "I'm here."

"W-why?" I want to hope. But I can't. Because he might leave again, and I don't think I'd survive him walking away from me a second time.

"Because I couldn't stay away. I love you, Stevie. I'm madly in fucking love with you. I can't function without you. In the shortest of times, you've come to mean more to me than anyone ever has before. You're on my mind constantly. I can't focus on anything but you. My life has gone to absolute shit without you."

He moves even closer, like he can't stay away, and I don't want him to.

He loves me. He's in love with me.

"What we have … it comes around once in a lifetime, babe. I'm not willing to lose this. Lose you. Leaving that morning … it was the hardest thing I'd ever done. I should never have left. I should have climbed back in that fucking bed with you, wrapped my arms around you, and never let go." He takes a deep breath. "I made that mistake then. I won't make it again. So … I'm here to stay. If you still want me, that is?"

Do I still want him? Is he being serious? Of course I still want him.

I part my lips, but nothing comes out.

"Babe, say something, *please.* I'm kinda out on a limb here."

"I … I just can't believe you're here." And then I do something so unlike me. I burst into tears.

His arms are around me a second later. "Jesus. Don't cry, babe."

"I'm sorry … I just … I've missed you so much and then you're here and I didn't expect it and you're telling me you love me and that you're staying here."

He takes my face in his hands, tilting my eyes up to his. He wipes my tears away with his thumbs. "So, the tears are a good thing?"

I bite my lip and nod my head.

Relief swims in his eyes. "Thank fuck for that."

Then, he kisses me, and everything is right again in my world.

He's here and he's staying and he's mine.

And he loves me.

"I love you," I tell him against his lips.

His answer is to kiss me deeper.

I wrap my arms around his neck. He picks me up, and my legs go around his waist.

And I don't even care that we're in the middle of the street. I want to stay here all day and kiss him.

The sound of a throat clearing behind me breaks us apart.

"As touching as this is, I've been driving for four hours, and honestly, watching you two make out has given me a boner, so I need to go jack off and then get some sleep."

"For fuck's sake, Cash," Storm groans, dropping his head to my shoulder.

Male laughter ensues behind me.

I can feel my skin getting hot with embarrassment. Clearly, I lost my head there for a moment, making out with Storm like that. But in my defense, I've missed him.

And he told me he loves me.

He loves me.

Storm puts me to my feet, and I turn to face the guys standing behind us.

Guys that I'm guessing are Storm's best friends. I recognize the name Cash from before when Storm told me about them.

"Guys, this is Stevie," Storm tells them, wrapping his arms around me from behind. "Stevie, this is Raze." Storm points to the guy on the motorbike, who gives me a smile that would melt the panties off even the toughest of girls. "Levi." Storm indicates to the dark-haired guy, who gives me a chin-lift greeting. "And this is Cash." He gestures to the light-brown-haired guy. "Don't worry; you'll get used to him."

"Hi." I smile, feeling a tad awkward. And then I wave.

Which is even more fucking awkward.

Jesus Christ.

"I can see why you wanted to come back," Cash says to Storm, a definite mischievous glint in his eyes. "I'd have come back too. So, Stevie"—he turns his attention to me—"you got any sisters?"

"Uh, no. I have a brother."

"He look like you? I've never gone guy, but I'd be willing to try if he's as hot as you."

I glance up at Storm, who just looks amused. I bring my eyes back to Cash. "Uh … no. He doesn't look like me. And you definitely wouldn't be his type."

"Fair enough. So, do you have any other relatives? Cousins? Actually, Storm, didn't you say Stevie has a grandmother?"

"For fuck's sake," Levi sighs. "We just got here, Cash. Don't scare her. You scare her off, and Storm will be in a mood for-fucking-ever. You know what he's been like this last week without her. Miserable as fuck."

So, he's been miserable without me. Good to know.

I slide my hand over Storm's, linking my fingers with his.

"Don't worry. I don't scare easily," I say. "And you're all staying here?" I glance back up at Storm when I ask this. "Not that I have a problem with it," I add.

Storm turns me to face him, keeping hold of my hand. "I'm here for good. The guys have just come with me while we do this album. We're going to finish writing it here and then record it at a studio either here in town or one close by."

I smile, my heart warming in my chest. "They came here for you?"

"Yep, we're awesome like that," Cash cuts in.

"Yeah"—I nod, taking my eyes off Storm—"I'm getting that."

So, these are his friends.

The kind of friends who would up and move four hours away from their home for the foreseeable future for him.

That says a lot about them and everything about him.

But then I already knew he was amazing.

And I'm getting that his friends are kind of awesome too.

"So, I'm guessing you all need a place to stay," I say to Storm. "I know this great B&B."

He pulls me closer to him, his arms wrapping around my body. "That so?"

I tilt my face up to his. "Yep. Thing is, there are only three rooms free. The rest are currently occupied. So, someone's going to have to share."

His brow rises. "And who would that someone be sharing with?"

I shrug, going for nonchalance. "I have a king-size bed."

"I volunteer as tribute," Cash calls out from behind.

And I laugh.

"Shut the fuck up," Storm says to him. "We're having a moment." Then, he lowers his mouth to mine and gently brushes his lips over mine. "So … I'm staying with you tonight then."

"Seems that way," I hum against his mouth.

"And what about all the nights after that?"

I pull back a touch and stare into his eyes. "You can stay for all of those too, if you want."

The corners of his lips kick up into a smile, and it lights up my insides.

"Damn fucking straight I want. I'm here to stay, babe. I ain't going anywhere ever again."

EPILOGUE

STORM

Four Months Later

"So, where exactly are we going?" Stevie asks me for the tenth time since we got in my car fifteen minutes ago.

"I just want to show you something."

"But why can't you tell me what it is before we get there?"

"Babe, that kind of takes out the element of surprise. Has no one ever surprised you before?"

"Of course they have. I have a brother who liked to surprise me with all kinds of shit when we were kids. I never got over the trauma of finding a skunk in my bedroom when I was ten. Hence why I'm not keen on surprises."

"Beck really did that?" I chuckle. "Put a skunk in your bedroom?"

She gives me a look. "You've met him. What do you think?"

"I think he's funny as fuck—but not as funny as you, of course, babe," I'm quick to say at her disgruntled expression.

"Good save," she says.

I grin at her. "I thought so."

I've been living in Lake Havasu for four months now, and I've never been as happy as I am here with Stevie. And I don't see that changing anytime—ever.

I've been staying with Stevie in her room at the B&B in the part of the house her family occupies. Raze, Cash, and Levi have been renting rooms in the main B&B.

We just finished recording the album, so technically, the guys should probably be heading back to LA because they were only here for the writing and recording of the album. But none of them seem to be making any moves to leave at the moment.

And I'm just happy to have them here.

I don't miss LA at all. But I miss everyone I left behind there.

Jake and Tru came to visit last month. It was good to see them. They absolutely loved Stevie, of course. She's awesome.

I said I'd take Stevie to LA to visit at some point. She still needs to meet Tom, Lyla, Den, Simone, Stuart, Smith, and all the kids.

Stevie's been in the studio a lot while we've been recording. She's been so fucking supportive, and I love that about her.

I played her the finished songs a few days ago. The songs she'd inspired. Which is basically the whole album.

She loved them, and she wasn't lying because she is nothing but honest.

She'd never blow smoke up my ass.

But she totally blew me after listening to those songs. And then I bent her over the mixing desk and took her hard and fast from behind.

The studio was empty at the time.

Stevie might have gotten a little more adventurous about where we have sex over the months that we've been together. But she's not into exhibitionism.

And I'm not into anyone seeing her naked but me.

But I sure as hell will never look at a mixing desk again without thinking of Stevie.

I drive the car up the dusty track that will one day soon be a driveway, and I park the car up in front of the building site.

I climb out of the car. Stevie gets out too.

I meet her round the front of the car, standing next to her.

"You brought me to see a building site?" she says.

"What do you think?" I ask.

"Well … it's nice. As far as building sites go. I've not seen many, but I'd say it's the best I've ever seen."

I chuckle. "Such a smart-ass," I say.

"Always." She grins up at me.

I lean down and press my lips to hers. I'll never tire of kissing Stevie.

I sling my arm around her shoulder. "One day soon, this building site will be a house, babe. With five bedrooms, six bathrooms, a double garage, and an outdoor pool. Six and a half thousand square feet of living space. With panoramic views of the lake and mountains."

She tips her head back, looking up at me. "Did you get a job as a realtor and not tell me? 'Cause right now, I feel like you're trying to sell it to me. Heads-up, it's like a million south of my price range."

"Try two-point-five million," I tell her.

She lets out a low whistle.

"And I'm not trying to sell it to you because it's already yours. Well, ours. Because I bought it."

Her mouth drops open. She's staring at me. Not blinking. And no words are coming.

Stevie is rarely speechless. She always has something to say. And when she doesn't, it's either really bad. Or really fucking good.

I'm praying for the latter.

"I know maybe it was presumptuous of me to go ahead and buy it for us. But I fucking adore you, babe. You're my best friend. The only woman I've ever loved. And you really do give great head."

"Oh, I know."

She smiles, and I can breathe. She's not mad that I bought it. Thank fuck for that.

My lips curve up. "You're also stunningly modest. And sexy as fuck."

"Also true."

"So, will you live here with me?"

"In the unbuilt house? It could get drafty. And if it rains, we'll be fucked."

"When it's completed, smart-ass."

"Oh, well, in that case, I'd love to move in here with you when it's completed."

I grin. Then, I pick her up, lifting her off her feet, and I kiss her stupid.

"I know I probably got carried away," I tell her when I finally let her up for air. "But I wanted to surprise you. I want you to know that I'm committed to you. That I'm here to stay."

She smiles softly. "I already knew that, babe. But five bedrooms though," she says, her fingers sifting through my hair. "There is only two of us."

"Well, I was hoping, one day, in the far-off future, we'd fill those extra bedrooms."

"With Raze, Levi, and Cash?" she quips, and I chuckle.

"More like I was thinking I'd knock you up in the far-off future, and we'd have lots of babies."

Her nose scrunches up in that cute way of hers that I love so much. "How many is lots?"

"Four. One for each of the extra bedrooms."

Her eyes widen, almost comically. "Four?"

"Okay, so maybe not four. Two or three. We'll probably need the other bedroom for Cash. He'll be with us for life. No woman will be crazy enough to live with him."

"True dat." She grins. "But call it two babies, plus Cash, and you've got a deal."

"Two babies, plus Cash, it is."

Then, I brush my lips over hers, sealing the deal.

"Storm?"

"Yep?"

"In this far-off future when we're having these two kids and adopting Cash, will we also be married?"

"Yeah, of course."

"How will you ask me?"

"You really don't like surprises, do you?"

"One word: skunk."

I chuckle.

"So, how would you ask?" she probes.

"Well … I'd probably buy you a half-built house. Drive you up to the half-built house. Sweep you up off your feet. And then ask you to marry me."

"Storm?"

"Yep."

"Are we still doing the hypothetical right now, or are you actually asking me?"

I put my hand into my jeans pocket and pull out the ring that I bought last week and have been carrying around with me ever since, trying to figure out when the right time to ask would be.

Seems the time is now.

"Holy shit," she breathes, staring at the ring. Her eyes flick back to mine. "You're really asking?"

"Yeah, babe, I'm really asking. And I know it's probably too quick and we haven't known each other for long. But, honestly, I think it's overdue. I'd have married you the day I met you. That lecture about the disposal of cigarette butts sold me. I knew in that moment that I'd marry you one day."

"Now, I know you're joking."

"Okay. I am about that. But not about marrying you. I fucking love you, Stevie. Like the crazy kind of love. The love that people like me write songs about. And I want to keep writing songs about you, babe. And loving you. Forever. So, marry me?"

She stares into my eyes. Then, she lifts her hand up, giving me the ring finger on her left hand.

I slide the diamond onto her finger. And it looks fucking perfect. Almost as perfect as she is.

I take hold of her hand and kiss the ring on her finger. Then, I kiss her beautiful mouth.

"So, I'm taking it, that's a yes?" I say against her lips.

She smiles, and it's the absolute best feeling ever. "Yeah, babe. It is unquestionably, definitely, one thousand percent yes. The easiest yes I've ever given."

PLAYLIST

"Purple Haze" by Jimi Hendrix
"The Monster" by Eminem, featuring Rihanna
"Thunderstruck" by AC/DC
"Enter Sandman" by Metallica
"Don't You (Forget About Me)" by Simple Minds
"Dreams" by Fleetwood Mac
"Love Shack" by The B-52s
"I Wanna Dance with Somebody" by Whitney Houston
"White Heat" by Madonna
"Paradise City" by Guns N' Roses
"Summer of '69" by Bryan Adams
"Afterlife" by Avenged Sevenfold
"I Don't Care" by Ed Sheeran and Justin Bieber
"Hysteria" by Def Leppard
"God Is a Woman" by Ariana Grande
"Don't Cry" by Guns N' Roses
"Is This Love" by Whitesnake
"Glory of Love" by Peter Cetera
"Home Sweet Home" by Mötley Crüe
"Love Is a Battlefield" by Pat Benatar

ACKNOWLEDGMENTS

Craig, Riley, and Bella—You are the best people I know. And considering I made the latter two of you, I'm taking all credit for your awesomeness. The three of you put up with my odd ways, my long working hours, and my random outbursts while I'm sitting, writing on my laptop. I know living with a writer isn't easy. Yet you all still love me. And I love you three like I didn't even know possible.

Jodi—I was literally shitting myself, sending the initial chapters of *Finding Storm* to you. Knowing how important Jake is to you, I was terrified that Storm would never measure up. Then, you messaged me and told me that you loved Storm and Stevie, and I knew I'd hit the jackpot with this story! LY, Bird.

Nicky, Natasha, Zoe, Jodi, Vic, Charlie, and ZoeElle—I laugh the most with all of you. It's great to be mates with a bunch of women who share the same weird sense of humor as I do. Bring on the next Venga Bus!

Jovana—You are the best editor in the whole world. A total editing ninja! You put up with my flaky, last-minute ways, taking it all in your stride. I honestly couldn't do this without you. So, don't ever leave me. Please.

Najla Qamber—You are quite simply awesome. The best cover designer I have ever worked with.

My agent Lauren Abramo, agent extraordinaire—I'm so lucky to have you. You handle my weird writer ways. My changes of plan. Taking away the worry and stress that I'm feeling with a few calming words. I get to see my books in stores, in foreign print, and hear them on audio because of you. You are fabulous. So, you can't leave me either. Please. Also, a big thank-you to Kemi Faderin for handling my foreign deals and keeping everything in line.

Wether Girls—As always, the best place on Facebook to be! Our group continues to grow but remains the exact same. In there, I am surrounded by wonderful, supportive women, and it warms my heart to see and helps to restore my faith in the human race daily.

Thank you to each and every member of the blogging world, who works tirelessly to help promote books without ask or complaint. We authors couldn't do it without you. You are truly appreciated.

And as always, to you, the reader—You are the reason I get to live my dream. And stay home and work in my pajamas! Thank you from the never-ending depths of my heart.

ABOUT THE AUTHOR

SAMANTHA TOWLE is a *New York Times*, *USA Today*, and *Wall Street Journal* best-selling author.

A native of Hull, she lives in East Yorkshire with her husband, their son and daughter, three large furbabies, and their small, grumpy cat.

She is the author of contemporary romances The Storm Series, The Revved Series, The Wardrobe Series, The Gods Series and stand-alones *Trouble*, *When I Was Yours, The Ending I Want, Unsuitable, Under Her, River Wild,* and *Sacking the Quarterback,* which was written with James Patterson. She has also written paranormal romances, *The Bringer* and The Alexandra Jones Series. With over a million books sold, her titles have appeared in countless best-seller lists and are currently translated into ten languages.

Sign up for Samantha's newsletter for news on upcoming books at: https://samanthatowle.co.uk/newsletter-sign-up

Join her reader group for daily man-candy pics, exclusive teasers, and general fun at:
www.facebook.com/groups/1435904113345546/

Like her author page to keep in the know:
www.facebook.com/samtowlewrites/

Follow her on Amazon for new release alerts:
https://amzn.to/2NEfdHI

Follow her on Instagram for random pics and the occasional photo of her:
www.instagram.com/samtowlewrites/

Pinterest for her book boards:
www.pinterest.co.uk/samtowle/

Also Twitter to see the complete nonsense she posts:
https://twitter.com/samtowlewrites

And lastly, Bookbub, just because:
www.bookbub.com/authors/samantha-towle

Printed in Poland
by Amazon Fulfillment
Poland Sp. z o.o., Wrocław

36190710R00179